THE LAST HAMILTON

THE LAST HAMILTON

A NOVEL

JENN BREGMAN

CROOKED
LANE

NEW YORK

Copyright © 2025 by Jenn Bregman

Published in the United States by Crooked Lane Books, an imprint of The Quick Brown Fox & Company LLC.

Crooked Lane Books and its logo are trademarks of The Quick Brown Fox & Company LLC.

Library of Congress Catalog-in-Publication data available upon request.

ISBN (hardcover): 978-1-63910-991-3
ISBN (paperback): 979-8-89242-224-6
ISBN (ebook): 978-1-63910-992-0

Cover design by Nebojsa Zoric

Printed in the United States.

www.crookedlanebooks.com

Crooked Lane Books
34 West 27th St., 10th Floor
New York, NY 10001

First Edition: February 2025

10 9 8 7 6 5 4 3 2 1

For Kaarin, Jerry, and Gwen,
with my love
and deepest gratitude

THE LAST
HAMILTON

PROLOGUE

S HE KNOWS IT'S there. She runs, skirting the barren bushes, weaving her way to the cellar door of The Grange. White and imposing, the colonnades rise in silent homage to the home's creator, Alexander Hamilton, a man of destiny who helped save a nation, but who, in the end, couldn't save himself.

The window she had left unlocked earlier in the day opens easily and without a sound. She climbs through the cellar window and into the basement, cringing at the thought the alarm could still be on. She pauses. Nothing. Feeling for the banister, she creeps carefully up the stairs and into the parlor where the piano sits dark and somber. The original instrument owned by Alexander Hamilton. Played with joy for many years by the Hamilton family, then with anguish by Alexander's daughter Angelica after the death of her brother, only to be left unused for over two hundred years. Alexander, suffering the agony of watching his daughter play day after day after Philip's death and sinking deeper into grief and despair from which there was no return.

She opens the lid, heavy and old, the hinges crackle and complain as they come into service. Using her low-light pen light, she looks inside at the strings, but knows, even before she starts, that it won't be in there. Nor in the bench or between the keys, all of which would have been reconditioned through the years. She steps back and considers the inlay. Running her fingers across the sides and top. But there is nothing loose. No indentations. No seams to gently pry.

The moon's cold light rearranges the shadows on the piano and on the floor, sending a thin triangle of light underneath and casting a tiny irregular shadow on a particular seam. She crawls underneath and feels its unevenness. Ever so slightly misjoined, it seems to soften at her touch. As she pushes harder, the pressure opens a slight space in the seam just large enough for a fingernail. She gently pulls at it, and a drawer about the size of a matchbox slides open. A key with scrollwork designs stands out boldly in the silvery shadows. She thrusts it deep into her pocket and quickly closes the drawer. But not before hearing the slightest buzzing sound. Someone is there. She turns slowly, raising her pen light as her only defense. But there is no one. The buzzing stops. She sighs with relief. It was just her imagination. The slight buzzing started happening weeks ago, when all this began. Now she knows that it's just a mind trick brought on by the anxiety of what those weeks had brought. But she is wrong. If she had taken off her glasses at that moment, she would have seen a tiny pin prick size video light on the front of the frames fading to black and turn off. She would have known that someone was watching.

3:15 AM

Quickly retracing her steps through the house and to the edge of the grounds, she pulls her coat tight against the frigid wind as she runs the three blocks to the subway. She has eight minutes before the train arrives and, at this hour, it's her only chance. She races down the stairs and through the turnstile. She can see the train's lights in the distance. She is going to make it with minutes to spare. She collapses onto the one lone bench on the platform, her breath exploding in jagged bursts, sobbing, holding herself tight. But she is not alone. A man steps from the stairwell's shadow and stands close to her. Too close. A second man comes down the far staircase and stops, blocking the steps.

She is trapped. The men start to advance. She frantically scans the platform for an escape route. She jumps up and runs toward the far stairwell hoping she can somehow get by the man at the end. But as she moves, he moves. He is fast and big and easily gaining on her. Glancing back the other way, she sees the first man approaching, closing the gap between them. The lights of the train are approaching rapidly. She can hear the whir of the wheels, see the rocking cars. The train is almost at the station. But one last glance tells her what she needs to know. It is too late. They will be on her before it arrives. In a split second, she knows what she has to do. She yanks her phone out of her coat, punches the last message sent and with brutal focus, texts "call ralph" before throwing it and herself in front of the oncoming train.

1

"GOOD MORNING, SARAH," Mr. Mandelman called cheerfully through the open water pipe shaft in the bathroom.

"Good morning to you," Sarah answered. Ever since the building had opened up the water pipe shaft to make some much-needed repairs, her neighbor in the downstairs apartment had taken to waking Sarah up with a 7:00 AM "good morning" voice alarm. Some mornings she hated it, but this morning she was already awake, bright, rested, and inexplicably happy. The bitterness and depression she had been living with for so long was finally starting to lift of its own accord, and she was grateful for any moment of feeling good again.

She lay for a few minutes more, savoring the delicious warmth of her bed before reaching for her phone. There was a text from Elizabeth at 3:23 AM: "call ralph." Ralph was Elizabeth's husband. Married less than a year, Sarah didn't know him well, but he was friendly and seemed nice enough. But 3:23 AM? Strange on a school night. Even so, it was too early to call. Sarah found her slippers and robe at the end of the bed and slipped them on. The apartment was freezing, and the pipes were cold. The boiler must be on the fritz again, Sarah thought, but she vowed not to complain. The apartment really was a steal even with all its problems. Rent control five-story walk up, just off the theater district, with a partial view of the Hudson River if you stood on your tiptoes. Perfect. She turned on NY1 just as the pipes started hissing with new-found steam. Good start to the day. Usual weather, traffic, and a lead story about a woman crushed by a subway early this morning in Harlem. She threw on some makeup, her typical black pants and top, and grabbed a bagel on her way out the door. Ten minutes. A new record for up and out. Even with the subways later than usual, she was at the office by 8:30 AM. Notably early by New York standards and her own personal best, but as soon as her coat landed on the chair, he was there.

"Good morning, Sarah," Pierce said with a smirk as he slid into her closest client chair. "I dropped off that stack of SEC documents along with my copious notes to Mr. Bardack last night. I probably should have given you a chance to make the corrections before Bardack saw them, but I thought it better that he sees them sooner than later, and I didn't know what time to expect you this morning."

Such a slimy jerk. Sarah squeezed her lips tight so nothing truly rude would pop out. In the three years she had worked at the Bank of Hoboken, she had been late once. Once. Granted, it had been a doozy. She had missed an important client meeting due to a combination of too much wine the night before, failed alarm clock batteries, and slow trains, but still. Mean. That's who Pierce was. Thin, slight, particular in dress, his skin was translucent and pale, even in summer, and his light blue eyes were watery and seemingly weak. She always thought of a jellyfish when she saw him. And she saw him a lot. He was presently one of the assistants to the Structured Finance group in the bank and he had designs on much more. Always busy. Either with his work or sucking up to various notables in the bank. He had been the liaison between the Structured Finance and Compliance departments for about eight months, and she had hated every minute of it. She couldn't wait until he took his Series 7 exam. At least she would be free of him for a few days.

"I'm sure your notes were time sensitive," Sarah said sarcastically. "Especially on such low level, form documents. And I'm sure Mr. Bardack won't mind spending his valuable time inputting the changes you could have done so easily yourself." Snap. Advantage Sarah.

Sarah picked up her phone indicating Pierce's clear dismissal as he humphed and grunted himself out of her office. Elizabeth's text popped up again. Not too early now.

But the moment Ralph answered, she knew something was horribly wrong.

"Sarah?" Ralph rasped. "Elizabeth's dead. She got hit by a train this morning. She's dead. She's dead." He started sobbing hysterically.

"No! No! Oh, please, no—Hang on, Ralph. I'm coming. I'll be right there," she yelled into the phone as she threw her coat over her arm and rushed for the door.

She was uptown in fifteen minutes and at the apartment in another five. Ralph was a mess. He lay on the cold wooden living room floor, curled up in a ball with his Wheaten Terrier, Bodie, at his side. Still in pajamas with an overnight growth of beard, Ralph was barely recognizable as the affable husband Sarah knew. She wondered why no one else was there. He must have friends closer than she, but when the doorman called to say the police were in the lobby, she realized he must have just found out. Asking them to wait a few minutes, Sarah helped Ralph into the bathroom where she splashed his face with water and made some sense of his deranged hair. Before she finished, the police were at the door.

"Hello," said a short, compact, police officer as she strode into the room. "I'm Detective Schwartz. This is Officer Durbman and Officer Striber. Are you Ralph Walker?"

"Yes," Ralph croaked out before the sobs overtook him.

"I'm sorry for your loss," Detective Schwartz said perfunctorily, moving closer to Ralph and pulling out her field notebook. "Do you mind if I ask you a few questions?"

Ralph gave a limp nod as Detective Schwartz took a seat on the couch. "And this is?" she asked, waving in Sarah's direction.

Sarah felt the detective's piercing green eyes shift toward her. "I'm Sarah Brockman, one of Elizabeth's best friends."

"Fine," the detective said making herself comfortable as she turned back to Ralph. "When did you last see Elizabeth?"

"We went to bed about ten last night. Early for us, but it was a hard week, and we were tired." Ralph started sobbing again but continued. "She got up sometime in the night and left. I didn't hear her. Bodie didn't hear her, and Bodie hears everything. I don't know how she did it."

"Do you have any idea where she went?"

"No."

"What do you mean it was a hard week?" the detective asked, looking at Ralph intently.

"Stressful. Elizabeth was short-tempered. Anxious. She acted like she was going to work every day but didn't. I'd call her office, and she wasn't there. And she was going to weird places. Not dangerous places, just weird. Like the Historical Society and the City of New York Museum. She even took the train to Montauk. I know because I went through her coat pockets. I found ticket stubs in there. I knew it was wrong, but I had to find out what was going on."

"Can you get me those?" Detective Schwartz asked, jotting some notes. "Where did she work?"

"Seidels midtown. Park and 48th."

"Wealth Management. I've heard of them. Do you know her boss's name?"

"Elaine Hornsbacher."

"What about her calendar? Did she keep a written calendar or online?"

"I know she used Outlook for work, and I think Google too."

"Anything else out of the ordinary?"

"Just all the stress. The weird places and the lying." Ralph pulled his legs up, squeezed himself into a tiny ball and closed his eyes.

"Okay," the detective said as she closed her notebook and stood up. "That's enough for now. Which computer is Elizabeth's?" Schwartz asked as she surveyed the PCs on the living room table. Is there a laptop as well?"

"This is Elizabeth's," Ralph said pointing. "She keeps her laptop at work."

"Fine," the detective said. "Officer Striber will take the computer with him now. Please give the receipts to Officer Durbman. He will take down some contact information from you and explain to you how this process will go. Generally, don't go out of the city without letting us know. And don't go out of the state at all."

Ralph turned to Detective Schwartz, startled. "What does that mean?" he asked loudly. "Am I a suspect?"

"Just routine police procedure" she said. "Get some rest, and we'll be back tomorrow." She turned to Sarah. "I would like to interview you as well. Is there a time you can come to the precinct this afternoon or would you like us to come to your home?"

"Ah, oh . . . I can come by the precinct this afternoon. What time?"

"4:00 PM will be fine," the detective said. "Officer Durbman will give you the details. I'll show myself out."

CHAPTER

2

SARAH TOOK DOWN the information from Officer Durbman as Ralph went to get the receipts. Within minutes, other friends began arriving, and she soon made her way out of the apartment, through the lobby, and into the cold, flat, November light. She couldn't make sense of what had happened. She knew she was in shock. She couldn't believe her friend was gone. Her eyes filled and overflowed with tears and then the sobs came. She sobbed as she walked. Up Broadway, crossing through the 90s, turning at 103rd Street to the park. Beautiful Riverside Park. The Hudson River roiling and churning as a cargo ship went by. Babies sleeping in strollers; dogs straining on leashes. The Palisades of New Jersey awash in midday sun. She hugged the stone wall tightly as she went down the steps and into the main section of the park. She found a bench and collapsed in a heap.

She cried until she couldn't cry anymore. She wanted to be alone. Those who looked her way and approached to help, she gently waved away. In New York, people did many private things in public. Apartments were small, roommates plentiful. She liked that about the city. Anonymity and privacy in a city of millions, if you wanted that. And today she did.

She thought about Elizabeth. Probably her best friend. She had met Elizabeth shortly after she and Sam had broken up or, more accurately, Sam had broken up with her. Elizabeth helped her get through it.

They had met at a Whitney Museum fundraiser. Not the most prestigious museum in the city and certainly not the Met Gala, but it was a museum with an eclectic offering of American Art and an inspired board of directors with drive and focus. Elizabeth had been the Master of Ceremonies and issued a warm welcome to the guests before cocktails were served. She was clearly connected to New York society or, at least, to New York's history. Many of the older patricians greeted her cordially and familiarly. Sarah had overheard many of them asking about Elizabeth's family. Later in the evening, they found themselves in the bar enjoying the same, rather inconspicuous Merlot. Pleasant conversation followed, and they made plans for lunch later the next week. But it would take many outings and almost a year before Sarah found out Elizabeth's lineage.

They had decided to treat themselves to brunch at Terrace in the Sky, an insiders' hidden jewel of a restaurant on the grounds of Concord University with spectacular views of the Hudson River. The waiter, one of the numerous Concord students who worked there, had peered inquisitively at Elizabeth after he took their orders.

"Pardon me," he said. "And I don't mean to be intrusive, but you look like a woman I was reading about in the *Concordian Times*. I'm doing a paper on the banking system in the U.S., starting with Alexander Hamilton, and so your story caught my eye. Are you really Hamilton's last descendant?"

Elizabeth seemed a little taken aback, but only a little. It was clear she had been at the end of this question many times before.

"Yes," she said kindly. "I am."

"He was a great man," the waiter continued. "Fascinating. Brilliant."

"Yes," Elizabeth agreed. "And a true patriot."

"Yes, he was," the waiter agreed. "I was just reading about The Grange restoration and how hard the house was to build in the first place, since he never had much money. No offense, but that seems really odd, since he was the Secretary of the Treasury and all. But we're all so happy they got The Grange restored and opened. I'm going next week. Everyone says it's amazing."

Sarah looked quickly at Elizabeth to see if she was offended, but Elizabeth just laughed and said: "Yes, you're right. It is surprising that Alexander struggled with money most of his life. He thought making lots of money unseemly, so he was relatively poor when he died after being shot by Aaron Burr in their duel. His friends had to help his widow, Elizabeth, financially so the family could even stay on in The Grange."

"Wow. Rough. And all those kids. Not easy for Elizabeth, I'm sure," the waiter said as he motioned to the table to their left. "Thank you for talking to me. Really nice of you."

"Well, that was a bit of a surprise," Sarah said as she turned to Elizabeth. "And you were planning to tell me when?"

"Oh," Elizabeth said with a smile. "I know it's all quite interesting, but people always seem to regard me just a little bit differently once they find out. And, you know, it's not like I did anything. I was just born into a certain family, and I haven't died yet. I'm just me. I like people to get to know 'just me' before they get to know 'the them.'"

"I hear you," Sarah said looking at Elizabeth anew. "You know, you don't look any different to me—oh, OK, maybe just a little smarter," she smiled as she sipped her drink. "And I hope you're better with money."

*   *   *

Sarah thought about these things as she sat on the bench. She thought about all the things they had done together—quick runs around the reservoir, street fairs on Fifth Avenue, drinks at The Boathouse in Central Park, that crazy weekend in Bermuda. All the heart-to-heart talks, the private, secret things revealed slowly, carefully, over time. Hours passed. The clouds came in and made the day even colder and still Sarah sat. A small branch blew off a nearby tree and landed next to Sarah with a thud. Startled from her thoughts, she finally looked at her phone. It was 4:15 PM. She was already fifteen minutes late for her interview at the police station, and she was still in Riverside Park. She hastily called the precinct and left a message for Detective Schwartz. Easily getting a taxi, she was there in twelve minutes.

"I'm sorry I'm late," Sarah said as she took a seat on the hard, wooden chair in the detective's office.

"Thank you for coming in," the detective said. "I know it's been a rough day." She eyed Sarah a little more carefully. "Would you like something warm? Coffee? Tea? You don't look too good."

"No, thank you," Sarah said. She felt cold, sick, out of sorts. She probably should have cancelled, but she was afraid the police would show up at her door either at home or at work, neither of which would be good. She had already received two messages from Pierce about something purportedly work-related even though she had her out-of-office response on. She could imagine how much he would love it if the police came to the bank.

"I'll be OK," Sarah continued. "Let's get started."

"Fine," the detective said. "So why would anyone want Elizabeth dead?"

Sarah's head started swimming. She thought this was going to be just a background interview, just learning about Elizabeth, not something like this. "I . . . I don't know," Sarah stammered. "What do you mean someone would want her dead? Didn't she just fall in front of a train?"

"Maybe," the detective said, "but why was she in Harlem in the middle of the night? Why was she at that subway station at all?"

"I don't know," Sarah said. "She seemed jumpy all week just like Ralph said. I didn't even see her, just talked on the phone. She was too busy. We tried for lunch a few times, but she canceled at the last minute. It just wasn't going to happen."

"Odd," the detective said. "Did you call her on it? Did you ask what was up?"

"Yes, I did. She said 'nothing.' She was really agitated. I'd planned to go to her office today just to see her, see if I could help."

"When did this 'jumpy' behavior start?"

"Two or three weeks ago, but it got really bad this past week. She seemed frantic and, I think, a little scared."

"Scared of what?"

"I don't know. But for every lunch we scheduled, she picked a restaurant that was out of the way. Not our usual places. Then she canceled anyway, but it seemed like she didn't want to be seen. It felt like she was hiding."

"When did you last see her?"

Sarah pulled up her calendar on her phone. "Almost three weeks ago. October 20th. Thursday. I remember thinking she was anxious even then. We only had thirty minutes, and she barely touched her food. I didn't know that would be the last time I'd ever see her."

Sarah fumbled for the Kleenex box as tears once again started streaming down her face.

"I'm sorry for your loss," the detective said standing up. "Thank you for your help. Go home and get some rest. Quite a shock, I'm sure." But as she walked past the credenza to show Sarah out, she glanced at the pile of pictures from the crime scene she had reviewed when they came in an hour ago, a picture of the key with the scrollwork designs was on top.

"Oh, one more thing, if you don't mind," she said picking up the picture. "Do you know anything about this?"

Sarah took the picture and studied it. The key looked old, but more than antique; it was bespoke and carefully made with beautiful scrolling designs on the bow, speaking to a different time. "No, I don't," she said, returning the picture to the detective. "It's lovely. Where did you get it?"

"Elizabeth had it in her pocket when she died. Forensics is running tests on it right now so I can't show you the real object, but if you might have any information about it, I'll get it for you to look at as soon as it's available."

Sarah didn't know what to say. It somehow felt familiar, but she couldn't say she had ever seen it before. And there was a big part of her that just wanted to touch it, to hold one of the last things Elizabeth touched before she died. "I'll think about it. Yes, I would like to see it when it's ready."

She left the precinct and turned down 82nd Street walking down the row of nineteenth century townhomes on her way to the subway. The key would fit one of these doors she thought absently as she made her way to the station. But as those thoughts flitted in and out of her mind, she realized the feeling of familiarity. The key *was* like a key that would fit into one of those keyholes. It was that style, it was that era, and Elizabeth had it in her pocket when she died.

Sarah knew she couldn't ask Ralph. Not now. Most likely not for a while although the police might ask him first. Ralph. Why was texting her to "call ralph" the last thing Elizabeth did? And why didn't she tell the police about the text? It didn't even occur to her *to* tell them. She paused. She didn't because it seemed too intimate, too private, to share just yet. It was Elizabeth's last communication, and it felt like it was meant just for them. She was exhausted and her mind was spinning. She somehow got on the right train and made her way home thinking all the while what it must have been like for Elizabeth. A train just like this one. Rushing over the tracks, wheels whirring, cars rocking, crushing her friend.

3

I T WAS AFTER midnight and the party was just starting to break up.

"You coming?" Pierce called to his friend.

"Can't tonight, Pierce," Camillo said with a gentle smile. "I've got a big early morning meeting tomorrow. Gotta' run."

"OK," Pierce said disappointed, but he understood. New York was even more about work than play if you were in the league. And the league was where he wanted to be—the big league. The league Camillo was already playing in.

The rejection, kind as it was, irked Pierce. Probably because it just highlighted where he was versus his friend. He was going on thirty and was just taking his Series 7 exams. He wasn't even a broker yet, for Pete's sake, the lowliest of lowly in banking, but a required step nevertheless. He was busy publishing articles in the *Financial Times* and other prominent publications, but that only boosted him so far in his climb up the banking ladder.

He had so much to prove, so much he wanted to do, to be and to have. If it wasn't for his project, he would probably be in the cuckoo ward now, made crazy by frustration. But he did have his project and, being still so ramped up from the party, he decided his best plan was to go home and work on it. He loved calling it his "project" because it made it seem small, most likely insignificant. And it was so not that. It was humongous. It was brilliant. It was brash. And it was his best opportunity to get into the big league. He tucked his raincoat under his arm and headed out to his town car. He knew he was making progress at the bank, since he not only had the usual car service but could also hold cars while he attended events. A notable perk in the bank pecking order. Within twenty minutes, he was at his desk in his apartment. Three monitors, encircling him, filled with graphs, arrows showing trends, rapidly changing data, spreadsheets, and numbers from markets all over the world. He hadn't done that well in college even in the finance classes needed for his major with one significant exception. Statistics. He had crushed it. He understood it better than his professor. He took advanced statistics as a freshman and got the highest grade on every test. He had some kind of savant understanding of it. He got it at more than a granular level. He got it at its core.

He pored over the data. Changing his spreadsheets with new assumptions, he watched the numbers roll into different combinations with surprising consequences. Striking consequences. He could see what he was after. He was watching the futures and currency trading and the overseas markets. He was watching gold. He texted his contact whom he knew would also be wide awake.

"Have you been watching it?" he typed.

"Yeah," came the reply. "Interesting fluctuations."

"I know, I've been watching it for a bit," texted Pierce. "Why?"

"Don't know."

"I'll look into it. The next buy is scheduled for market open," typed Pierce. "Do we need to delay?"

"No," came the reply. "It should still be within the spread. We're OK."

"That's what I thought too," texted Pierce. "I'm working on a global spreadsheet. After this buy, and one more, we're there."

"Excellent. Right on schedule. Talk later."

Pierce turned back to his screens, he double checked his numbers, charted the trajectories, and saved it all into one massive, encrypted spreadsheet. After adding lock-down codes and a vapor antivirus bug, he was done for the night. At 4:00 AM, he could still get a few hours of sleep before heading to the bank by a respectable 10:00 AM starting time. He closed the blackout shades, slid under his weighted blanket, and went quickly to sleep.

4

SARAH HAD SLEPT fitfully and awoke with a start, her sweat-soaked nightgown encasing her like a shroud. She struggled to sit up, to quiet her racing heart, to stop the nightmare still playing in her head. Wheels whirring, cars rocking, frigid wind coursing through the tunnel as a train approached. An ear-splitting screech as the emergency lever was pulled. Hellish silence. It was dawn. She got out of bed and let her feet guide her—to the bathroom, the coffee maker, to open the soft muslin curtains bathing the room in gray. She got dressed rapidly, conscious of the time. She simply couldn't withstand Mr. Mandelman's cheery 7:00 AM wake-up call this morning. She called her supervisor and gratefully received the day off, then let herself out of the apartment quietly, going down the stairs and into the day. She began to walk. And as she walked, she considered everything she knew about her friend. Strong, smart, sometimes intense, often funny, but always a person of character, integrity, and consequence. Eventually, Sarah made her way back home, no wiser and no closer to any understanding of what had happened to Elizabeth. Only a clingy, dark guilt that she hadn't seen her friend last week when she knew something was wrong.

A box with her name on it greeted her when she pushed through into the vestibule. It looked a bit old, and somewhat tattered, which struck her as an unusual thing to think about a box even though true. The writing on the label was visible but, again, lacked the clarity of fresh ink. Small enough to carry upstairs, Sarah put it on her kitchen table and carefully began to open it. A handwritten note, no larger than a postcard spilled out of the top. It was from Elizabeth. Sarah felt her heart catch in her throat as she recognized the writing.

"Dearest Sarah," it began. "If you are reading this note, I am dead. I am either dead from natural causes or not, but dead, nevertheless. I have instructed my attorney to leave this for you in this eventuality."

Sarah squeezed her eyes tight to keep the tears from blinding her as she read on.

"As you know, I am the last Hamilton. Medically there can't be any more. The line dies with me as it, sadly, just has. But the legacy cannot. I am sending this to you in the fervent hope that it does not." A hastily scrawled "Elizabeth" at the bottom was all there was. Sarah turned the note over, but there was nothing more. She reread the note, hunting for clues, for context, for explanation, for a more human piece of her friend, but there was nothing. She put it down with a sigh.

Next in the box was a piece of paper. So obviously old that Sarah hesitated to touch it lest it crumble in her hand. Worn almost into nothingness at the edges with a large smudge in the middle, the script was thin, scrawling like a spider across the page, and so faint, it was almost invisible. It began:

My Beloved Family:

To Elizabeth, my loyal and devoted wife, to Alexander, Jr., James Alexander, John Church, William Stephen, Eliza, Little Phil, to Angelica, with prayers for your full recovery, and in loving memory of Philip who still holds my heart in his in Heaven, and for whom this derives. And to all the descendants that shall come after them until there are none:

My life will soon be over. My last breath will be drawn. All the forces of goodness and justice have commingled with those of evil and I am afraid for the future. I feel the forces coming after me, especially that of Aaron Burr and his ilk, seeking self-interest above democracy, equality, and fairness. Caring not for the mantle of liberty for which we fought nor the moral ideals before which we laid our lives. I call upon you, when I am gone, to fight the forces that threaten America and to keep America free, just, equal, moral. I entrust this to you.

You must make a secret society, comprised solely of you, my heirs, to protect this country that I love. You must use your voices to shout down those who seek to tear and destroy and when the forces become so strong as to rend the institutions of justice asunder, you must act swiftly with force and passion and purpose. You must rise up and crush those forces and redeem these United States.

For this noble purpose alone, I have acquired and stowed for your use a vast sum. Not with any desire to line my own pockets, but with right, and with pure and true purpose, to save liberty.

My customs agents and revenue cutter captains, loyal to me since the inception of my Revenue Cutter Service, have always kept a piece of that which was gained, and saved it in trust for me, to protect these United States and save her liberty. Upon my death, these sums I will pass to you, also in trust, to do the same thing.

Sarah breathlessly turned the page, but there was nothing on the back. She looked for another page in the box, not sure that there was another though, as it seemed to so tidily end. She began to unload the rest of the contents of the box. She carefully withdrew two heavy, thick, loose leaf books. They looked like the kind used in years past that were adjustable. You could add pages and remove them. The first book was dusty like the letter, the thick yellowed pages held together with a dark rose ribbon that threaded through each page and then tied in the back. It had an embroidered vase on the front filled with an explosion of spring field flowers, each embroidered with meticulous skill and care. Sarah gently set the book to the side and withdrew the second book. Although about the same size and weight, it was much more modern in design, its pages still white, using a notebook style metal ring to hold the pages. A sepia picture of New York graced the cover.

Sarah set that book to the side as well and looked deeper into the box. She turned on the flashlight on her phone and scanned the bottom. There in the corner was something so tightly folded, it lay, almost flush against the bottom. Sarah drew it out and gently opened the creases, smoothing them flat with her hands. Small and square, it was a fine linen handkerchief with a large carnation pink "A" embroidered in the center and nothing more. The cross-stitch was tiny, perfect. It was hard to imagine how any human finger could have created something so sublime, but someone had, and someone had left it in this box.

Sarah sat down heavily and pulled the oldest book toward her. Her hand trembled as she brushed the dust from the cover, her fingers lingering over the delicate embroidery. She didn't want to open it. She didn't want to know what was inside. She didn't want to be part of anything that had gotten her friend killed. Yet she knew her friend loved her. She knew Elizabeth wouldn't ask if she didn't have to ask. She knew she had no choice. The black, bold, calligraphic writing leapt off the page.

WE ARE ASSEMBLED:

On this date, August 6, 1804, let it be recorded that the following persons convene the first meeting of our society directed to be formed by our beloved husband and father, Alexander, at his bequest and with his purpose, to preserve and protect these United States from tyranny and oppression, to defend justice, and uphold liberty for which war was waged and won and for which war will be again waged should it be so required.

Elizabeth Schuyler Hamilton

Angelica

Alexander, Jr.

James Alexander

John Church

William Stephen

Eliza

Phillip, also known as "Little Phil"

The names were set forth in a thin spidery hand, noticeably different from the preamble, more similar to the words penned by Alexander. Sarah paused. Hamilton's children were so young when he died. Alexander himself was only forty-seven years old. Yet another element of the profound tragedy of his death, Sarah thought. The oldest surviving child couldn't have been more than twenty years old, maybe less; that was Angelica, who became mentally incapacitated after the death of her brother Philip. That left Alexander Jr. as the most likely scribe. She thought Elizabeth was probably the author of the preamble, written in such a strong hand, and identifying Alexander first as a husband and then a father. She read on. The entry continuing in the same spidery script:

> We have come together as directed, in love and in grief, to mightily assume the yoke handed us. Elizabeth Hamilton, Alexander, Jr., James Alexander, and John Church have discussed our understanding of what we have been entrusted to do, William, Eliza, and Little Phil being too young to engage. We have determined that we will conduct a meeting, periodically as set by agreement, or urgently if required, to discuss the occurrences in the nation.
>
> To take measure of all the forces affecting these United States and her citizenry, both within and without her borders. To weigh them, with scrupulous care, against the standards of justice, equality, and liberty and if any is found to be in the path of grave harm, or danger of usurpation, then to take all necessary action to quell the foe and extirpate the threat. We hereby reaffirm the sacred pledge of our Declaration of Independence:
>
> "With a firm reliance on the protection of the divine Providence, we mutually pledge to

each other our Lives, our Fortunes, and our sacred Honor."

All had signed, although those too young, by proxy. Sarah studied the script. The signatures were spidery, with looping Js reminiscent of John Hancock, the sole exception being Elizabeth. Bold, raven black, unmistakable, hers was the hand that had penned the preamble. It must have given her great satisfaction to be visible at last, to step forward onto the world stage in which she had been holding the curtain for so long. Sarah read on:

> After long and deliberate discussion, and with unanimous opinion, we hereby determine that there is no imminent threat to the liberty of these United States requiring this society to take action. The cruel threat posed by Aaron Burr and his followers, expressly noted by our father and husband, is greatly diminished, if not expunged, by his own savage hand. Vilified by all, he has silenced his own voice and run from New York like a coward. And, as the beloved, righteous orphans of which we now are, we pray for his just and ignominious end.

The date was affixed at the bottom, and all had, once again, signed the entry intending, it seemed, to make it more authoritative and correct, which it accomplished. Except, of course, for the last sentence, which belied the officiousness of the document and opened the window, if only an inch, to the anguish the family must have felt upon the loss of Alexander. What must it have been like for them, Sarah thought, to have him taken from them so early and by a duel no less? Did they find any significance in the parallel deaths of their beloveds? Both Philip and Alexander, by duel, in the same location in Weehawken, New Jersey, shot with the same weapons in almost the exact place over the hip? What was it like for Elizabeth to have spent her whole life living a legacy, keeping such a secret? Sarah's life felt small in comparison.

She started turning the pages gingerly, praying they wouldn't disintegrate, knowing what she was doing was wrong. She knew she should take everything to the police station. Immediately. Not only were they monumentally important historical documents, but they might be relevant to solving Elizabeth's death. But she also knew that she wouldn't. Elizabeth had chosen her. Of all her friends and acquaintances, most much more significant than she, Elizabeth had chosen her.

A large part of Sarah hated that she had. She had already lived that life, unwittingly thrust into a crime that had almost killed her. It had taken five years to get through and over that and she was sure she didn't want to do that again. Elizabeth knew that. Why would she put her through that another time?

What if she did just deliver it all to the police? No one would fault her. On the contrary, she would be doing the right thing, especially since keeping the documents was, most likely, some kind of a crime anyway.

She was angry. And guilty that she was angry at her dead friend. She hated all of it, and she hated Elizabeth for it.

She closed the book. The late morning sun caught the prisms in the juice glasses drying on the counter and sparkled purples and blues, greens and light orange around her tiny kitchen. She watched them dancing on the ceiling. She thought about why she had been chosen. It was precisely because she had already done this. She had already uncovered, investigated, and solved a huge case. She had already pulled the rabbit out of one hat, and now she would have to pull it out of another.

She thought about her friend. She thought about Alexander Hamilton and his legacy. She thought about liberty and justice, and about her obligation as an American.

But she also thought about what she had been through, how nice it was to be coming out on the other side. Taking on the contents of the box, and all the unknown consequences that would follow, wouldn't bring Elizabeth back. Her friend would still be dead.

She didn't know what to do. For the moment, she decided not to turn in the box to the police, and that was enough.

Her phone started buzzing on the table, as if on cue. It was Ralph.

"Hi, Ralph," she said.

"Hi."

"I'm sorry."

"Me too." His voice was rough, raw, painful to hear. "Why did she text you to call me? And right before she died?"

"I don't know," Sarah said.

"I think it was the last. It was right before she fell in front of the train. Had to be. It was seconds before."

"What do the police say? Was that the last one on the phone?"

"The phone was crushed by the train wheels. Completely smashed. I don't think they'll be able to get anything from it."

"They won't be able to retrace anything? Especially the last week?"

"That's right," Ralph said, his voice beginning to fade. "Unless they can pull it from other sources, I guess." Sarah could hear other voices in the background.

"Hello?" It was a woman's voice, a mature voice. "This is Ralph's mom. Who is this?"

"Hi, Mrs. Walker. It's Sarah Brockman. I'm so very sorry for your loss." The words hurt coming out.

"Hi, Sarah. I'm sorry for your loss too. Thank you for coming over yesterday to see Ralph. He's not doing very well. I'm glad he has friends like you."

Sarah mumbled something, not wanting to tell Ralph's mom that they weren't really that close, but that she was the first to find out.

"I think we'll hang up now," Mrs. Walker continued. "Ralph is exhausted and not thinking clearly. If he can sleep now, that would be good."

"Yes, of course," Sarah said quickly. "Talk later."

5

Pierce had been in the office since 10:00 am, after just a few hours of sleep, and was still racing around trying to get everything done at the bank before he stepped out for a few days to take his Series 7 exams. By 2:00 pm he was done. He walked out into the brilliant day and crossed the street to magnificent Bryant Park. He never failed to notice it regardless of what was going on in his life. But he never would have shared that private thing about himself either. For a man on the rise in finance in New York, the fact that he noticed the beauty of a park was not something anyone needed to know. And today, awash in fall colors, the park was a picture postcard of the city. He took a window table at the Bryant Park Grill and waited. He loved hiding in plain view.

Within minutes, a man in a plain, rather drab business suit approached from the hostess stand and sat down. He could be anyone. Not a local, of course, but he could be someone from the United Nations just down the street, or from any number of governmental offices housed in the city, or even from the insurance industry, famous for bland. But he was none of those things.

"Hi, Timothy," Pierce said as he rose to shake his hand. "So good to finally see you. You're looking fit." Pierce had started saying that to everyone lately whether they looked fit to him or not. It was always well-received, and he had decided to keep it in his social arsenal.

"Wonderful to see you too, Pierce," came the reply as they settled into their usual seats. "Yes, I started working out again. Nice of you to notice. We've both been so busy, but still hard to believe we haven't seen each other for a few weeks.

"I know," Pierce said. "I've missed you, also sorry about all the computer issues we've been having lately. It's been quite disturbing to me. As I mentioned to you, I thought my whole system had been hacked. And since we can't keep backup, I was worried."

"Understandably so," Timothy agreed. "I was really concerned about it myself. I'm glad we were able to get it all resolved. You're comfortable now, aren't you, Pierce?" Timothy asked with a sideways glance. "No worries?"

"Yup, I'm fine. I love the buy we got under the wire this morning. It really moved the dial."

"I agree. Strange market fluctuations. I'm glad you texted me to make sure we could go forward. The buy got in within the spread as we thought, so we're good. Just one more buy and we're done. I wanted to hand deliver the new account numbers though, just so there wouldn't be any confusion from my end, especially with all this computer nonsense going on. We need to be careful, so nothing blows up before the project is finished. The political fallout would be disastrous."

"Fatal," Pierce replied. "It would take a lot of people down."

"Yes. No one would stop to ask any questions; they would point fingers and blame. Just the word 'gold' gets people excited, in all kinds of ways—some kind of primal attraction, I think. Anyone who wanted to hurt and blame could do all the damage they needed in sound bites alone. The press would have quite a romp, for a long time, and all at the expense of the current administration. Not the best scenario for our heroes, right?" Timothy acknowledged, turning to Pierce. "And, on that rather solemn note, here are the new account numbers, so we don't need to worry about any of that."

Timothy handed Pierce a small slip of neatly folded paper and turned to the menu.

"I hear the monkfish is particularly good lately," Timothy said, "although a bit spicy."

"Yes, it is," Pierce agreed, pocketing the folded paper. "And spicy is exactly how I like it."

* * *

At 2:00 PM, Detective Schwartz had just finished a tuna fish sandwich at her desk. She took a sip of iced tea as she studied the additional crime scene photos that had come in, loving the sugar rush she got as it hit her system. She placed all the photos in sequential order around the room to get more of an in-time feeling of what the event had looked like while it was happening. Then she read the reports from the officers who were first on the scene and all the forensics reports that had come in. The angles. The trajectory. The way the body had been crushed and where it had been thrown, all pointed to a suicide. There were no witnesses, at least none that had come forward, and she knew that the chance of any witnesses at that hour was almost nil. Other than Elizabeth's entrance, at 3:20 AM, the closest turnstile fares recorded were at 2:08 AM and then again at 4:34 AM. But the turnstiles were the older, easy to jump type, so that didn't say much. Of course, there was no video footage of the platform since the cameras had been broken and gone unrepaired for years. Added to all that was the fact that the victim's cell phone was useless, having been run over by the train, so they needed to do everything via third party sources, which took longer and involved more headaches. And what did it mean that the victim used the turnstile at 3:20 AM and was dead at 3:23 AM? Did that point to a suicide or a crime? Schwartz wasn't sure.

Then there was the key. They had needed to send it to Reginald Davies, the curator of the American Wing at the Met to get proper dating. Mr. Davies had seemed excited about it and eager to help, so hopefully they would return a dating within a few days, but she knew "urgent" meant something very different to intellectuals than detectives working a hot case, so she wasn't holding her breath.

She was just finishing up the last report, when Matt McNally popped his head around the door.

"Hi, Detective," he called. "Got a minute?"

"For you, always," Detective Schwartz said with a smile. She liked Matt. Nice guy. Hard working. Funny.

A little yippee-skippee, but she liked that about him. There was no such thing as too much enthusiasm in her view. She thought he was a huge asset to the department and was still so pleased they had lured him away from LA.

"It's the Walker case. The guys dumped a bunch of evidence bags on my desk yesterday, and I'm just about finished with them. It took longer since it was mostly junk from the railbed—old nuts and screws, greasy dirt, random pens, food wrappers. You know, stuff like that. But then I found this."

He held a tiny electronic part in his palm and offered it to the detective. "I sent it to the new lab for dusting," Matt said. "Nothin' on it."

Detective Schwartz took the small piece in her hand and looked at it intently. "It looks like some kind of micro camera. Is that the lens?" she said pointing to a small part at the top. "Really damaged. And what's this hard plastic? Is it a metal fragment around part of it? Is it brown or black? I can't tell."

"Right," Matt said excitedly. "I wanted you to see it before we pulled it apart. There were some crushed pieces of glasses close to where this was found. Here," he said as he pulled a picture out of the stack he was carrying. "See? In this photo? It looks like a piece of these glasses. Same color, same material." He looked at Schwartz expectantly. "What do you think?"

The detective studied the tiny piece and the picture. "It could be." She nodded. "Do you have the rest of those glasses? Farfetched, but the color looks right, and it looks like the same material."

"The glasses weren't in any of the bags on my desk, but the guys are bringing the rest of the bags in an hour or so. The glasses should be in one of them. Here's the real kicker though," Matt said, delighted he had saved the best for last. "Elizabeth Walker wore glasses just like those."

Matt pulled some other pictures from his pile and showed Detective Schwartz close-up headshots of Elizabeth. "I blew these up so they're easier to see."

"Wow!" Schwartz said. "They really look the same. Great work, Matt! Let me know when you get the electronic piece pulled apart and when the glasses come in. This could be huge."

"I know, right? I have one more stop on the Upper West Side, then I'm going to head back over to the lab. The guys did a great job collecting. I'll tell them. They may really have found something."

"Yeah, thanks. I'll tell them too. One of the worst parts of this job, and they knocked it out of the park. You too," she said as Matt headed for the door.

"Thanks," Matt said. "I love this stuff."

"Me too." Schwartz called after him as he scurried down the hall. She grabbed the closest stack of reports and started thumbing through them looking for the victim index and photos. The index had no listing of eyeglasses on the person of Elizabeth Walker. And, as difficult as it was to look at the photos of the victim, she confirmed that it didn't appear as though Elizabeth was wearing any glasses in the photos either. She made a note in her interview books to ask Ralph Walker and Sarah Brockman whether Elizabeth wore glasses and add that to the warrant for the apartment.

Both theories made sense. Either Elizabeth was so emotionally disturbed that she took her own life or someone killed her by pushing her in front of the train. But what if there really was some kind of recording device embedded in her glasses? Either Elizabeth had installed the device herself to record things she wanted to record surreptitiously or someone else was doing the same thing. Both were plausible. The detective studied the close-up shots of Elizabeth's face and also those in profile. The glasses were tortoiseshell, an elongated square with metal designs in the front and on the arms. As small as the device was, it looked like it could be built into the arm and the recording lens then easily concealed in the front of the frame's metal design. She knew the spy business had only become more robust since the Cold War ended and significantly more so in the last few years. This installation should be an easy project for anyone in the spy world. She decided to make sure.

"Hi, Gavin," she said as he picked up the phone. "It's Deb. How are you?"

"Super. You?"

"Same. Great seeing you at the conference last week. I'm glad they're finally starting to do more interagency get togethers. So stupid to teach the same stuff over and over again just to different agencies."

"Yeah, no kidding. Plus, it's fun to share war stories. But did you hear Baker go on about the Nemmer bust? He's such a cocky SOB. I'm getting really sick of him."

"Yeah," Deb said. "I want to punch him every time I see him. But, you'll see, he'll get his. They always do. Do you have a minute? I have something to run by you."

"Yeah, sure, go ahead."

"I was wondering how small anyone is building cameras these days. And do they make a kind of reverse cone lens that would have a pin prick opening at the front and expand to the back to record?"

"Oh yeah, easy," Gavin said. "They've been doing that for years. You can hide them almost anywhere, providing you have just a little bit of space in the rear to build out the lens. It makes the cover lens almost impossible to see. There's still a tiny red light and a very slight humming noise, but that's it. They've been mainly using them for corporate surveillance, but that's because they're so expensive. Governments are mostly stuck with the larger, older models."

"Right," Deb said. "Thanks Gavin. Appreciate your help as always."

"My pleasure."

Detective Schwartz hung up and turned to the ticket stubs. The Museum of the City of New York was dated last Tuesday, and the Historical Society was Wednesday. She emailed her authentication documents to the police contacts at each location and then called the museum to see if she could get through. Ms. Laemle picked up on the first ring.

"Good afternoon, Ms. Laemle, this is Detective Schwartz at Manhattan, 20th Precinct. I just emailed my credentials."

"Yes, good afternoon, Detective Schwartz. I received them. I was expecting your call."

"Thank you. I was hoping to do this over the phone to save time, but let me know if you would prefer an in-person visit so you and the museum are comfortable."

"No, it's fine. I've been the police liaison for many years. I'm familiar with the process. Please proceed."

Detective Schwartz liked Ms. Laemle's laconic style immediately. "Thank you. What is the status of your video surveillance and public archive access?"

"The cameras are brand new and excellent. We were fortunate to receive a significant bequest two years ago for the 'museum's best purpose,' and we used it to completely redo the surveillance equipment. As you know, we've had a few thefts over the past five years. We'll do everything in our power to not have any more. There are cameras at the entrances, in the stacks, in the basement, on the grounds, and even in the staff areas, as it was thought that some of the thefts might have been engineered by insiders."

"That's terrific news. I need copies of the tapes from the last month, last week's being the most crucial. I'll send a subpoena over."

"Fine."

"Also, what about the stacks? The person we're investigating visited the museum last week. We're trying to find out why. We think she came for research versus visiting an employee or meeting someone at the museum, but don't know."

"That's more difficult," Ms. Laemle said. "The museum has been in the process of digitizing all the objects in our collection for preservation purposes and for ease of access. The ones that have been digitized are found in the Collections Portal. But there are many not yet digitized. They can be searched in the Archival Collections and with help from our Collections department."

"So, is there any record if someone just uses the Collections Portal to research objects?"

"No," Ms. Laemle said. "There will only be a record if they purchase a print or license an image using the portal."

"OK, thanks. I will add that to the subpoena," the detective said. "So, if someone visited the museum for research, what does that look like?"

"They would come into the museum if they couldn't find what they were looking for online in the Collections Portal. They would want to check the collections presently housed in the museum, so they would search the stacks and the exhibits. They might also send an email asking for further assistance from our research department or even make an appointment with one of our curators to help with research. We are a transparent organization tasked with not only preserving objects, but with helping people understand, celebrate, and interpret New York. We handle numerous requests for assistance every day."

"Are there records of any of this process?" Detective Schwartz asked.

"Yes. Any emails to the research department or curator appointments, of course, and if any document was removed from the stacks for further viewing, that would be logged in as well. We don't 'check-out' materials from the museum for personal use outside of the museum, but people can take them to private rooms for further study if they like."

"Thank you, Ms. Laemle. I'll add that to the subpoena as well."

"Of course."

"I also need a list of the employees who were at the museum on Tuesday, November 5th starting at 10:00 AM. I will send a plain clothes officer over later to interview any employees who might have seen her or helped her. She was quite striking looking. They might remember her, even if they didn't help her. Can you think of anything I'm missing? Is there any other process or technology utilized at the museum that would help us find out why she visited?"

"No," Ms. Laemle replied. "I can't think of anything else. I will check to see whether the employees who were here on November 5th are here today. If not, I will let you know."

"Thank you, I appreciate your help," Detective Schwartz said. "I will send the subpoena over as soon as I get it."

"My pleasure, Detective. I hope you find what you need."

Detective Schwartz replaced the receiver and found the stub for the Historical Society. Dated November 6th, it had a time stamp of 1:53 PM. She grabbed her coat. The Historical Society was on Central Park West, just a few blocks away, and she knew the fresh air would do her good. She arrived just as a large school tour was leaving and made her way to the Society director's office. The door was open, and Ms. Sullivan was enjoying a cup of tea.

"Hi, Doris," Detective Schwartz called out from the doorway. "Do you have a minute?"

"Hi, Deborah. Nice to see you. I just received your authentication email; I was hoping you had time to pop by. Care for some tea?" she asked, moving to the tea pot on the credenza.

"Oh yes, thank you," the detective replied. "It's cold today. A little warm tea will sure hit the spot."

"I couldn't agree more," Doris said pouring the tea. Schwartz once again noted the way the director moved. Like a gazelle. And she looked like one too—long and lean. Doris was twenty years her senior with long silver hair that she always kept neatly tucked up in a bun. She had been Division 1 in track and field in college and had almost made the Olympic team. The detective suspected Doris could still easily take her in a sprint or even walking up the stairs for that matter.

"We're investigating a woman who came here last Wednesday at 1:53 PM. We found the stub with that time stamp on it, but that's all we know. Here's the subpoena that basically covers everything we might need to review: video footage, digital and written documents, you know, the typical things."

"Thanks," Doris replied as she accepted the subpoena. "Who is it?"

Detective Schwartz didn't even bother to give the director the admonitions about nondisclosure in ongoing investigations since Ms. Sullivan most likely knew them by heart. Before becoming the director of the Historical Society, Doris had been a vice president at the Metropolitan Museum of Art and had handled all the higher-level security issues there. Although the Met was in a different precinct, Detective Schwartz had been brought in on occasion to handle overflow work concerning the Met, so they knew each other quite well and had become friends.

"It's Elizabeth Hamilton Walker," the detective said.

"Oh no," Doris said placing her teacup down with a clatter. "Is she OK?"

"Do you know her?" the detective asked.

"Oh yes, I do. Socially. I wouldn't call us friends, but we have run into each other fairly often at political or social events. She is a charming and cultured woman. Did you know she's the last of the Hamilton line?"

"No, I didn't. What does that mean?"

"Just that. She's it. If she doesn't have children, the line will die with her."

Which it just has, Schwartz thought. She wasn't sure why, but she decided not to tell Doris that Elizabeth was dead.

"I didn't know that. Thank you for telling me." Schwartz picked up her cup and took a long thoughtful sip.

"Elizabeth came here last Wednesday. Did you see her? Did she stop by to see you?"

"No," Doris said. "And that's unusual. She's come by the Historical Society frequently through the years, especially in the last few years since *Hamilton* hit Broadway. She was a source of some media coverage as a Hamilton descendant. Not a lot, she told me and more on the scholarly side, but interviewers would sometimes have angles that required a little research on her part. She never wanted to disappoint them, or anyone for that matter. She would always drop in and say hello to me though. I never knew her to come here and not stop in."

"Well, unfortunately, she didn't stop in last Wednesday."

"She's not in any trouble, is she?" Ms. Sullivan asked with a sideways glance at the detective. "I mean, why don't you just ask her?"

"No, she's not in any trouble with the law," Schwartz said truthfully. "We just want to investigate more quietly to, perhaps, flush out some evidence." The detective didn't really know what that meant, but it sounded good, and the director was ready to move on.

"I'll get the video recordings right away," she said. "But let me make a few quick searches in our database and see if she accessed any materials in the Klingenstein Library. You know patrons have to make appointments to view anything from there, and that's one of our largest holdings."

A few quick keystrokes later, Ms. Sullivan had the appointment records up on her screen, one of which was a 2:00 PM appointment made by Elizabeth.

"Yes, there it is. Brayden helped her. He will have logged in everything she looked at while in the library." Doris searched again and opened Brayden's file for that day.

"I will, of course, give you a printout of these entries, but it looks like she was reviewing all kinds of drawings and paintings with dates around 1790 to about 1804 and also looking for pictures and descriptions of places frequented by Manhattan's elite at that time. I see Fraunces

Tavern and The Bridge Cafe. Also a few other taverns close by. There's the Battery. There are searches for interior pictures of Hamilton's Grange and 122 William Street, which may have been Hamilton's former residence before he moved to The Grange. I recall it was in lower Manhattan and may have been on William Street. Also, pictures of the thirteen trees that Hamilton had planted at The Grange in honor of the thirteen original colonies. She also searched for any drawings or paintings of the Hamilton children. It looks like she found a few portraits of the older Hamilton children and a couple of drawings of them set at The Grange. Angelica, Alexander Jr. and James Alexander. Nothing of Philip though, probably because he died so young. It looks like she finished with a painstaking search for architectural drawings of The Grange, but I wish she'd asked Brayden about that and not wasted her time. There are no authenticated architectural plans of The Grange. She ended her search there, or at least paused it. There's no record of a follow up appointment and she finished twenty-five minutes before the library closed for the day, so she probably found what she was looking for."

"Is Brayden in today?" the detective asked. "Can he show me the materials Ms. Walker found?"

"Yes, he's in," Ms. Sullivan said. "And yes, he can find them easily."

The director made a call and within minutes, Detective Schwartz was seated in a private room adjacent to the Klingenstein Library looking at digitized documents and some actual documents and paintings. This part of an investigation always felt weird to the detective, like she was an invasive time traveler, going backward, some-times into very private places, to put together the "how" and the "why" of a crime. The "what" being typically obvious. But the objects were just as Doris had described, and there was nothing that struck her as significant. She made a note to check Elizabeth's calendar for any upcoming interviews in the hope that might yield some clues. Within an hour, she was on Central Park West winding her way back to the precinct, the unusually cold November wind swirling the fallen leaves on the stoops she passed by. Classic brownstones, over one hundred years old. Protected as historic landmarks, with their facades intact, they remained a tribute to that era. Many still had original outer doors, or convincing replicas. Some, she noted, even had locks that could fit a certain key with scrollwork designs.

6

I T WAS GETTING dark as Sarah stood up from her chair at her kitchen table and stretched. She had spent the entire day with the box. She had read every entry in the books, except the very last. She knew who had met and when. She knew when a new heir had been born into the society and when someone had passed away. She had read the usually brief entries for the quarterly meetings and the extended discussions when the United States was in crisis. Credit Mobilier Scandal, the Whiskey Ring, Tammany Hall, Gould & Fisk and Black Friday—they were all there. The Civil War, Trail of Tears, Internment Camps, McCarthyism, Watergate. Crises almost too numerous to mention. Stories of greed, deceit, fraud, and rapacious lusting for power. Over two hundred years of grasping, clawing, lying, and cheating by men who had lost their moral compass. Yet the United States had not lost hers. The institutions of government had continued to function. Hard questions were allowed. Voices, even when ugly, had retained a forum. A forum that was free, open, and exposed to the light of day. The rule of law had ultimately prevailed. In two hundred years, the society had considered acting to protect the United States and preserve her democracy in only a few situations in which the institutions of justice seemed to be floundering. Situations where the checks and balances didn't appear to be working, where individual corruption was smothering the process, where justice, liberty, and equality were battered, seemingly, beyond the point of return.

Sarah studied these times. Of all the terrible things that men had done, often in the name of righteousness, one had been closest to activating the purpose of the society. It wasn't the most obvious, but to the society, it was one of the three crises where action had been one vote away. She now understood why the Japanese internment camps had caused such grave consideration. One hundred and seventeen thousand mostly American citizens, jailed without evidence, without due process. In retrospect, almost uniformly agreed to be one of America's most atrocious violations of civil rights. But civil rights had been violated many times before in many different contexts. The difference here being that few questioned the method and all seemed to concur with the underlying assumption that the best way to prevent espionage in the United States was to incarcerate thousands of Japanese citizens, including children and the elderly or disabled, for years with the sole evidence being that they were at least one-sixteenth Japanese. It was a conspicuous, monumental product of racism that went unquestioned and unchallenged, at least until it was.

But as the society debated action, thin green shoots began to rise from the dry racist soil. The American people, who had been consumed and confused by fear and the horror of war, regained their feet and reclaimed their voice. They brought America back from the brink. They restored her moral compass. And the society stepped back.

Sarah was ready. She turned to the final entry. It was in Elizabeth's hand and dated two months prior. In a black pen, the script was thin and spidery. Some words so lightly drawn, they were almost invisible. It reminded Sarah of Alexander's script and those of his sons. It was as if Elizabeth was affirming her legacy:

> As the unhappy result of the death of Jessica Hamilton Madison two months ago, I am the remaining descendant of Alexander Hamilton and the sole member of this society.
>
> As an active member of this society for my entire adult life, I have watched carefully over the comings and goings of this country and its leaders. I have studied information from the society's monitoring systems, and I have immersed myself in media and content of every persuasion.
>
> I have been concerned about the direction of these United States for quite some time—about the increasing numbers of those who oppose human rights and human dignity, who disavow science, who increasingly plunder the earth's resources. A group who believes in divides and

polarities, instead of "United" States. A group that is growing.

The core has shifted. The moral compass of the United States is tilting, and I don't know if it's coming back.

Yet there is more that is sinister afoot. Something that threatens not only our moral fiber, but America itself.

In the year prior to her death, Jessica Hamilton Madison and I observed and discussed what appeared to be unusual financial patterns in the world market for gold. Someone was accumulating gold, and in massive quantities that could corner the world's negotiable gold. The buys were being done in such miniscule amounts that we were not sure if the Fed or the International Monetary Fund was aware of the aggregation. And, even if they were aware, it is not illegal to hold gold, even vast amounts of it.

Ms. Madison and I first noticed the gold trading patterns as a result of information gathered by the society's financial monitoring system. We then became aware of the extent of the gold aggregation when Ms. Madison was able to replicate some of the gold buy models and graph them by applying algorithms she had designed through her years in international banking and finance.

It became evident to us that there was a gold hoarder somewhere. It also became clear that the buys were coming from within the United States on behalf of someone outside. And that the buys were escalating. We didn't know why, and I still don't know, but I do know that a menacing threat is rising, looming over this country, and that I am filled with foreboding and alarm.

I look to the words tasked to this society by my beloved forefather Alexander Hamilton over two hundred years ago:

"You must use your voices to shout down those who seek to tear and destroy and when the forces become so strong as to rend the institutions of justice asunder, you must act swiftly with force and passion and purpose. You must rise up and crush those forces and redeem these United States."

Redeem these United States. This duty has fallen to me. Accordingly, and fully aware of the significance of this decision, I hereby activate the purpose of this society.

May God help me.

CHAPTER

7

September 8, 5:30 PM

ELIZABETH CLOSED THE logbook gently, fully aware that this might be her final entry. The last sentence twisting in her head. She never thought it would come to this, but time had run out.

She had to pick a successor.

A wistful smile crossed her lips as she thought about Ralph. Love had been evasive for her. Through the years, she had dated many men. Almost made it to the altar on two occasions, but at the last minute, knew they weren't right for her. She was waiting for true love, and it seemed that she couldn't settle for less.

She met Ralph through friends at a gender-reveal party. Handsome and well-built, he wasn't her usual type, preferring, as she did, more bookish academics. But something clicked. He was gentle and kind, funny and inquisitive, using his finance background as a gateway to bigger, more creative things in business. She liked his dog, and soon, she loved him.

They were married just eight months after meeting, knowing each other deeply, better than she had ever known anyone. The time with Ralph had been the best of her life. Still in the honeymoon phase, they spent most of their free moments together and alone, not wanting to bring others into their cocoon quite yet. Sarah was one of the few who had met Ralph, and the only one who knew they were trying to start a family.

When all this started, she felt her heart had been ripped from her chest.

Ralph. Kind, beyond measure. Gentle. Resourceful. But lacking the shark instinct, the steely edge that might be required. She knew he could do only part of what might need to be done.

Who else? Of all her friends and acquaintances, there was only one whom she thought had the strength and character.

Only Sarah.

Sarah was tough, fair, and loyal. Elizabeth admired how she volunteered her time to fight for the rights of the underrepresented and marginalized at the battered women shelters of New York City. Even at the bank, as institutional as they come, Sarah made her voice heard. She was often bloodied by the conflicts, but she never gave up and never gave in. She was a study in courage and conscience. Elizabeth wondered if her own intuition had brought them together, meeting so randomly at a museum fundraiser, somehow knowing that Sarah would be needed in the future. The reason why they had become friends so quickly and irrevocably.

But Sarah would need help too. Elizabeth thought about how hard it had been for her after Jessica died even though she had been part of the society her whole life. She wasn't sure Sarah could do it alone. She would need Ralph's resourcefulness and his creativity. She would also need his comfort and support when she was gone.

The best chance they had was together—fighting for America and helping each other through their inescapable grief.

She wiped the tears away and considered. She would throw them together. She would give them each pieces the other needed. They would need to come together to find the way.

But it was a terrible risk. What if it didn't work? Why do this to them anyway? Why put those she loved most in danger? For what?

To redeem these United States. Nothing less. If it came to this, Sarah and Ralph were her best chance to save America and the best way she had to care for them after she was gone.

It was time. She tore a piece of paper from her notepad and wrote to Sarah. Her signature, a heartbreaking scribble at the end, fulfilling her destiny in the only way she knew how.

And what would Alexander have thought about a successor not of the Hamilton line? Would he have faulted her for waiting so long for true love to knock at her door jeopardizing the possibility of an heir?

No, not Alexander. He who had lived a life defined and directed by passions, of all kinds. Love being one—both a blessing and a curse. He would have understood.

She opened the logbook one last time. Outlining the last sentence. Making it bold and raven black. Like the Elizabeth before her.

May God help me.

8

BODIE NEEDED TO go out for his evening walk. Ralph took the leash down from the hook and went to the closet for the box of extra dog bags. It wasn't in its usual place. Strange, Ralph thought. Elizabeth was fastidious about everything relating to Bodie. She always had back-up supplies for Bodie and always in the same place. He teased her about how she treated Bodie better than she treated him. He wiped his eyes with his sleeve and dug into the closet. He still couldn't find the box. Pulling his cell phone out of his pocket, he turned on the flashlight to reach the far recesses in the back. He finally saw it tucked under Bodie's old dog bed.

Ralph scooted in and grabbed the box. Pulling it into the light, he yanked the extra roll of bags out of the box, but there was something wrapped around it. Gingerly unrolling the scroll, Ralph stretched the paper flat and turned it over. It was a drawing, or most likely a copy, of a young woman seated at a small, antique piano or maybe a harpsichord, music on the stand, a handkerchief delicately dabbing at the corner of her eye. She was pretty, Ralph thought, but looked a little pensive and sad. She wore a long dress with a tightly fitting bodice. It reminded him of the pictures he had seen of revolutionary times, someone like Abigail Adams or Betsy Ross. It could be Abigail, he thought. The handkerchief had an "A" on it. But why had Elizabeth put it here? It was clear she had. They didn't have a dog walker, and no one else had access to their apartment excluding the superintendent, of course, in emergencies. It almost seemed to him that Elizabeth had put it there for him to find. And only him.

Bodie was pawing at the door now, so Ralph grabbed a bag and walked to the park, preoccupied with the drawing. He didn't know if it was some kind of clue to her death. He didn't know if he should call Detective Schwartz. He searched for her card, still in his pocket, but something didn't seem right. Elizabeth had clearly left that drawing for him. In a private place, where no one else would find it. He put the card away.

By this time, they had arrived at the dog run, and Bodie leapt joyfully into the fray. Ralph sat on a bench and watched. He didn't know what to do. But he knew he wanted to do something. He needed to know what happened to Elizabeth. Did she fall in front of the train? Did she kill herself? Was she pushed? It had all gotten surreal. He knew he wasn't thinking straight, but he knew he didn't want to tell the police about the drawing. Who could he trust? Sarah.

Sarah was the only person he could show the drawing to. He still didn't understand why Elizabeth had texted her right before she died, but she had. Elizabeth trusted Sarah. He would too.

Sarah picked up the call on the first ring. "Ralph?" she said. "How are you doing? I was just about to call you."

"Not good Sarah. I feel like I'm in a twilight zone. Everything is moving in slow motion. Like cartoon cars."

He sounded tired and forlorn. "Is there anyone with you?" Sarah asked.

"No," Ralph said. "Just Bodie. I sent my mom home. She was just getting more and more upset. I think I'm better off by myself."

"Where are you?" Sarah asked. "I'll come meet you."

"I'm at the dog run across from Hudson Beach. Bodie needed some exercise."

"Good. I'm home. I'll be there in twenty minutes."

"Why don't you come over?" Ralph asked. "I want to show you something."

"OK." Sarah hung up and started getting ready to go. She put the notebooks and handkerchief back in the box, closed it, and put it high in her bedroom closet. She didn't know why she felt like she had to hide it, but she did.

It was almost dark. She walked into the hubbub of the city at dusk. People scurrying from work, racing to catch trains home. People with families to see, children to hug. She looked at them but didn't see them. She was still absorbed in another time. She could imagine figures huddled around a table. Candles flickering, voices subdued, inkwells, quill pens, and papers strewn about.

Men and women shoulder to shoulder talking quietly about justice, equality, and liberty. Embracing the task entrusted to them by Alexander, wherever it led.

* * *

Sarah arrived just as Ralph and Bodie entered the lobby. Bodie barked happily and ran over to greet her. She rubbed Bodie's favorite spot right behind his ears as he thumped his tail madly and rolled over on his back for more. Sarah scratched him a few times then gave Ralph a hug as they walked to the elevator.

"Cold for November," Sarah said, feeling awkward. "I think it's supposed to snow tomorrow."

"Yes," Ralph said absently.

Sarah tried not to stare at Ralph's transformation. In less than forty-eight hours, he had gone from handsome to haggard. She was sure she must look the same. Death can do that. She kept her eyes down in the elevator not wanting to catch his gaze.

"I was looking for extra dog bags right before taking Bodie out and the extra bags weren't where they usually are," Ralph started as soon as they were seated. "You know Elizabeth was a fanatic when it came to Bodie, right? She always had extra supplies, and everything organized. Well, I couldn't find the extra dog bag box, and used my flashlight to dig around in the closet until I found it. This was wrapped around the roll."

Ralph carefully pulled out the drawing from between books where he had been trying to flatten it.

Sarah took the drawing carefully in her hands. The paper was new, so it was clearly a copy. It looked like a drawing set in revolutionary times. It reminded her of paintings and drawings at the Met, in the American Wing. It was a simple scene of a young woman, seated at a pianoforte, whose practice or performance had just been interrupted for capture in the drawing. She was clearly of an upper social station. Her dress was fine, and she displayed a delicately embroidered handkerchief demurely dabbing her eye.

"It's a beautiful drawing," Sarah said. "Quite period."

"Yes, I know. It looks like Revolutionary times. I've seen pictures of Martha Washington, and it doesn't look like her but maybe Betsy Ross or Abigail Adams. It could be Abigail Adams. Do you see the handkerchief?"

She looked closely. It seemed so familiar. She brought the drawing into the kitchen where the light was better. She could now see what the embroidery was in the middle. It was a large, carnation colored "A." She gasped.

"What's wrong?" Ralph asked, rushing in.

"I have this handkerchief! This exact handkerchief. It was in a box I was just going through from Elizabeth. It was delivered to me this morning. I've spent the whole day reading everything in it." She stopped short when she saw Ralph's face.

"What do you mean a box from Elizabeth?" he asked, his face screwed up in pain. "Why did she send you a box? Why not me? What was in the box?"

Sarah realized what she had done. She hadn't really decided anything about the box other than not to show it to the police just yet. She hadn't decided to share the box or even acknowledge its existence, but she had just done both. She looked at Ralph. What did she know about Ralph? Not much. Just that Elizabeth loved him enough to marry him and that Elizabeth trusted him enough to lead him to this drawing. She had also trusted him enough that she used the last second of her life to text Sarah to call him. Maybe this was her way of bringing them together. In trust. Each of them having a piece of the puzzle the other needed.

"OK," Sarah said. "Sit down for a minute while I tell you about it and then we'll go back to my apartment, and I'll show you what I'm talking about."

They sat for a few minutes while Sarah gave Ralph a thumbnail sketch of the contents of the box and how she came to receive it. Ralph, although still upset that he hadn't been entrusted with the box, brightened when Sarah pointed out that Elizabeth had entrusted him with the drawing. In twenty-five minutes, they were back at Sarah's apartment seated around the table.

"It looks so beat up," Ralph said. "Elizabeth must have carted this box around with her for quite some time. I wonder why I never saw it in the apartment."

"She probably kept it in a bank safe or some other secure location. She wouldn't risk having it destroyed in a fire or somehow stolen."

"Yes, that's true and then she probably just delivered it to her lawyer."

Sarah guided Ralph through the box, showing him the separate books and letters. She showed him the handkerchief, which they compared to the drawing. It was obviously the same.

It was getting late, and they were both bleary eyed. They decided to call it a day and revisit in the morning.

Ralph held the handkerchief gently in his hand. "It's so beautiful," he said. "Exquisite. Every stitch is perfect. Hard to see how any human could make such a thing."

"I know," Sarah said. "Divine, like an angel made it."

Like an angel made it, Ralph thought as he made his way down the stairs, gripping the banister tightly, not trusting his legs to navigate the steps. He felt the whoosh of the outer door slam behind him as he entered the street. At 11:00 PM, the post-theater crowd was starting to thin. Clusters of people were winding their way to the subways and cabs. Couples were tenderly saying goodnight. He paused for a moment to drink in the cold, damp November air. He had never been so exhausted, drained to his core. He was so tired he didn't see a man, big and bulky, sitting on the stoop next door. He was so tired he didn't see another man hail a cab right behind his cab.

As the cabs pulled away, the man on the stoop pulled his collar up and his hat down, bracing against the cold night air, settling in to wait. He took off his right glove, tucked his hand deep into his pocket and found the two metal balls, surprisingly cold, the steel hard and familiar. He started rolling them, this way and that, turning them over and over again in his pocket. The sharp angular cut he had made in one of the balls caught his skin as he rolled it, tearing his skin just enough. Every cut calming him, soothing him, bringing him back from the edge. He left when her light turned off, and made his way back uptown to a small, dark, underground apartment on the Hudson, stopping at the corner bodega for two large pepperoni pizzas on the way. Even after months, the blackness of the apartment still unnerved him. Without windows, it had a thick, gluey feel to it that overwhelmed and unsettled him the moment he walked in. He often tried to secretly coordinate his return time with the others so that he wasn't the first one back, but with this contract, it was frequently impossible. Tonight though, every piece of surveillance equipment was up and running and the blinking lights and occasional muted beeps pushed the disquiet from his mind.

He lit up another cigarette and sat down to watch. The targets were still in their apartment buildings and the street traffic was dwindling. This was all the information they had, but it had to be enough for now. He couldn't let that huge mistake gnaw at him anymore. It was his fault they were so far behind in surveillance installation and everyone knew it. He had one more chance to redeem himself, just one more, and he had to get it right. He cracked open the pizza box and pulled a slice. He could hear the others coming down the outside stairs to the apartment.

"Good evening, *Team Leader*," Yugov said with a sneer. "Were you able to keep track of your target, or did you let that one slip through your fingers too?" Such insolence, Dmitri thought. He knew he had lost all credibility with his team after the mistake and, most notably, with Yugov, who had been there on the subway platform that night. They had been watching the feed all day. They had seen Elizabeth retrieve the key and put it in her coat pocket. Yugov had arrived first at the subway station and had wanted to just shoot her with his silencer and get the key, but he had said no. He thought they could corner her on the platform and force her to not only hand over the key but tell them any information she had about the trove to save her own life. He never thought she would jump. The consequences of this spectacular misjudgment had been dire. Everything blew up. The cops were in, the Metro Transit Authority, maybe even the FBI, and all were investigating. The profile of what had been a small, almost private surveillance operation had fully exploded.

"Enough!" Dmitri said gruffly. "Get some pizza. Viktor, make sure you are on Pierce by 6:00 AM tomorrow. He's got an early morning."

Viktor nodded and made his way to the pizza box. Yugov still had that infuriating smirk on his face. Dmitri wanted to reach over and slap it off but forced himself to turn back to the monitors. The streets were quiet, the targets, hopefully, in for the night.

9

A T 8:00 AM, Pierce had already arrived at the testing site. He was as prepared as anyone could be, ready to complete this technicality and continue his climb up New York's financial ladder. Finally, it was "go time"— time to enter the examination room. He eyed the other aspirants sitting in the cubicles, each in front of a testing center computer. Some looked scared, some bold, and some even drowsy, but none had the focused energy he had. He was ready.

He sat down in his appointed cubicle, checked his computer's functionality with the tutorial presentation and waited for the proctor to commence the exam. When he did, Pierce was off. Breezing through the first eleven questions, he knew all the material, was sure of the correct answers. He was on a roll.

But just as he thought that, he felt a familiar niggling in the back of his mind. He started getting anxious. He could feel tension creeping into his neck, his palms starting to sweat. His mouth became instantly dry. His mind, crystal clear a few moments before, started scampering all over his brain. It was happening again. He looked at the screen. He could hardly focus long enough to read the question, let alone figure out an answer. He started to panic. Sweat that had beaded on his forehead now began the long trickle downwards. He thought he might pass out. He got up and stumbled to the proctor at the front of the room.

"Restroom. May I use the restroom?" Pierce squeaked.

The proctor eyed him suspiciously. Only twenty minutes into the exam, and he wanted to use the bathroom? But the restrooms were secure and there was another proctor stationed outside.

"Of course," the proctor said magnanimously as he waived toward the exit. "It's right down the hall."

Pierce made it to the bathroom and into the closest stall, his legs collapsing as he hit the seat. His head was spinning. He gripped the walls as a wave of nausea washed over him. He began to gulp air, hoping the oxygen would somehow revive him but knowing, from experience, that it wouldn't. He started to sob uncontrollably. His entire future rested on this one test. This one stupid test. He had always had problems with testing. No one had ever been sure if it was a form of anxiety disorder, but it had haunted him throughout school and now into his professional life. He had dealt with it as he dealt with most things, with unwavering persistence and focus, like the Wall Street bull. He had always done what he needed to do to get what he wanted, and he wouldn't let what he viewed as "technicalities" stand in his way. Cajole, manipulate, bribe, even cheat. It was all fair game for him. But this test was getting the better of him.

At last, the nausea passed. His sobbing subsided, and his mind began to clear. He stood up. His legs still felt a bit wobbly, but he could handle that. He splashed water on his face and started to feel better. He had no idea how much time had passed, but suspected it was about fifteen minutes. Although that much time would be difficult to make up with a test of this difficulty and length, he thought he could do it. After all, he probably knew the material better than most people in that room since he'd already been through the test before. His mind raced back to that terrible time. Same test, same complete breakdown. He had run from the room and ended up at one of Wall Street's favorite bars. A testament to poor judgment as he might run into someone he knew, but it was early and just a few patrons were there. One being Timothy. He had often thought that, perhaps, the test incident was pure providence since he did meet Timothy, a man he never would have met in any other circumstance.

He had taken a seat at the bar with open seats in either direction. Timothy had been the closest on his right. They were both drinking a particular blend of whiskey, currently favored on the Street and in financial branches of the government, and it was natural that they struck up a conversation.

They were both glum. Pierce due to the exam and Timothy due to difficulties at work. But after a few more whiskeys, their troubles were far behind them, and they were the best of chums. They lambasted the financial system and plotted its just overhaul. They revised the compensation structure for themselves and other tireless peons in their industries, and they considered the macro and micro financial structure of the world. Timothy seemed particularly keen to understand Pierce's view of the world and his place in it. Pierce was delighted to share his grandiose plans for his future and his own Machiavellian bent for achieving them. Timothy was delighted.

At the end of the evening, they had exchanged contact information and, within weeks, had seen each other three or four times. They became confidants and friends. They were both dissatisfied with where they were in life and in their careers. They had a lot in common.

Yet here Pierce was again. He shook those thoughts from his mind and squared his shoulders. He was ready to go at it once more. He emerged from the bathroom and walked briskly down the hall. He would look quickly at the clock upon reentering the testing room and make a plan for finishing the exam. He expected it would be 10:35 AM or 10:40 AM at the very latest. Plenty of time to finish the 125 questions in the three hours, forty-five minutes allowed.

He opened the door. Everything seemed strange. A few test-takers looked up from their cubicles, the proctor seemed surprised. It felt like he was in some kind of time warp. Pierce looked at the clock. It said 11:50 AM, but it couldn't be. His eyes must still be clouded. He looked again. 11:51 AM. 11:51 AM! That would mean he had been in the bathroom for over an hour instead of fifteen minutes! No one could make up an hour on this test. No one.

The clock must be wrong. He made his way to the proctor.

"Excuse me, it appears as though the clock is wrong. Can you tell me what is the correct time?"

The proctor, so highly suspicious before, seemed to bend and soften a little.

"That is the correct time, sir. It is 11:51 AM."

Without a word, Pierce withdrew his locker key from his pants pocket, reclaimed his cell phone and wallet, and walked out the door.

10

DETECTIVE SCHWARTZ HAD just returned to her office after the morning's precinct meeting when Matt popped his head around the door.

"Hi, Detective. Sorry I didn't call ahead, but I knew you'd want to see this ASAP," Matt said as he walked in and placed an evidence box on her desk. "It's the Walker case."

"I figured. Nice to see you. Coffee?"

"I'm good, probably had too much already. Let me show you what we found," Matt said as he took the lid off the box. "The guys brought in the last of the evidence bags from the railbed and then went back and did an even more thorough scrub. They found the rest of the glasses," Matt said excitedly.

"Look, here," he said, withdrawing the glasses from the box. The majority of the pieces of the glasses had been carefully reassembled, leaving only a few missing parts around the bridge.

"Do you see this tiny hole?" Matt said, pointing to the left arm. "This is where the camera fits in." He sat down, took a tiny electronic piece out of a small, cushioned box with tweezers and placed it in the hole.

"See?" he said. "It fits perfectly. We were right."

"Oh, yes!" the detective said, pulling out her magnifying glass to get a better look. "Yes, you're absolutely right. It fits perfectly. I've never seen anything like this in person. Just in some of the surveillance training classes we've had. It's really something."

"I know, right?" Matt said.

"Do we know for sure they're Elizabeth's glasses?" the detective continued.

"I think so. I'd give it about a ninety-nine percent chance that they're hers," Matt said. "I found a lot more pictures online. She was a bit of a celebrity, you know. Plus, I'm sure we can get some better pictures from the family. But look at these," Matt said as he held out the pictures to Schwartz.

"Yes, they sure look like hers. Pretty unique glasses too. Not cheap. Yeah, I think they're hers. We'll run the DNA of course, but all the grease and industrial chemicals on the railbed might have degraded it so I'll go ahead and get some pictures from the family as well. Even without though, I feel pretty good with a "yes" right now."

"Me too. So what does that mean?" Matt asked. "Why would she have a camera in her glasses?"

"I don't know," the detective replied. "I don't know. Really weird. Did you get any kind of make on the camera? Any idea where it came from?"

"No. No markings on the electronics. I have a call into my CIA buddy to follow up again, but all he said originally was that these kinds of mini electronics are generally made in China and sold all over the world. I don't think we're going to get much more than that."

"Gotcha'" Schwartz said. "Thank you so much, Matt. You did an amazing job and quickly. I think I'll keep the box here if that's all right with you. I may want to run the glasses by the family and see what they know."

"Absolutely, Detective. I'm off. I'll be back at the lab in an hour if you need me," he said as he darted out the door.

Detective Schwartz sat back in her chair, studying the glasses. Pretty ingenious way to record things without anyone knowing. But was it Elizabeth wanting to record things she was seeing surreptitiously or someone else wanting to do the same thing?

The detective made a mental note to look for video feed on Elizabeth's computer. That was the weaker choice in her mind. It was more likely that someone wanted to record what Elizabeth was seeing, what Elizabeth was doing. But that would be hard. Attaching a camera to a shoe or coat button was relatively easy but getting a miniature camera in a pair of glasses was something quite different.

Since the camera was built into the glasses, the only way anyone could have done that would be to switch the old glasses for a new pair that had the camera inside. Really tough. The logistics were overwhelming. It seemed almost fanciful, Schwartz thought. Who would be able to pull that off?

Only someone with a real need to do it, the detective decided. And someone with a lot of capital. These mini electronics were expensive, not to mention the new pair of glasses and correct prescription. Tough, really tough.

She decided to check in with Mr. Davies at the Met to see if he'd learned anything about the key. He picked up on the first ring.

"Oh hello, Detective Schwartz. Nice to hear from you," the curator said.

"Sorry to trouble you, Mr. Davies. I was just wondering if you had learned anything about the key I sent you the other day?"

"Oh, yes. I did," he replied. "Sorry, I didn't get back to you yesterday. I felt a little chill coming on so I thought it best to spend the day in bed."

Detective Schwartz decided to hide her irritation at the delay and move on. "Not a problem," she said quickly. "What did you find out?"

"Well," Mr. Davies said. "It seems to be a steel key with the most likely dating being the early 1800s. The steel keys were thought to be the best and most durable keys of the day. To me, it looks like a product of the Bethlehem, Pennsylvania, locksmiths but my esteemed assistant thinks it was made in Boston by Day & Newell, famous at the time for designing specialty keys and locks that were virtually unpickable. You might recall the Bramah Safety Lock challenge? Well, A.C. Hobbs, from Day, was the one to pick it. But I digress. It's definitely late 1700s, early 1800s. I'm going to go with Bethlehem because some of their scrollwork designs on the bows look similar and the heavy weighting is also more like Bethlehem."

"Thank you," the detective said. "Quite a thorough analysis. The police department thanks you, and I am especially appreciative."

"Anytime," said the curator. "I enjoyed the process. Rather cloak-and-dagger, you know? I felt a wee bit like Sherlock Holmes. Not so dry as my usual day."

"Oh, I almost forgot, do you think it has any value just as a key or is the value what it might open?"

"A fine question," Mr. Davies said. "Values can range all over the board depending on quality and rarity, but generally fall between $800 to $1,000. I would value this one at about $1,000. It isn't that rare. There are still many steel keys of this vintage circulating in the world. The only thing that makes it more unique is the scroll-work design on the bow, which is a bit unusual and beautiful, which also counts with collectors. That's why I'm inclined to give it the higher $1,000 estimate."

"Well, thanks again Mr. Davies. I appreciate your help," Detective Schwartz said.

She finished entering her notes and considered what she had just heard. Elizabeth probably wasn't carrying around the key for its value. She must have been searching for the lock that fit it, which made this a classic case of trying to find a needle in a haystack. So many locks that it might fit in New York alone. Manhattan, Brooklyn—all the boroughs had locks that might fit this key.

Was that what Elizabeth was looking for at the museums? The lock? Was she looking at old pictures and drawings trying to find the lock? Farfetched was putting it mildly. Then what was she looking for in the drawings? She took another sip of coffee just as the phone rang.

"Good morning, Ms. Laemle. Thank you for acting on the subpoena right away. I sent it as soon as I received it, but it was still a bit late last night."

"Not a problem at all, Detective," Ms. Laemle replied. "We were already able to access the video tapes, and we also found an online purchase of a drawing that is responsive to your subpoena. My colleagues are working on the other matters contained in the subpoena."

Schwartz could barely hide her excitement. "Are you able to email me an image of the drawing that was purchased? I'll be over shortly to look at the surveillance, but I would love to take a quick look at the drawing if you can email it."

"Oh yes, no problem. It will be in your inbox in just a minute. What time can we expect you?"

"In about an hour, give or take. Thanks so much. I'll see you soon."

Detective Schwartz saw the email come in. She opened the attachment to see a drawing of a young woman, seated at a small, antique piano, music on the stand, a dainty shoe extended beyond an elegant long dress with a handkerchief delicately dabbing an eye. Looks like the Revolutionary period, she thought. It could be Martha Washington or one of the founding mothers in her youth. Someone with the initial "A" she concluded, noticing the handkerchief. But there was no lock or key in the drawing, or any door for that matter.

She had no idea why Elizabeth would have wanted a copy of this drawing.

A few more emails were coming in from Ms. Laemle containing background information and the description. It was a picture of Angelica Hamilton at her pianoforte, dated 1800, by Matthew Harris Jouett. Well, of course, that would make sense. Doris said that Elizabeth regularly visited the museum to research requests by the media. A reporter had, most likely, inquired about Angelica as part of some kind of article about the Hamilton family and Elizabeth had added a picture to the mix. The detective felt her enthusiasm evaporate just as quickly as it had appeared. Nothing sinister or even interesting there. She closed her computer and put on her coat. She would head over to the museum and see what else they had found and then, probably, head over to the husband's apartment. At least she might be able to confirm the glasses.

"**Y**EAH, HE HAD a complete melt down again," Timothy said. It was cold and blustery, and Timothy had to cup his hand over his iPhone's microphone so he could be heard. "I agree," he continued. "I think it's a good thing. It just makes his commitment to us stronger since he won't be able to move up the ladder by the more usual means. I gotta say though, I feel sorry for him. It's got to be crushing. I mean, he knows the material like the back of his hand. After his first flameout, he told me it's some kind of hereditary thing. Like his whole family has it. Once in a while it skips a generation, but then comes back. They can trace it in his family line all the way back to the 1800s although they just called it a mental weakness then. Personally, I think it's more along the lines of an anxiety disorder."

"Have you seen him or talked to him?"

"No, he just texted 'Flameout' at about noon yesterday. I figured I'd give him a little time to freak out and do what he needed to do. I'm on my way over there now to make sure he's OK."

"Good," came the reply. "You can help him refocus on the prize at hand. Do you think the bank will fire him though? That would be problematic."

"No," Timothy said. "They really love him. He's such a suck-up. He got invited to McArthur's Christmas party last year and he's got a town car. I think he's safe for a while. Don't know what will happen when he flunks Series 7 again though. Everyone's got their limits."

"Luckily, we don't have to care about that."

"Right. Good thing." Timothy hung up and continued his cold walk to the subway. Still quicker than a cab at this time of day, he thought, but frickin' freezing.

*　*　*

He should have taken a cab. Pierce was nowhere close to being home. In truth, he wasn't close to being sober. He knew all the best spots in the city, all the tony spots, all the places the beautiful, powerful people went. He had been to some, aspired to all, but was about as far away from those places as anyone could be. He had gone home to his old neighborhood. Back to the tiny, wood clapboard row houses on Staten Island. Where he was raised, to the place he grew up. Back to the bar he knew best.

He was there drinking by 2:00 PM yesterday and still drinking at 10:00 AM today. Friends had come, stayed, gone home. New friends had come, stayed, gone home. He had slept for a few hours in the booths. He had told his troubles and listened to troubles. He was waiting for his father.

"Hi, Pierce," his dad said, taking a seat next to him in the booth. "I'm sorry it took me so long to get here. I was driving the turnpike."

"Thank you for coming," Pierce said, grabbing his father in a strong bear hug, tears flowing down his cheeks. "I'm sorry I'm such a mess. I'm sorry."

Mike looked at his son carefully, up and down, taking in all the disarray and all the anguish. He had never really understood the things Pierce wanted, which were so different from what he himself wanted now, but he could remember back to a time when he had wanted something different too, back when he thought it was possible.

"Did it happen again?" his father asked gently.

"Yes," Pierce said, his eyes welling up with new tears. "All the prescriptions, psychotherapy, acupuncture, nothing helped. I only made it twenty minutes before it was all over. I don't think I'm ever going to make it. I don't think I'm ever going to get through this."

He was curled up next to his father, looking every bit like the four-year old child his father remembered when the anxiety disorder first appeared. It was in the spring. He was reading the Sunday paper at the kitchen table, and Pierce was on the living room floor building a Duplo Lego set. It was quiet in the living room for some time, and he went in only to find Pierce frozen, staring at the picture on the box, a Duplo block in his hand. Pierce was sweating and seemed to be having trouble breathing. Mike raced over to him to see if something was stuck in his airway, if he was choking, but he was just frozen. Unable to move forward or backward, stuck in the stress of the project. Mike gently removed the block from his hand and tried to gather him in a hug, but Pierce was rigid, as if his limbs were frozen too. Tenderly, he laid him down on the floor, put his head on a pillow, and covered him with a blanket. He sat with him for over an hour, not saying a word.

At last, Pierce began to emerge from his stupor. He sat up and smiled. He asked for water. It was as if nothing had happened except that he refused to pick up a Duplo block ever again.

And that was just the beginning. Mike had prayed since the moment he knew he was having a child that it would skip Pierce. He, himself, had it so bad that it had kept him out of college, crushed his dream of becoming an economist, and thrust him into life as a truck driver.

But it didn't skip Pierce; it hit him particularly hard. He suffered all through school, while his dad took him to one doctor after another trying different prescriptions, behavioral therapy, psychotherapy, even meditation and diet, but nothing worked. Pierce found ways to trick it in certain circumstances, and he would even cheat when he needed to get through. The cheating didn't bother him. He justified it by studying hard, by knowing the material as well or better than any "A" student. Pierce's situation was even more heartbreaking for Mike than his own had been because Pierce wanted so much. From an early age, he had loved finance, statistics, numbers of every kind. He wanted to be a banker. He didn't want to give up like his dad had done. He wanted to succeed, and he wanted to succeed wildly.

Mike stayed next to his son, holding him, comforting him, wiping the tears from his eyes and his own, not saying a word.

Pierce eventually fell asleep, curled up in the booth, his head resting in Mike's lap—all the pain from the last few days temporarily forgotten. Mike thought about the wasted hours and the wasted money spent trying to find a cure, or at least a work-around, and that was just in his lifetime. His mother, himself, Pierce—it hadn't skipped a generation for a while. In fact, it seemed to be getting stronger with even more pronounced effects later in life. His mother had become increasingly anxious in her last years. First, she had stopped driving, then she stopped going out of the house. She stopped seeing her friends or any people for that matter other than him. She stopped reading the newspapers, stopped watching TV. She kept shrinking her world, smaller and smaller, until, in the end, she lived only in her bedroom and bathroom with prepared meals coming through a hewed-out hole in the door, which she then covered quickly with an old pillowcase. He was afraid that would happen to him and was afraid that something even worse would happen to Pierce.

Mike had decided to continue the work he had been doing. Clearly, there was a genetic aspect to it. He felt that if he could just look backward far enough into his family history and put the pieces together, he would be able to cure his family and eradicate the family curse, and the shame of it, forever. He thought back to the first recorded reference of the disorder in the family. It was in the early 1800s. Much reference was made in letters and diary entries to a pervasive "restlessness and irritability."

Could symptoms of anxiety be described as "restlessness and irritability" by those of another generation? Perhaps, or perhaps the disorder had changed into more of an anxiety disorder over time. Was the disorder responsible for the "untrustworthy" and "unprincipled" epithet that had dogged the family for over two hundred years? Tarnishing the family name, and all those who carried it? He was, once again, overwhelmed by the breadth of the task before him. But maybe he didn't need to do the historical, forensic research. The thought appeared in his mind beaming like a star of hope. Maybe the best key was right before him, in himself and in Pierce. Maybe a DNA analysis of each, that they could compare to both, would provide the missing link and open the door to salvation. He shifted in his seat excitedly, inadvertently jostling Pierce awake.

"Hi, Dad," he said.

"Hi, Son," Mike said giving Pierce a hug. "I just had a thought that might help us. They do so much with DNA these days and one thing we know is that this is a genetic issue. Maybe we could have our DNA tested and see if there is anything that comes up. Maybe there is some kind of peculiarity that could be treated. Since Mom passed, it's just us, but it *is* just us. Two of us, different generations. Worth a try. What do you think?"

"Yes, I think it's a great idea," Pierce said excitedly. "We're in New York City after all, we should be able to find somebody who is working in this area."

"I don't know why we didn't think of this before. I guess we were just so focused on trying to cure the symptoms, rather than go to the cause. But with all this genealogical stuff they're doing now, there's a lot of activity in this field."

"I know," Pierce said. "Most of it is just genealogical tracking, but I bet there's a lot more money going to DNA research labs as a result. I have another day off from work that I was going to use to celebrate, but now I guess I can use it to, hopefully, find us some help."

"Sounds great to me," Mike said. My computer is pretty good, and my hook up is fast. I have two days off until my next trip. Do you want to come home and work? Maybe we could work together."

Pierce looked at his dad. His beautiful, smart, kind, loving dad. There was nothing he'd rather do. "Thank you," he said. "I would love to."

An enormous smile spread across Mike's face as he gave Pierce a huge hug. "Super! Let's get some breakfast and get you cleaned up a bit and then dig in."

"Coffee."

"Lots of coffee."

* * *

Timothy had been waiting in the lobby of Pierce's apartment building for over two hours. He'd had the doorman call up twice in the hope that Pierce was still asleep, but now it was becoming quite clear that Pierce wasn't home. From the extensive background checks they'd done, Timothy knew Pierce didn't have a significant other, or others, so it was unlikely he spent the night with a friend. It was also unlikely that Pierce had already gone out, but since he wasn't picking up Timothy's calls, anything was possible. It might have been a mistake, he thought, not going over last night right after the flame-out. Maybe Pierce really did have a meltdown. Maybe he was hurt or in trouble. Timothy grimaced at the thought.

"Sir . . . sir?" asked the doorman finally getting Timothy's attention. "Is there anything else you would like me to do for you?"

Timothy understood doorman-speak and quickly gathered his coat and gloves. "No, thank you. I appreciate your patience. I'll try back another time," he said as he stood up and moved toward the door.

Where was he? Timothy was getting anxious. Maybe he really had screwed up by not going over last night. His phone rang again. Same number. He decided he better pick up.

"Yes, hello. No, I'm sorry, I had my phone in my briefcase and didn't hear it," he lied. "No, I haven't talked to him yet. I expect he's running errands or at the gym. No, I don't think there's a problem. And, even if there was, we're just one buy away, we would hobble through somehow."

"Hobble through somehow? Hardly," came the icy reply. "Pierce is perfectly situated. He does what he's told, and he keeps his mouth shut. He sees his shot at redemption, not just for himself, but for his family, and he's going to get it. Your job is to keep him doing what he's doing. There's no 'hobble' about it. Understood?"

"Understood," Timothy said as the line went dead. What a jerk. He really hated that guy, but it wasn't too much longer. And it would be worth it. He would be set for life. He decided to check in and get the status on the accounting.

"Hi, Macky, it's Timothy. Thanks for picking up. I just wanted to check in with you and see how the accounting is going and that it's still within the parameters we were expecting. I know you're wrapping up today. You haven't found any large, previously unknown, bins of gold, have you? I just don't want any surprises."

"Oh, yeah, hi, Timothy. Don't worry. No big bins of gold. I can't believe how much work this is. You know there really hasn't been an audit at Fort Knox since 1953? And all this business with the vaults, sealed compartments, and permanent seals that somehow aren't. It's a nightmare. Just getting into every storage container has been the problem. Not actually counting the gold since there isn't a whole lot. We're not going to get to the exact amount, but we will be able to come close. Close enough for government work. Ha, ha! Get it?"

"Yeah, Macky. Super funny. We don't need complete accuracy, just not too far off. I know you haven't had the time or team to do an official audit. We just wanted to know as specifically as possible how much actual gold is in the depositories. The Denver Mint and West Point have reported in. You're the last. But before you yell, I know you're the biggest so just finish today and you're golden."

"Funny, Timothy. Will do."

"Keep up the good work, Macky. Chat in a few."

"Over and out."

* * *

Timothy. Pierce had forgotten all about Timothy. He looked at his phone—texts, calls, voice messages. Timothy must be worried sick that he couldn't find him.

"Timothy? Hi, I'm so sorry I didn't call." Pierce could hear the relief on the other end of the line. "I had a few drinks. I felt so bad about it all. And then I had a few more, and some more, and before I knew it, it was this morning. I'm really sorry."

And he meant it. He and Timothy were good friends. They had bonded over basic life troubles, but then advanced into a deep friendship, based on mutual respect and trust. Nevertheless, when Timothy came to Pierce with a seemingly incredible request, Pierce looked at it carefully, at a distance, and with his eyes wide open.

It was about four months into their relationship. They had spent so much time together and knew each other so well that Pierce felt Timothy was the brother he never had. Timothy certainly seemed to feel the same. He was also an only child. On occasion, Pierce felt his own emotional floodgates open as Timothy shared personal things about growing up that he had never been able to share with a brother. It was an unexpectedly intimate relationship to form in adult life, and Pierce was grateful for it.

They had returned to Pierce's apartment after a particularly challenging tennis match. A few beers and burrito bowls later, Timothy turned to Pierce.

"I have something I want you to consider," he said. Timothy had put down his beer and was staring right at Pierce.

"You want another doubles partner?" Pierce joked uncomfortably as he turned to face a serious Timothy.

"Look," Timothy said. "You know I've been in Treasury a long time. Almost made it to the top. And you know, through the years, I've made some friends, a few enemies, but mostly friends, and I guess folks there think I'm trustworthy and can keep a secret because that's what they asked me to do."

Pierce was over his discomfort and was listening intently, his untasted beer warming in his hand.

Timothy continued. "What I'm going to tell you isn't illegal, but it is privileged, and it is private. I probably should have you sign an NDA, but I have the call on that, and I don't think it's necessary." Timothy looked at Pierce for confirmation and Pierce nodded "yes."

"Do you know anything about the Treasury's gold reserves, Pierce?" Timothy asked.

"Not much. I probably should know more, being in banking and all, but I know that the government has vast amounts of gold bars in Fort Knox, and other places, I'm sure. From what you just said, I guess they're held by the U.S. Treasury."

"Yes, that's right insofar as the government holds gold reserves in the name of the U.S. Treasury and the reserves are held in Fort Knox, and also in Denver and West Point, plus a small amount in the vaults of the Federal Reserve bank of New York. What you're not quite right about is the 'vast amounts' of gold part. Apparently, no one really knows how much, if any, gold is actually there. Sounds incredible but it's true. You see, Treasury hasn't permitted any kind of audit since 1953 despite all kinds of requests by various governmental agencies, politicians, and even citizens. And the 1953 audit wasn't even complete, so it's accurate to say that there has never been an audit of the gold reserves. Even more surprising because private gold holdings are routinely audited. There are lots of people across the nation, and even the world, who think the amount of gold stored in the vaults is not what is claimed, or that that gold bars are of inferior quality, or that, even if all the physical gold in the vaults is accounted for, it is completely encumbered by third party obligations such as leases or swaps meaning that America's gold reserves are no longer even owned by America.

"And here's where the NDA comes in," Timothy said looking intently at Pierce. "Do you promise not to reveal any of what I'm going to tell you to anyone at any time or do we need the writing?"

Pierce wriggled in his seat. Having no intention of revealing State secrets ever and in any context, it still made him uneasy and, he had to admit, quite excited to be hearing them.

"No," he said. "I will never reveal anything you tell me at any time, to anyone, ever."

Timothy studied Pierce closely, knowing full well that an NDA only goes so far anyway. You could never contract trust. "OK," he said. "Here goes."

"The truth is, there is very little physical gold in any of the U.S. depositories and, of the gold that is there, much of it is poor grade, having been melted down from coins. There are few high-quality gold bars remaining. Treasury does not have even close to the gold it has been claiming for decades."

"What do you mean?" Pierce asked, sitting straight upright. "Where did it go?" Pierce had been anticipating something cloak-and-dagger, maybe a little bawdy, but not outright theft. "Isn't that millions and millions of dollars missing?"

"More like billions," Timothy said. "The book value is billions."

"Are you talking theft?"

"No, it's not like the guards have been swiping gold bars. It's the government in cahoots with the Federal Reserve. Probably first to help pay the bills for World War II and the Korean War, then the debt piling up from the Vietnam War, and recently, probably just unchecked government spending or maybe even as payments to China to cover our debts. The buying and selling doesn't have to be approved by Congress, it's controlled by Treasury and the Federal Reserve. There's no public oversight. The Fed and Treasury can do just about whatever they want."

"And I guess they have."

"Indeed. Plus, other countries have gold in our vaults too. During World War II, gold was sent for safekeeping from Eastern Europe, France, and Great Britain and, during the Cold War, from Germany as well. Which brings up the question: 'Whose gold is whose?' And a further question: 'Why did it take four years to repatriate Germany's own gold from the United States? And why did the gold bars repatriated by the Bundesbank have different labels?'"

"And what were you saying about bank securitization?"

"Oh, yeah," Timothy said. "There are many people who believe that *all* the gold has been encumbered, maybe even two or three times over. So, even if there is any gold, it's no longer even owned by the United States."

"This sounds bad. I still don't understand why there can't just be an accounting. That's what accountants do—count things. It doesn't seem like it would be such a big deal to count bars of gold. Although, I admit, tracing encumbrances would be more challenging."

"Yes, exactly. There hasn't been an accounting because the government doesn't want an accounting. If the truth came out, it would be a disaster for everyone involved."

"Yeah, I can see how that would play out in the news. 'Government Steals Gold.' Not a great headline. Definitely not a plus for Treasury and the government. I expect people would freak. Governmental trust would go down the toilet."

"Exactly," Timothy said. "So we're trying to get ahead of this one before it blows up and takes us with it. And this is where you come in. We need to replace the gold that has gone missing, but we need to do it in a way that doesn't come to the attention of any of the watchdogs. There are a bunch of suspicious gold bugs out there who are already spouting lots of conspiracy theories. And, between us, of course, with good reason. They would love to jump on this."

"I ran across some of their blogs during one of my investment classes. They write really exciting stuff that makes you buy in. It's hard not to believe it."

"Yeah," Timothy said. "And then there's the fact that they're right."

"Oh yes, that," Pierce nodded. "I can see how this would all go. Not good for anyone."

"Correct. And it would probably go all the way up, although Treasury hasn't said a word about it. At this point, it's still just in Treasury and the Fed. The White House claims it doesn't know anything about a gold shortage, which is most likely true, although the executive branch would sure take the hit if it came out."

"I agree," Pierce said. "It would backflow up to the Oval Office."

"And this is where you come in," Timothy said pointedly, locking his eyes on Pierce. "We need a cover for the buys. We need a way to replace the gold in all the depositories now so if there is an audit in the future, we'll be clean. But we need to make the buys in a way that's untraceable to us. Otherwise, all the alarms will go off and the world will know what we were doing. It's a little complicated, but we figured out a way to do it that should be fail-safe. We just need someone like you. Someone in a bank position who is a finance whiz. Someone who is trustworthy and who understands that there is no wrongdoing here, it's just what happened over the years, under many Treasury heads and Federal Reserve governors. It's just what is, but it doesn't need to stay that way. There's time to right the ship."

"I understand," Pierce said. "As you know, I'm not really a judgy person. Things happen. It doesn't sound like a bad gig for the person making the buys. That is what you're asking me, right?"

"Yes."

"Yeah, well, so I hate to be crass, but what's in it for me? It's going to take some work on my part and some kind of hiding the ball, I'm sure, even though it's for a good cause, right?"

"Yes, you're right. You will get the satisfaction of knowing that you'll be helping shore up the financial system of the United States, helping the administration, Treasury, and Fed governors, and also . . ." Timothy looked at Pierce for emphasis, "yourself. You will be compensated handsomely."

"Again, I hate to be crass, but what does that mean exactly?" Pierce asked, practically salivating at the thought.

"It means one million dollars. U.S.D. Not gold bars, but a whole bunch of greenbacks."

Pierce could feel the blood drain out of his face. That was a handsome payday indeed.

"Plus," Timothy went on. "You will have the undying appreciation of some of the biggest wigs in government finance. The only people who will know who you are and what help you have given will be the guys and gals at the top. The ones who matter. And they will remember you, I'm sure, when it comes to future advancement in your career."

It was almost too good to be true. A big money payout and a big boost to his career. He was so excited; he could hardly breathe.

"The only thing is," Timothy said quietly. "I don't know what would happen if somebody caught wind of this—if the gold bugs did, or if the media did, or even if someone who hates the administration did. I don't know what that would look like, and no one is willing to discuss it. I don't know if they would hang you out to dry or if they would step up and take the blame. They're all political animals and all survivors. I don't know what they would do. I had to tell you this, Pierce, because I'm your friend. But you need to know it all if you're going to make a decision about this." Timothy turned to face Pierce and saw the gratitude etched on his face. Yes, just as he thought. Timothy silently congratulated himself. He knew if he fed Pierce a tiny tidbit about possible risks, Pierce would be even more trusting. He could see that Pierce had taken the bait. Now if he could just get him to swallow it.

"Such providence," Timothy said. "What a strange set of circumstances that put us together in such a random way. Kismet, I guess they call it." He could see Pierce nod in agreement as he said that. Although not a piece of that meeting was random. What Timothy failed to tell Pierce was that he had investigated and tracked Pierce for months along with two other possible candidates, but Pierce had always been his first choice. Pierce had a personal chip on his shoulder in addition to the one from his family legacy. He was driven. He was focused. Timothy had seen him notch a win in a bank situation where others would have failed either for lack of inventiveness or lack of courage. He had always thought Pierce was the one, and now he was sure.

"Well, what do you think? Timothy asked. He knew if he could press the point and get a decision in the excitement of the moment, he had a better chance of closing the deal.

He didn't need to worry. Pierce was already at the finish line spending his million dollars and vaulting to the top of the banking hierarchy. He was in.

"Oh yes," Pierce said. "I would love to help the government fix this bungle. And, as you know, I've been doing some commodities and currency tracking at work. I've developed programs that might help with timing the gold buys."

"Well, that is an added benefit," Timothy said. "Trying to time the market in terms of price for the buys is helpful, but what we really need to do is time the quantities of the buys so no alarms go off anywhere."

"My programs can do that too. They're designed to chart the most miniscule trends, either up or down, so you can flow your buys into the market in smaller increments, thereby avoiding attention. It's like a dripping faucet. Buys go in drop-by-drop and nobody takes notice."

"I like that," said Timothy. "A lot. I thought that's what you had been telling me about your programs. I knew you were a smart guy, just biding your time at the bank. This should be something really good for you."

"I know, Timothy. Thank you. Thank you for thinking of me for this project. It's going to be a big success."

And there it was, Pierce was thanking him, Timothy thought, instead of the other way around. He looked at Pierce, flushed with excitement and greed. He certainly had made the right choice.

12

H E FINISHED THE last lap of his swim, his body gliding smoothly, seamlessly through the water. A daily two-hour swim, weights, and occasional hockey kept him fit and fighting ready. He was proud of his discipline, the ubermanliness he was able to maintain now into his seventies, and the indurate way he wielded his authority. He disdained the weak, in mind or body, and privately mocked those sharing the world stage who lacked his discipline and control. But he valued them as the useful pawns they were, to move at will and do his bidding.

He drank his first cup of coffee along with his favorite Kefir from Vladikav, and alerted the translators that he was ready for his call.

"Good evening, Mr. President" he said. "Yes, indeed, such a pleasant day here as well. How are you? And your family? Very well indeed. Yes, thank you."

Dual translators always made calls like this difficult, but it was still preferred. Nothing to trace. No emails or texts to find. His years in State Security had taught him that.

"I understand things are going quite well. Even a bit ahead of schedule. The market is being cleared. Soon there will be very little to trade in the market at all. Our mines are producing in record amounts, our supply channels are running smoothly, our banks will continue to buy, and we will continue to stockpile. There will be little left for anyone else. When the United States comes under pressure, there will be no gold to buy. We will have it all. And, as we have discussed, other countries will not sell to them, because they will need it for the new financial standard as well. The new financial order of the world. They will horde their gold to keep their economies going. They will not be caught without."

"Yes, thank you for mentioning that," he continued. "Germany's repatriation was quite a surprise. They are smart over there and decisive. But we all saw how long it took, and that was just what the news reported. I think we can be sure it took even longer. They must have had to buy gold to replace the German gold they had stolen." He listened for a moment and then continued.

"Did she tell you that? Did she really say 'untrust-worthy?' The dollar standing on a pyramid of debt. I guess that's why Germany acted so quickly. They must have felt that their gold was at risk in the United States vaults. So much debt and bloat. So undisciplined. They keep printing money to cover their whims and fancies. Paper money. Based on nothing, but trust and faith, which is eroding even as we speak. Venezuela, the Netherlands, Austria have already repatriated significant sums.

I talked to Paris and London last week. They are also concerned. There is discussion about repatriation as well. Even the great state of Texas has built its own depository and would like to bring its gold back from New York." He chortled as he poured his second cup of coffee.

"Yes, a welcome surprise. I agree. Their requests for repatriation will be part of the first wave of runs on the banks and the vaults. Everyone will be scrambling to get their gold out of America, but there isn't any gold to get. The vaults are mostly empty, and the strings attached to the few bars left could wrap around both our countries threefold." He listened again carefully to the translator as he savored his second, and last, cup of coffee.

"Yes, it is a good plan," he continued. For us to achieve world domination and control. To strip away the power of the United States, to break the dollar's stranglehold on the rest of the world and crush the United States all at once without firing a shot—brilliant. With our gold-backed currency, we will, at long last, replace the dollar as the world's dominant currency, and extinguish America's financial dominance. The dollar will devalue against gold at a rapid rate. There will be panic. Pandemonium. Runs on banks to exchange dollars for gold, but there will be no exchange because there is no gold. The government will turn to the depositories in Fort Knox, West Point, New York, and Denver, demanding the gold, but there again, is only a pittance. The government will frantically try to buy gold, but there will be very little gold in the market as we have made sure, and no one will want to exchange gold for U.S. dollars. There will be no time to wait for U.S. mines to produce. Inflation will skyrocket, the dollar will devalue swiftly and precipitously, and the United States economy will collapse, taking all with it."

He smiled again when he said that. He still couldn't help it. He had said it so many times in his head and just a very few times out loud. It was most likely unseemly to smile at the demise of a country and its millions of citizens, but he had been underfoot too long, disrespected and denigrated by such an arrogant nation and its pompous and simple-minded leaders. He could hardly wait. Just a little longer, until everything was in place, until every tiny detail was perfect. Then, and only then, would he spring and exact his revenge.

13

D AY FOUR? WAS it day four or day five since Elizabeth had died? Sarah didn't know. She was in a terrible, painful fog. Her head hurt, her body hurt, her soul hurt. She struggled out of bed and glanced at the clock: 6:59 AM. Mr. Mandelman would be calling up the water pipe shaft in one minute. She couldn't bear the thought, but she was too exhausted to do anything else.

"Good morning, Sarah," Mr. Mandelman called cheerily through the opening.

"Good morning, Mr. Mandelman," Sarah returned.

"You'll pardon my asking, but you don't sound so good this morning, Sarah. Is there anything wrong?"

"Yes, Mr. Mandelman. There is. There's a lot wrong and I don't know how to fix it."

"I'm sorry, Sarah. To say you don't know is always the hardest part," Mr. Mandelman said gently. "But it is the opening God needs to hear you."

"Thank you," Sarah said.

"And Sarah?" Mr. Mandelman said. "God always hears you."

She rolled over in bed, pressing her face close to the lightly frosted windowpane. Cold, she thought. Cold for November. She took in the hustle of the city below. People rushing here and there, busy with their lives, buying coffee, selling newspapers, rushing children to school. Unaware that there was anything amiss, especially as stark as Elizabeth had painted. Why was Elizabeth so concerned about someone buying gold, even enormous amounts of gold? How was that a threat to the United States? How was it such a huge threat that Elizabeth felt she had to activate the purpose of the society—and for the very first time? Why didn't Elizabeth say what she was doing in her last entry? What was Elizabeth looking for?

Her head was killing her. She took some aspirin and turned on the coffee maker. She went back to the kitchen table and lifted the handkerchief gently out of the box. It was so beautiful. She could imagine a woman, or perhaps a girl, smoothing the fabric, expertly weaving the carnation-colored thread into the cursive, capital "A." How she would check the evenness of the stitches with a fastidious eye, wanting it to be perfect. And it was.

She sent a quick email to her boss asking for one more day off. She knew it was a stretch as there were deadlines tomorrow, but she was sure Pierce was working on the materials. As irritating as he was, he was always reliable. Except when he wasn't. Which was now. Her boss sent back an emphatic "No." Apparently, Pierce had taken yesterday off after his exam, and no one was working on their projects. She knew she had to get herself to the office as quickly as possible, but she couldn't let go.

She considered what she knew so far. Not much. Logbooks and letters, a picture, a handkerchief, the key. What about the key? Elizabeth had it in her pocket when she died. She decided to contact Detective Schwartz and see what she could find out. Schwartz had said she could see it. Now it seemed as though seeing it, touching it, and holding it, were the most important things she could do.

Schwartz answered on the first ring. "Good morning, Detective Schwartz here."

"Good morning, Detective. It's Sarah Brockman. I'm sorry it's so early. I figured I'd just be leaving a message."

"Oh, no worries at all, Ms. Brockman. I've been here for an hour already. Busy time."

"Yes, I'm sure," Sarah said, the words catching in her throat. "I was thinking about the picture of the key you showed me that Elizabeth had in her pocket when she died. Is it possible to see it now?"

The detective paused. Interesting request. "Why yes, Ms. Brockman. Forensics is finished with it; you can drop in and see it anytime."

"Thank you, Detective," Sarah replied. "Would it be possible to see it today?"

"Yes, of course. What time?"

"Nine?"

"Fine. See you then."

A text was coming in just as Sarah hung up. Ralph. "Are you up?" he asked.

"Yes. I just arranged a meeting with Detective Schwartz to see the key. I woke up and knew that was the next step to take."

"I wish you'd waited to ask me," Ralph texted. "I want to see it too. I don't think we can both go in, or Schwartz will know we're doing something."

"Sorry, you're right. I wasn't thinking."

"OK, thanks. I'll go in tomorrow and see it. Why don't I come over and work on the box while you see the key?"

"Good idea. See you soon," Sarah replied, placing her phone on the table. Strange that they were somehow in this together now. She considered again whether that final text from Elizabeth was meant just for this purpose.

Sarah made coffee, took a quick shower, and was just popping a bagel into the toaster when Ralph arrived. She buzzed him into the lobby, and within a few minutes he was at her door. He looked much better than last night, and the circles under his eyes had lightened, if only a little.

"Morning, Ralph," Sarah said. "Did you sleep?"

"Yes, some. You?"

"Same," she said.

"I feel better," he continued. "Now that we know she didn't kill herself. The box proves that. Somebody was after her. Somebody didn't want her to find what she was looking for."

"That's right," Sarah said. "I never really thought that anyway."

"Me either. Plus, I feel like she wants us to do this. She gave you the box. She gave me the picture. If she had wanted the police to have these, she would've sent these things to them. But she didn't. She sent them to us. She wants us to figure this out. Maybe she thought we'd be the best ones to do it—to figure out what's going on and find out who killed her."

"I agree, Ralph. She did send them to us for a reason, and I don't want to let Elizabeth down. But I also don't want to die. We have no idea where this is going to end, and I'm not sure I want to risk my life, which is in the cards Ralph, by the way, for some grandiose idea of saving democracy or the United States or whatever it is."

They stared at each other. *Neither of them had put any of this into words before.* Sarah's bagel popped out of the toaster startling them both.

"Bagel?" Sarah stammered, clumsily fishing the bagel out with a spatula.

"No, I'm good."

Sarah pressed the cream cheese into the bagel, wrapped it in a napkin and put on her coat. Her racing thoughts crisscrossing her mind. She paused at the door and turned to face Ralph.

"I just don't know Ralph. I've already been there. I already risked my life once, and it's taken me almost five years to get over it. You know that right, Ralph? Did Elizabeth tell you about that big insurance fraud case?

Did she tell you how Sam and I were like David against Goliath? How we solved the case and put the bad guy in prison? And did she tell you how Sam left me after that? Did she tell you that?" Sarah stopped. Her eyes welling up with tears.

"Elizabeth picked you," Ralph said quietly. "She picked me. We can't let her down. And yes, Elizabeth told me a lot about you. I don't think you could ever forgive yourself if you didn't do this. If you didn't do this for our country. If you didn't do this for Elizabeth." He looked carefully at Sarah. "My life is over. When Elizabeth died, she took me with her. But this thing I can do for her, to honor her, her courage, and her legacy. I can do this for Elizabeth."

Sarah sighed. A long, deep sigh. Her life passing through her mind. She saw the big insurance fraud case, felt again how good it felt to have good triumph over evil. She saw the grateful faces of the clients she had served in her personal injury law firm years ago. Clients who never would have had a chance at justice without her. And she thought about her family and her values. Growing up without much money but grateful, hungry to pay it forward and pay it back.

"You're right, Ralph. I don't want you to be right, but I know you are. I don't want to do this, but I could never live with myself if I ran from it, if I said no." She pulled her gloves from her pocket and opened the door.

"OK then," she said. "I'm going to the precinct to take a look at the key and talk to the detective."

"And I'll go back through the box and then head over to my apartment to see what else I can find. There are some drawers I haven't gone through yet and some boxes. Now I have a better idea of what we're looking for."

"Good," Sarah said heading out the door.

"Good."

14

AT 9:00 AM, the precinct was already bustling with the day's activities. Blue uniformed police officers, plain clothes detectives, clerks, and even a few reporters trying to corner a detective and catch a quote. She checked in at the desk and was escorted to Detective Schwartz's office.

"Good morning, Ms. Brockman," the detective said as she rose from her desk. "Thank you for coming in."

"My pleasure," Sarah said extending her hand.

"Coffee?" Schwartz asked.

"No, thank you. All set."

Schwartz motioned to the cushioned chair in front of her desk, directing her away from the hard, wooden chair she had employed at their first meeting days before. "Do you mind if I ask you a few questions before we get to the key?"

Sarah had expected this once she made herself available at the precinct. She was prepared. "Of course, go ahead."

"We understand that Elizabeth wore glasses. Do these look like the glasses she wore?" Detective Schwartz showed Sarah a picture of elongated rectangular Barton Perreira tortoise shell glasses.

"Yes, I think so," Sarah replied. "It's hard to tell with just a picture of glasses, but I remember the brand. Elizabeth loved their glasses and wore them for about the last ten years. There's an optical store right in Grand Central that she frequented. They do free repairs."

"Thank you," the detective said. "Does this look like the frame material?" she said, handing a few broken pieces to Sarah.

"Hard to say. It looks like it, but I can't be sure."

"Thanks," Schwartz said putting the pieces back in the evidence bag and making a note to herself to visit the optical store in Grand Central.

"Do you know if she was working on anything outside of her job? I understand she would frequently help reporters or academics with research for articles and that kind of thing."

"Yes, she did. Often. She felt it was her responsibility as the last Hamilton. You knew that, right? The line has just died with her." The words caught her off guard, and she fought to hold back the tears. "I . . . I don't know if she was working on anything special now. But maybe that was why she was going to all those museums."

"Yes, exactly," the detective said handing her a box of Kleenex. "That's what we think, but all we've found so far is this. She purchased this online from the Museum of the City of New York last week." She reached in another file and pulled out a picture of a woman, seated at a pianoforte, embroidered handkerchief in hand, daintily dabbing at her eye.

Sarah could hardly breathe. The detective looked down for a moment, restacking the papers in the file. Sarah knew she had a few seconds to calm herself or the detective would know the picture was familiar. She tried to slow her breathing, but she could feel her face getting hot and her palms starting to sweat. If she could somehow just get to the bathroom before Schwartz noticed anything, she'd be OK. She moved the Kleenex box to the desk and prepared to stand up, just as the phone started ringing.

The detective looked down at the number and motioned to Sarah that it would be just a minute. Sarah pushed herself back in the chair and took a deep breath, and a few more. She pretended to study the picture. By the end of Schwartz's call, she was fine.

"This is all we have from the museum right now, although they're looking for more," the detective said. "Nice period picture. Angelica Hamilton sitting by her piano. I remember she played, and I understand, almost obsessively after she became deranged following her brother Philip's death. I read that in a brochure when The Grange reopened. Sad tale."

"Yes," Sarah agreed, her mind scrambling to make sense of what she had just learned. Angelica Hamilton. The "A" on the handkerchief. The "A" so perfectly formed and the handkerchief apparently so favored by her that it was memorialized in a portrait that held her favorite object—her pianoforte. The picture could easily be part of research Elizabeth was doing for an article or to help some reporter, but why would she have left the picture for Ralph to find?

"Do you know anything about this picture?" the detective asked.

"No, but it does seem like a picture that could relate to some research or helping some reporter."

"Yes, that's what I thought too. Although I can't see how it's related to Elizabeth's death other than just the timing. She bought it from the museum days before she died. I don't have any other questions just now. Would you like to see the key?"

"Yes, thank you."

Schwartz took the key from the evidence bag on the credenza and handed it to Sarah. It was beautiful. Scrollwork decorations on the bow, the weighting and balance comfortable and tactilely satisfying. She could feel Elizabeth holding the key, rubbing the contours, warming it with her touch. She studied the decoration. Nothing hinted at a location for the keyhole or purpose for the key. It seemed, for all purposes, just like the picture—a nice period piece, exemplative of an era and nothing more.

Sarah held it for a few moments more, savoring the feeling of touching one of the last things Elizabeth held before she died.

"Thank you," she said eventually, standing up and handing the key back to the detective. "It's lovely."

"Do you know anything about it?" Schwartz asked. "Have you ever seen it before?"

"No," Sarah said. "And I've been racking my brain since you showed me the picture. Unfortunately, I've never seen it before."

"Thank you for coming in, Ms. Brockman," the detective said, escorting Sarah out of her office and to the door of the precinct. "We'll talk soon."

Sarah waited until Detective Schwartz started up the stairs before signing out on the precinct log sheet, afraid that her shaking hand might give her away. Within minutes, she was free. She walked quickly down the street and into Central Park. She needed to clear her head and a brisk walk across the park to the Number 4 Lexington Avenue express subway line would get her into the office just about as fast as using the Upper West Side trains. Plus, she knew the shortcuts. Through years of running the park in all seasons and all times of day, she had learned the way the footpaths navigated the park to a depth that bested most New Yorkers. She was walking rapidly by the time she approached Delacorte Theatre and Belvedere Castle and making good time. She decided to sidetrack, just a little, to view the beautiful fall colors of the Ramble. It had been such a spectacular fall, and she had missed most of it due to work and, in retrospect, numerous trivial distractions, but she let herself enjoy it now. She loved the crunch her boots made as they moved through the fallen leaves. She loved the nooks and crannies of the Ramble and the wilderness feel to it. On days like today, she was all alone, all alone in the woods.

She paused for a moment to take in the quiet and was surprised to see a man, a hundred feet or so behind her. Unlike her, he hadn't made any sound as he walked up the leaf-strewn path. He was big, and bundled up against the cold, he seemed even more conspicuous. She decided to let him pass and stepped off the path to give him more room. He passed without a greeting or a nod, but a hint of musty cigarette smoke followed him, as if it had been trapped in his coat for a long time. He must be foreign, Sarah thought, smelling the smoke as she resumed her walk on the path through the Ramble. Although she was moving at the same rapid pace, she didn't see him again. Emerging from the Ramble, she continued up Fifth Avenue, cutting in at 86th Street for the subway stop. The station was packed with commuters jockeying to get on the Number 4 express train to Midtown and lower Manhattan, but she managed to squeeze on and found a spot to stand near the back of the car. She pulled her phone from her pocket and started scrolling through the most recent emails from the bank compliance deals that were due the next day. The work that had to be done by tomorrow was staggering. Where was Pierce and why hadn't he touched any of it? Still celebrating? She couldn't hide her consternation. Her mother said she had a scowl that could sink a thousand ships but she would likely up the count by another thousand if she saw her daughter's face now. Sarah jammed her phone back into her pocket and looked up just as the train arrived at her station. She squashed, squeezed, and apologized her way out of the train just as the doors closed behind her. But as they did, she caught a slight whiff of the kind of musty cigarette smoke she had smelled earlier in the Ramble, but just a whiff, and then it was gone.

15

PIERCE SMELLED THE coffee brewing downstairs and heard his dad clanging through the pots and pans in the cupboard, hunting for his favorite frying pan. He had been at home with his dad for two days. Working together on research, calling and emailing various experts and labs. It was exciting. He was starting to feel a glimmer of hope that this huge obstacle could be overcome, that this problem might be fixed, for the first time since he could remember. He checked his final numbers, the graphs, and trajectories. If he wasn't mistaken, the final buy would be completed in the next few days. He would check in with Timothy today to make sure, as well as apologize for going AWOL.

He still felt so bad about it all. The flameout, the way he had broken down. The way he had let himself down. The embarrassment he knew he would feel when he returned to the bank. But the time with his dad had been some of the most precious days of his life, and for that he would be forever grateful.

"Good morning, Dad," he said as he came down the steps. "Coffee smells good."

"Right? All the fancy coffee blends and nutso prices, and Folgers is still the best."

Mike poured coffee into mugs and handed one to Pierce. He looked at him closely. "You're leaving today, aren't you, Son?"

Pierce looked down at the floor, the linoleum had peeled in a few places and there were stains by the stove and refrigerator, but it was still in pretty good shape after what had been almost a lifetime in this house.

"Yeah," he said. "It's time. I've got to get back to the bank. I've got to try and fix the mess I've made for myself there. I've got to step back in." He sighed and looked at his dad.

"I love you, Dad. I've loved this time together. I know it was a gift and I appreciate it." He let the tears roll. He never had to pretend for his dad, and he could tell him almost anything.

"I love you too," Mike said, his eyes welling up as he gave his boy a big hug. "It's been great. I know you need to go. I have to drive later today anyway, but I'm so happy you were here. So happy."

"We're going to get this figured out Dad. I know we will."

"I know we will too." Mike grabbed his boy in one last bear hug as Pierce reached for his coat.

"See you next week, Dad."

*   *   *

Pierce walked into the cold, early morning sun. Everything looked different. Crisper. Less muddled. It was as if he was seeing the world with a fresher eye. He boarded the ferry and, within minutes, was stepping back into Manhattan. Back where he belonged. He made his way to his apartment to clean up and then headed to the bank. Everyone would know what had happened. He had told too much to his boss, and he knew he couldn't count on any degree of confidentiality, but when he walked into his department, it was as if nothing had changed. No one stared or said anything other than the usual pleasantries. He began to think it wasn't going to be too bad. He got to his office just as his cell phone started ringing.

"Oh, hi, Timothy. Yes, I just got in this minute. You were going to be my first call. I wanted to tell you again how sorry I am about all this mess. I'm sorry I didn't tell you what was going on. I'm sorry I didn't keep you in the loop. My apologies."

"No worries, Pierce," Timothy said. "I was just concerned about your safety, but you sound good. Are you OK?"

"Yeah, disappointed, but OK. It's just so ridiculous, this thing I have. I know everything on that test, hands down. I could teach it for goodness' sake, but I was working with my dad on some research related to DNA, and we might have some leads, so I'm starting to feel hopeful for the first time ever."

"That's exciting, Pierce. I'm really happy for you."

"Thanks. I wanted to check with you and see where we were. I think we're one buy away, right? And then we're done?"

"Yes. One and done."

"Fantastic. I think my programs have really paid off. I can't imagine anyone has been able to put these buys together as coming from one source, let alone tied to the government."

"I agree, Pierce. I don't think any bells and whistles have gone off. Too ingenious. I don't think anyone would think to trace them. You've done a really good job."

"Thanks, Timothy, but I wasn't looking for compliments. I'm just thrilled that we're almost done and that it worked. I think we'll all feel more secure knowing that the United States has the gold we say we have. It's more stable, of course, financially, but it also feels like the right thing to do."

"Of course, you're right, Pierce. For all those reasons. Maybe you should think about running for office. You're smart and you have a lot of integrity. Sorely needed right now, I admit."

"Thanks, but no thanks, Timothy. My forefather already did that, and it didn't really work out too well for him. I'd rather stay in business and work my magic from here."

"I understand. Well, you will certainly be in a good business position when this is all wrapped up. I guess this would be a classic case of a 'win-win.'"

"Yeah, definitely," Pierce said. "Can we go for lunch this week? It would be nice to catch up."

"Absolutely. I'll call you tomorrow."

Pierce hung up and started fishing through his inbox, looking for anything that needed his immediate attention. Lots of spreadsheets and documents relating to the projects that were due tomorrow. He opened a few. Nothing had been done. He checked for cc's to Sarah. Yes, she was on every document, but she hadn't started any of the work. He was glad he had made it to the office when he did. Maybe she was sick. She didn't pick up when he called her office, so he decided to go by and see if she was in. They had a lot of work to do in one day, and it would be best to make a quick plan for getting it done. He saw her coming through the door just as he rounded the corner.

"Good morning, Sarah," he said briskly. "I thought I'd come by and see how we can get all this work done today. It looks like no one has done a thing on this," he said pointedly.

Sarah was fumbling with her phone and trying to hide her irritation at the same time. Pierce was such a jerk. And she hadn't even been able to enjoy the days when he was out since she'd been out too. Now they were in this squeeze play.

"I was out on family matters," Sarah said turning to face him. She decided not to ask him about his test since it had clearly gone fine based on the arrogant confidence he was showing. She certainly was in no mood to have to congratulate him. "Well, let's get on it," she said instead. "Meet me in the small conference room in five minutes. Print out the global spreadsheet from Reggia and bring it. You know which one?"

"Yeah, see you in five." Pierce was surprised Sarah hadn't asked about the test, but he was surprised no one else had asked about it either. Maybe he wasn't as big a deal as he thought. Maybe no one was really that interested in what he was doing. The thought was like a knife to his ego, but, in this case, he was glad no one was asking and making him relive it all again. He hustled back to his office, printed out the spreadsheet and some other documents he thought might be useful, and was waiting in the conference room when Sarah appeared.

"OK," she said. "This is where the rubber meets the road. These deals are looking shaky on compliance. And I am compliance. If they don't make it, no matter how close they are, I'm not going to green light them." She looked Pierce in the eye. "No matter how badly you want them through. I am not going to green light them," she said again. "Understood?"

"Of course," he said snappishly. *Nasty woman*, he thought.

They worked through part of the morning and then Sarah excused herself to take a break. She went back to her office to privately check in with Ralph.

"Hi, Ralph. How are you doing?" She tried to sound more cheerful than she felt. She could imagine him, cramped in her small apartment, musty documents strewn about on the kitchen table, the weak autumn light just barely passing through the windows, trying so hard to put together pieces of what had happened to Elizabeth.

"I'm OK, thank you," Ralph said quietly. "I haven't found anything. Not one thing. It's all just historical stuff. Nothing that points to what Elizabeth was chasing. Why didn't she leave us more clues?"

"I don't know," Sarah said. "Just the picture and the key. That's all we have. And it's been how many days? We're still nowhere."

"I know. I'm beyond frustrated. The picture is the strongest lead, but it still doesn't go anywhere. I'm sure Schwartz would be interested to know that we have the same picture."

"No doubt."

"I'm going to go home now and take Bodie out. I'll look through more things at home and see what I can find on the computer. I'm at a dead end. I'm feeling so sad. Hopeless."

"Me too."

Sarah hung up and reached for a Kleenex. She dried her eyes and forced herself to turn back to the project at hand. The work had to get done, plus she couldn't think of anything to do to help Elizabeth anyway.

She studied the programs Pierce had used on the deals and the financial models. She knew Pierce had tweaked some of the programs with his own applications, but they were solid. Quite advanced. He really did know what he was doing. He could go so far in finance if he wasn't such a jerk. Thankfully, she didn't have to care. She continued to study Pierce's programs and their application to the deals. The way they funded was ingenious. More like a small trickle than the usual spigot on-and-then-off approach of most large banks. They were much more nuanced. Disbursements were made in miniscule amounts to take advantage of the subtle, undulating movements in the market thereby capturing the greatest value.

It made her think about the gold buy models Elizabeth had referenced in her letter that had been replicated by Jessica Hamilton Madison. The models that had enabled Elizabeth and Jessica Madison to spot what they believed to be a massive, if subtle, gold accumulation.

"Hi, Ralph, me again," she said, happy to catch him before he left her apartment. "When you get home, can you check something for me on Elizabeth's thumb drive?"

"I'll try. I still feel so stupid about letting the police take her computer. I wasn't thinking clearly that first day. But at least I found her thumb drive."

"Yeah, well I was there too, remember? We both weren't thinking clearly, and I think the police took advantage of that. That's the main reason they came right over. Not to talk to you so much as get the computer."

"Smart. On their part. What do you want me to check?"

"I've been running across some refined and highly nuanced programs in the projects I'm working on right now for the bank. The programs work to fund structured finance deals by way of a subtle trickle, rather than the spigot on-and-off approach that banks have been using for decades. So, in essence, because each funding is so small, the bank or the borrower, depending on who has bought the advantage, gets the benefit of the smallest movements in the markets. It seems almost like a rounding error when you look at one transaction, but when you add them up, it turns into quite a large number. It may be that Jessica Hamilton Madison had developed something like that as well, and that's how she discovered what she did."

"It's certainly possible, Sarah. I don't know my way around Elizabeth's computer very well yet, but I will get to it as soon as I get back with Bodie."

"Great. Thank you. I really don't know what we're looking for, but I think the best place to start is any spreadsheet files she has, especially connected with emails to Jessica Madison. Probably Excel but could be something proprietary too. All those numbers would have to get into spreadsheets one way or another."

"I agree. Will do."

"Thank you, Ralph. Hang in there."

"I'm trying. You too."

16

PEOPLE DO THINGS for all kinds of reasons, Timothy thought as he added the finishing touches to his coffee. Many of them complicated and profound. But not him. He never lingered on those kinds of questions. He liked to think of himself as straightforward. Simple, in a way. He wasn't doing anything he was doing to upend the world's political or financial order, although that would be the likely result, but rather, to just retire and have a very nice life, unencumbered by worries about money and security. Just lie on a beach and enjoy his days. He was smart and charming, good with people of every persuasion. He could have made more of himself and probably should have, but he just didn't care. He had never wanted to climb the highest peak; he was happy to rest in the valley. So, when this opportunity presented itself, he studied it carefully and then leaped, quickly and decisively. Now he was almost done and his future almost secure. He took a sip of coffee and dialed in.

"Good morning, sir, Timothy Murphy here."

"Good morning. Nice buy."

"Yes, the micro buys ticked in perfectly. Probably the smoothest one yet."

"Last buy probably tomorrow, correct?"

"Yes. I'm heading to work now to finish the paperwork."

"Good. Send me your wire transfer info later. Where was it again, the Cooks? Caymans? I don't remember where you decided. In any event, I know you plan to head out right after close. Let me know."

"Of course."

"All right then, we're set."

"Good-bye."

"Bye."

Timothy hung up and moved around his apartment, gathering his various security clearance lanyards and ID cards, putting on one of his boring, government-appropriate suits. He had some trendy clothes and nicer everything, but he always left those in his New York apartment. His DC apartment was just for government work. He didn't think anyone knew he had apartments in two cities or that he led a double life. The people he knew in New York City and the people he knew in DC never seemed to cross, which was unusual for these cities where everyone was interwoven in some way. And this wasn't a new thing; he had been doing it for years. He enjoyed being both Timothy Murphys and the secrets he kept. It made him feel dangerous and alive. He wondered why he was so interested in giving up that life and turning instead to such a bland and uninspired existence. He didn't know. He suspected there was a lot he didn't know about himself and never would. But again, to be fair, it was really of no consequence to him. His was an unexamined life, and he intended to keep it that way.

The only thing that bothered him just a little, if he stopped to think about it, which he rarely did, was what this would do to Pierce. He liked Pierce. At least as much as he liked anyone. Pierce considered him a friend. What would happen to Pierce was not something a friend would do. Still, Pierce was a big boy, he told himself whenever he had those kinds of thoughts. Timothy had told him about the risk, or at least some of it, and that was enough for him. He took another sip of coffee and felt that little nudge to his conscience clear. He was good to go.

17

D ETECTIVE SCHWARTZ STUDIED the drawing in the early afternoon sun. What was it about that picture? It was beautiful, a bit stilted and posed, but captivating, nonetheless. She studied the information that had been returned from both museums in response to her subpoenas. All Elizabeth's searches in the last week before she died were about Angelica Hamilton. They were either requests for pictures of her, places she might have frequented, or pictures of Hamilton Grange. It must be the case that Elizabeth was working on some kind of research involving Angelica. But why did she only purchase this picture? There were others of Angelica in the collections. She looked carefully at the picture. It looked like it was set in a family home, possibly The Grange. She felt the hairs on the back of her neck stand up. The Grange. It was The Grange. She had seen pictures of the home and grounds coming through in the evidence folders. She quickly scanned through the photographs and drawings. There was a picture of the salon with a pianoforte in it that looked just like the one in the picture. It could be the same one. She matched the address of The Grange to the subway stop map. Elizabeth was killed at the subway stop closest to The Grange, at 3:20 AM. Whatever she was looking for at The Grange she either found or it found her.

The detective tossed her coat over her arm and hurried to the subway. She loved being anywhere she wanted in the city in minutes. She took the Number 1 uptown to the 137th Street station in Harlem and walked the few minutes to St. Nicholas Park, approaching The Grange from the long yard stretching out in front of the home. It was majestic and commanding, even more so in its day, designed to let everyone know that the owner had made it. Not even Alexander Hamilton, revered for his humility and lofty democratic vision, could escape a little self-aggrandizement.

She walked briskly to the park entrance, showed her identification, and was quickly given access to walk around The Grange and grounds. Her first stop was the parlor. The moment she entered, she knew it was the pianoforte in the picture. The instrument looked the same and, surprisingly, the placement in the room was almost identical. She stooped to read the description card:

Sheraton Mahogany Pianoforte

Count: 1

Date: c. 1795

Artist: Clementi and Co. (Manufacturer)

History: The piano was given to Alexander
Hamilton's daughter, Angelica, by her aunt,
Angelica Schuyler Church (Mrs. John B. Church)
in 1795. In 1942, the piano was given to the
American Scenic and Historic Preservation Society
by Mrs. J. Jenks, a great-great granddaughter of
Alexander Hamilton.

Although the public was allowed into this room as
part of The Grange tour, there was no one in the room
right then. Quickly scanning the room for surveillance
cameras and seeing none, Schwartz skirted the red velvet
ropes and made her way to the pianoforte. Up close, it
was even more beautiful. The polished, rich grain in the
mahogany captured the warm lighting in the room,
turning the parlor into, what must have been, a welcome
sanctuary from the cacophony of colonial political times.
Stealing a look behind her, she crept closer and inspected
the pianoforte. Fearful of smudging the polish, she put
her gloves back on and ran her hands over the instrument. Joints held firmly, there was no warping in the
wood. Everything seemed well preserved and in good
order. She quickly moved over the instrument, gently
touching, prodding. She knew this might be her only
chance to get this close to the piano since getting a
search warrant with such speculative evidence would be
a stretch. She heard tourists in the next room, finishing
up. She just had a few moments. She stepped back,

imagining what an evening in the parlor would have looked like in 1795. Elegant ladies and cultured gentlemen standing and sitting about, perhaps enjoying a glass of madeira, listening to Angelica play. The light dust that covered the furniture only added to her musings. As a National Memorial, its funding was tied to the whims of Congress, so there was never enough money to keep the building in top shape. But the dust under the pianoforte seemed to have been disturbed. She looked closer. There were a few small wooden filings almost indistinguishable from the dust. She quickly crawled under the piano and could easily make out a small drawer, about the size of a matchbox, that was open and empty. A drawer that could easily have held the key.

She stood up and rushed back across the red roped barrier just as the next tour group came in. She was breathless with excitement.

"Stunning, isn't it?" the tour director asked, mistaking her breathlessness for admiration.

"Yes," Detective Schwartz said. "Yes, indeed."

She practically ran back to the subway and made it to the platform just as a train was arriving. She felt as if she was stepping into Elizabeth's shoes, that this must have been how it was for Elizabeth except that Elizabeth was here, alone, in the middle of the night with someone after her. Elizabeth had found what she was looking for at The Grange and those following her knew she had too. The case was now, unquestionably, a murder.

Schwartz was back at the station in twenty-five minutes and immediately retrieved the key from the evidence bag. The key would fit perfectly in the matchbox drawer. But when was it hidden there, and by whom? It looked like the matchbox drawer had been built into the piano when it was ordered by Angelica Church. It clearly was not an add on from a later time. But if Angelica Church requested the hidden drawer, it could be for her sister Elizabeth or Alexander. It could even be for someone else who lived at The Grange. She considered the key anew. It was not a child's plaything. It was a substantial key, made to last a long time—even centuries. It was meant to be secret, hidden from all eyes except a knowing few, all of whom had taken the secret with them when they passed into history.

18

R ALPH HAD BEEN opening and closing files, searching for what he wasn't quite sure of on Elizabeth's thumb drive for hours. Folders, files, documents, spreadsheets, graphs. Thousands of them, tidily organized, but still daunting. He glanced at Bodie sleeping in the sun. He was still spending his waking time pacing the apartment looking for Elizabeth, but for this moment he was a warm, contented dog. Ralph's phone started buzzing. It was Sarah.

"Hi, Sarah, how's it going?" He found it surprising that he could still put comprehensible sentences together when all that was in his mind was gibberish.

"Fine. Still working on all this compliance stuff, but Pierce, that creep I told you I'm working with, has been helpful for a change. Really good on the numbers. Quick on the models and his own weird workarounds. Kind of a numbers savant."

"Well, that's good. Maybe you'll get out of there sooner."

"Yeah. How's it going on your end?"

"Goose egg. There are so many files and spreadsheets. I've done tons of searches using 'Jessica Hamilton Madison,' but barely anything's come up and nothing tied to spreadsheets."

"Ugh. This is so frustrating. That seemed like the best first step."

"I did find one email with spreadsheets from Jessica Madison that describes the financial model she was trying to replicate, so we know there's some truth in all this, but there's no follow-up, it just seems to stop there."

"Well, send that one to my personal email. Maybe it will trigger something on my end. Are there any encrypted files, if you can tell?"

"Not so far, but I'm not that deep into it yet. OK, just sent it."

"Thanks Ralph. Talk later."

Sarah flipped to her personal email and opened the document. It began:

Dear Elizabeth,

This work is the result of our discussions about the subtle pattern of global gold buying.

I found the article I remembered about some new financial models that was published in the *Financial Times* from the Bank of Hoboken in New York.

I've been trying to replicate the modeling described and, with some help, was finally able to do so. I then graphed the gold buys using some algorithms I had designed when I was in banking. The short answer is—we were right.

Someone is aggregating gold in vast amounts using a "raindrop" technique. Instead of typical large block trades, this strategy uses innumerable frequent buys, almost miniscule amounts, like raindrops instead of a torrent, so no single trade gets noticed. But the raindrops turn into oceans. Take a look at the attached. The picture's thousands of points tell a singular story.

Sarah opened the attachment and was greeted by a flurry of dots that had been connected into graphs. It looked more like a blizzard than a rain shower, but the simile held. She glanced up as Pierce noisily drew himself to his feet.

"Lunch," he announced as he headed for the door.

No pleasantries from that one, Sarah thought. No offer to bring in anything for her either. She went back to the spreadsheet. It looked familiar. Like some Pierce had up on his computer. She stood up and made her way to his screen. Yes, she was right. She had never been much of a whiz in statistics, but it looked very much like the same financial model to her.

"What are you looking at?"

Sarah spun around to find Pierce glaring at her from the doorway.

"Ah, ah, nothing," she stammered. "Just wanted to see if I could understand where that spreadsheet fits into my summary. I thought you were going to lunch."

"Forgot my frequent flyer card to Pret. I'm almost at a free sandwich."

He moved past her to his suit coat pocket and pulled out a punch card, his eyes resting on her screen as he walked past.

"Well, OK then, have a good lunch," Sarah called cheerily as he made his way out of the door. She waited a minute to make sure he wouldn't reappear and then went back to her computer and began browsing through spreadsheets of other projects they had worked on. As a lawyer in compliance, her job was to perform the global overview of a project and stamp projects as compliant, reject them, or send them back down for more work. Pierce was tasked with crunching the numbers, modeling outcomes, and all the financial minutiae that attached. Even though she disliked him, she had to admit he was good at his job and always a value add. He saw patterns and trends that others couldn't see and had, on a few occasions, discovered faulty deals that would have been a big headache for the bank.

She pored over the spreadsheets for a few more minutes and then reverted to their current project just as Pierce returned, sandwich in hand.

"What did you find?" he asked curtly. It was clear he had been thinking about what had happened. "What were you looking at on my computer?"

He seemed disproportionately upset, based on whatever alleged crime she had committed, and she was, once again, on the defensive.

"Nothing," she said. "I told you. I was just trying to see where that spreadsheet fit in."

"Did you? Did you find where it fit in?"

Sarah could feel his eyes boring into her. "Yes," she said a bit too forcefully. "I did."

"Good," he said caustically. "I'm glad."

What he hadn't told her, was that he had not just seen the spreadsheet on her screen when he passed by but had also seen that the spreadsheet was in a personal email, open on her screen. She wasn't looking at work; she was looking at something else.

It looked like his model. It even looked like one of the gold buys. But how could she possibly have one of his gold models? Ludicrous. He was just being paranoid. He knew he was on edge right now with one more buy to go. One more buy, then this whole project would be finished, and he would be on his way to riches and glory. He smiled secretly at the thought and decided to relax. He thought how proud his dad would be, and how he would feel, finally achieving that which should have been rightfully his for years. He thought about his family and his family's legacy. He dared to consider how this might rectify the past, or at least, redeem the future.

"OK," Sarah said, disturbing his thoughts. "Let's get on with this."

They worked in silence for what seemed to Sarah to be a very long time. Every time she looked up, Pierce was looking at her, studying her. She felt squirmy, uncomfortable, and decided that was probably his intention. Just the kind of thing Pierce would do. But Pierce, for his part, really wasn't attempting anything of the kind. He was thinking about other things, grander things. He was fully submersed in his future, in the luminous treasures that were within his grasp. He wasn't seeing Sarah at all.

"I'm going for a bite," she said as she headed for the door. She stopped by her office and picked up her laptop, stuffing it in her bag as she walked. She was at Hale and Hearty within two minutes and eating within six. She snagged a small table toward the back and popped open her laptop. She accessed the bank's secured portal and expertly moved through the last projects she had worked on with Pierce. She went straight to the spreadsheets. Most were typical line and block graphs, but every so often she ran across what she now called the "rain" spreadsheet. She remembered thinking they were unusual when she and Pierce were working on the projects, and she knew that Pierce had designed them himself. She had never asked Pierce about them for fear of appearing stupid. Now they jumped out at her like a blizzard in July. She called Ralph.

"Hi, Ralph. Having any more luck? I think what you found may be significant."

"What do you mean?"

"I just had the weirdest thing happen with Pierce. He's so creepy, but like I said earlier, he's a numbers savant. I would never tell that arrogant SOB, but I've always admired his way with statistics and models. He built a few models that the bank approved for use in compliance analysis and one of them looks exactly like the spreadsheet you forwarded to me from Jessica Hamilton Madison. It has the same flurry of dots and graphing. It looks like the same model to me but, as you know, finance is not really my strong suit. I would love for you to use your finance brain and look at examples from some of the bank projects and get your take on them. This is, of course, confidential bank work product. But I don't think I need to tell you that. Can you take a look?"

"Of course, Sarah," Ralph said. "Send everything."

"I'll send them through my portal. The access code is 48937."

"OK, got it. I'll revert as soon as I can."

"Thanks Ralph," Sarah said as she gathered up her things to return to the office.

*   *   *

Dmitri took another long drag on his cigarette as he studied Sarah through the large pane window. She had been talking to someone, probably the husband. He should know who she was talking to, and he should know what was being said. Idiot. How could he have been so stupid to not have known Elizabeth Walker would jump in front of the train? Or that she would have left a trail for others to follow? And now, here he was unprepared, with very little surveillance, trying to track these two on foot. Flitting to her apartment, to his apartment, to the precinct, across the park. It didn't look like they were on to anything, let alone anything as significant as he had been told, and he knew he had been told only a small portion of what was really going on. He didn't believe these two amateurs could be a threat to even that small portion but, he had to admit, he had been fatally wrong before.

His mind slipped back to that terrible time. He had been given a straightforward assignment from SVR (now SVR, but forever KGB in his mind), a simple hit on an easy target. He quickly found her the first day he arrived, walking along the Seine River just north of Pont Neuff. Long legs. Thick, curly chestnut hair that reached to her waist and swung from side to side as she walked. She was a beauty. He watched from the bridge, and, when she got too far away, he took out his binoculars and watched some more. Tomorrow was soon enough he thought. He would watch her just a little more today. But he couldn't leave well enough alone. He found himself watching her, stalking her. What should have taken a day was taking two, then three, then four. He couldn't help himself. He was obsessed with her, with everything about her. How she looked, how she moved, how she laughed, how she brushed her hair. The old impulses he had buried years ago started bubbling back to the surface. He took out his tool kit. All the knives were still razor sharp. He started leaving little surprises for her. Nothing big, just pieces of little things he had cut. She screamed when she found the last one on her doorstep, and he especially liked that, another new part of her to experience. He thought he would leave something even more interesting the next day, but Sergei was calling again. Sergei was texting. Sergei was trying to reach him as he had every day all day for the past few days. He didn't respond. He couldn't. He had to keep doing what he was doing.

It's not hard to get kicked out of the SVR.

In retrospect, he knew he should be grateful he wasn't immediately killed by the agent sent in to replace him. He was lucky just to be kicked out, especially when they couldn't find her. She had apparently left during the night when he was sleeping the few hours he slept a night. No one could find her and, last he heard, no one had. He was secretly happy about that. She was still his, his in his memory. He was the last one to possess her, to dominate her, to be intimate with her, watching from afar.

He turned back to watch Sarah. She was walking back to her office. Sarah moved like *she* moved. She didn't look like her, but she had the same cadence to her walk. She tossed her hair the same way; she had the same uneven smile. He swallowed hard and reached deep into his pocket and found his metal balls. He switched them to his left pocket and started turning them over and over again, the angular cut in the ball tearing his skin just a little. He could feel some of the tension evaporate, but not enough. His phone was vibrating.

"Yes?"

"We are in place, *Team Leader.*"

Team Leader. Such impudence. Dmitri hated Yugov and the poison he was injecting into his team, but he was powerless to do anything about it. The team was already in his pocket. Yugov had wanted Dmitri's job for a long time and, after "the mistake," as he had taken to thinking about it, Yugov sprang into action. Not only had Dmitri caught Yugov saying vile things about him to the team, but he suspected that Yugov had promised them all bigger, more powerful positions in his new world order. No doubt with bigger pay checks. The harder he tried to turn the team back around, the more vicious Yugov became. He started to wonder if Yugov had a direct line to Sergei, since Sergei knew things he otherwise couldn't have known and was becoming increasingly critical of Dmitri. He couldn't wait until the contract was completed and he would be rid of Yugov forever.

"Thank you, Yugov. You three can take it from here," Dmitri said through gritted teeth.

"Thank you, *Team Leader*."

Dmitri was livid. He walked to the park and sat down on a bench for a smoke. After a few puffs, his tension started to recede again, but only slightly. He reached for his metal balls, but even they didn't seem to work. He saw the number come in even before he felt the vibration.

"Hello, Sergei."

Good day, Dmitri. How is the work going?"

"Fine," Dmitri lied. "On track." He hadn't told Sergei that most of the surveillance equipment had not yet been installed or that he had no idea what Sarah and Ralph were up to.

"What have you learned? Time is running out."

"Yes, I am aware of that. They haven't found the trove. In fact, they haven't made any headway toward finding it," Dmitri said not knowing if that was at all true.

"Good. I want tapes and transcripts of your surveillance. I want to see for myself."

The line went dead. Sergei didn't believe him. He knew Dmitri didn't have any tapes or transcripts. He must know they weren't yet installed. Probably because Yugov had told him. Dmitri could feel the tension rising higher and higher in his body. He had hoped that good work on these non-SVR contracts Sergei threw him from time to time would be his ticket back into the SVR but now, after "the mistake," he only hoped to stay alive. He took another long drag on his cigarette and rolled the balls faster and harder in his pocket, tearing his skin. He could feel the warm blood starting to drip on his fingers and palm. Dmitri checked his phone. He had an hour before anyone was expected back at the apartment. Assuming a twenty-minute subway ride, he would have forty minutes alone in the apartment. More than enough time to do what he needed to do to bring himself back from the edge. He caught the uptown Number 1 and was in the apartment twenty-two minutes later. He walked quickly to the bathroom, removed his hidden knife from under the cabinet, and with one swift, experienced cut, temporarily set himself free.

19

H E FINISHED HIS Kefir and coffee and saved the last of his pistachio ice cream, thoroughly enjoying one of the few treats he allowed himself as he adjusted his robe, reviewed his notes, and alerted the translator.

"Good evening, Mr. President. How are you and how is your family?"

"Very fine, Mr. President. We are well. Beijing is beautiful this time of year. How are you and your family?"

"We are also in good health and enjoying this lovely fall weather. I understand that the last gold purchase will likely be tomorrow, which will, at last, clear the world market of gold. Is that your understanding as well?"

"Yes. It has been a long journey. I believe everything is in place on my end. How about for you?"

"Yes, I will alert Treasury as well as our media department. We can begin work on a joint statement for the media now in advance of our press conference."

"Yes, we will craft a bilateral statement from our two countries. It need not be adversarial. After all, it is just business. The business of the great world countries. Our countries."

"Indeed. I wonder how long it will take America to understand what has happened."

"They will be stunned and at a great loss to grasp what has happened to them. So quick and fatal. Like a financial nuclear bomb. Our gold-backed currency will crush the dollar and the economy of the United States. The citizens will run crying to the banks trying to exchange their worthless dollars for gold, but there is no gold in their banks. They will run to the government, but there is no gold in their depositories. They will try to buy gold on the world market, but again, there is only a pittance. We will crush the United States not with might, but with our intelligence and cunning. Intelligence that is sorely lacking there. When the government understands what has happened, they will rage. They will panic."

"They may even call us to plead and to beg, but we will say nothing, do nothing."

At that, both men smiled. A lust for power, narcissism, arrogance. These things, they could understand and condone. But weakness? This they never would.

"Good-bye for now, Mr. President.

"Good-bye. We will see each other soon."

The president finished his last bite of pistachio ice cream and unzipped his burner phone from his satchel.

"Good evening, Sergei. Any update on when the last buy will occur?

"Good evening, Mr. President. Yes, sir. We are looking good for early tomorrow morning."

"Excellent. And what about Dmitri? Should we be concerned? He made a huge error. A sloppy, unforgivable error. I'm not sure we should wait until the contract is over to dispatch him. I am inclined to hit him now for that mistake."

"I agree. It was a serious mistake, a fatal lapse in judgment. How could he not have anticipated that she would jump? If he knew her as well as he claimed, he would have known that's exactly what she would do. But I know he's being especially careful now. He knows he's on borrowed time. He thinks he'll survive if he gets this right. He doesn't know he's already dead. Plus, he, Yugov, and his team are already in place and, we think, presently unknown to the Feds. It would be difficult to get someone in place quickly now. All they are doing anyway is minding Elizabeth Hamilton Walker's husband and her best friend as they wander about the city trying to figure out who killed Walker. Class A amateurs. I'm sure those two need to go through this exercise to put their consciences at rest, but a pure waste of time. I think we let Dmitri finish the contract and then kill him. More of a deterrent for others than anything else."

"Fine."

20

"THANKS FOR RETURNING my call so quickly, Doris," Detective Schwartz said. "Do you mind if I talk to you about the Elizabeth Walker case? I'm kind of stuck. With your intelligence and expertise, I thought you might be the best person to help with this."

"I'm flattered. Thank you and, of course, my pleasure."

"I hate to tell you this over the phone, but it will be in the news shortly so I thought it should come from me first." Schwartz took a deep breath and continued. "Elizabeth was the 'unidentified woman' killed by the subway train in Harlem a few days ago."

"Oh no!" Doris gasped. "I heard about the accident on the news. How did it happen?"

"I understand the media is going to say it was an accident, but it wasn't. Elizabeth was murdered. It wasn't an accident, and she didn't kill herself. She was pushed in front of the train. We don't know by who. But someone was after her. They trapped her and pushed her.

I think they were after a key that was found in her pocket. We have it. Over two hundred years old. It was authenticated by one of your colleagues at the Met, Mr. Davies. I think you know him."

Doris murmured "yes" as Detective Schwartz pushed on.

"Well, I was just at Hamilton Grange, and I found where the key had been hidden. It was tucked into a small, secret drawer under the piano in the parlor."

"Oh, oh . . . ," Doris could hardly breathe. "What does all this mean? How did you find it?"

"I was looking at some of the materials that you and the Museum of the City of New York had sent in response to the subpoenas, including a picture of Angelica Hamilton from the museum that Elizabeth had purchased. It struck me that the picture was of the piano in the parlor at The Grange, so I went to The Grange and found the dust underneath the piano disturbed, plus there were a few small wooden filings mixed into the dust. I reached underneath the piano and found a drawer open, just big enough for the key to have been wedged inside. The subway station where Elizabeth was killed was the closest one to The Grange. She must have gone to The Grange that night, slipped inside, and found the key. Unfortunately, the killer or killers found her too. I suspect they were tracking her somehow, watching her every move."

As she said it, she knew it. Of course, that's how they did it. They must have used the camera inside Elizabeth's glasses to track her. Its placement insured that they saw everything she saw. They went everywhere she went. They knew when she found the key, and they knew where to find her.

"This is just horrible and heartbreaking," Doris said. "What a horrific way to go."

"Horrible."

"How can I help?" Doris asked.

"The main piece of evidence we have so far is the key, and it really is 'the key' to finding Elizabeth's killers. We think Elizabeth was first trying to find it and then find where the key would fit. All the documents, all the research she was doing seem to point to that. She found the key, but did she find where it fits? We don't know."

"That sounds right. She was looking at drawings and paintings of places in a very narrow time frame."

"Yes, around 1790 to about 1804. I had copies of the key made and some of my officers are checking the key holes of the buildings she was looking at in her research that are still standing, but it seems like a fool's mission to me."

"Worse than a needle in a haystack."

"Exactly. I just emailed you a picture of the key," Schwartz said.

"Beautiful," Doris said as she studied the picture. "Bespoke. Such an elegant time in many ways, brutal in others of course."

"What was happening in history then with Alexander Hamilton or the family?" the detective asked. "The key was placed at The Grange, so it has to have something to do with the Hamiltons. And why that narrow time period? I know the Hamilton–Burr duel was fought about that time with Hamilton dying a few days later, but that's about all I can remember."

"Yes, you're right. I think that was when Hamilton's U.S. Mint was established and the Revenue Cutter Service, which became the U.S. Coast Guard. They have a wonderful museum with some original Revenue Cutter artifacts in Montauk that I visited last year. Really marvelous."

Ms. Sullivan quickly pulled up Wikipedia on her computer and continued. "Yes, the Mint, Cutter Service, were in the early 1790s and then came the Reynolds Affair and the whole mess with the 1800 presidential election. But these are all just historical facts that anyone can easily find online, so Elizabeth must have been looking for something more."

"Yes. But what? You are one of the foremost experts on early American history. Is there something you see that we can't?"

Doris glanced out the window to the park. Circles of dry leaves swirled around the trunks of bare trees before being whipped away by the wind again. Cold. November. There was something right in the front of her brain, a barely formed thought. More like a mist than a thought. She stared hard at the cold landscape again and then she knew.

"*Root cellar!*" she almost yelled into the phone. "It's the root cellar! I know it. Last month, the Historical Society received some old architectural plans as part of a bequest. Apparently, the documents had been in the family for generations and had just been shuffled between apartments, storage lockers, and various family members in the city. Finally, one of the younger heirs decided to make some sense of all the boxes, and he conducted an inventory. He categorized them and determined which ones were part of the bequest. Then, thankfully, sent them to us. It's quite a substantial box, and we have been going through them very carefully, authenticating them and, in some cases, just trying to figure out what they are. We've been working especially hard on one set of documents that appear to be partial plans for a root cellar, dated somewhere in the late 1700s. But here's the exciting part. It may be the plans are for a root cellar at Hamilton Grange. If this is the case, it would be the first architectural plan of any kind to be found of The Grange. It would be a significant historical find. Of course, it would also be of great significance to the Historical Society, so we are approaching authentication carefully and conservatively. We can't afford a misstep. We are also proceeding quietly with our process so as not to bring premature media pressure to bear. Only a few people in the Society even know we're working on this. That's why Elizabeth's database search for architectural plans of The Grange didn't yield anything. There's nothing to find—yet."

"That's exciting!" Schwartz said. "But why do you think the key would fit the root cellar?"

"It's exactly the kind of key that was used for root cellars at that time. Vegetables, pickled vegetables and fruits, dried foodstuffs—all these things were quite valuable. Food was often scarce and expensive, especially in the winter. Having a secure root cellar could be the difference between making it through the winter or not.

Later, when these items became more plentiful, people ceased even locking the cellars, but in the early 1800s, security was important."

"That makes sense. Because it was so valuable, hiding the key in the piano, away from the probing eyes of the servants would be a good idea, but retrieving the key and putting it back, probably every day, would be difficult."

"Yes, it would," Ms. Sullivan agreed. "You're right. It wouldn't work. Either Elizabeth or Alexander would have to go into the salon, close the door, fish underneath the piano for the key, use it, and then return it. The servants would certainly note that over time as would the children. It would become an open secret quickly. Plus, there's no root cellar at The Grange now, and there's no record of The Grange ever having a root cellar, even though it would be a common addition for a house of that size."

"What else? Can you think of any other important keyholes?"

"It could be the key for the iron chest. Alexander must have had one either at The Grange or at his law offices. In fact, he would probably be remiss if he didn't have one for clients' documents, even if he didn't use it for his own."

"That's a good thought too, but any iron chest would be long gone I expect."

"Yes," Doris said. "And Elizabeth would have known that too. If she was looking for a key, her focus wasn't on the key, but on what the key fit into. It's the thing the key fits that Elizabeth was after."

"Right."

"I can't think of anything else. If it was for Alexander's personal strongbox, that is certainly gone as well. And what if it wasn't Alexander's at all? The drawer was placed at the behest of Angelica Schuyler Church, Elizabeth's sister. Isn't it more likely that it was something owned by Elizabeth? Maybe a strongbox of her own?"

"Yes, absolutely," Detective Schwartz concurred. "More likely." She sounded glum. Instead of moving the ball forward, she felt like the other team just got a safety in her end zone. "Everything you've said makes sense. Maybe we need to focus on the killers. Most likely it's more than one. They must have known what Elizabeth was after, or at least have had a good idea, otherwise they wouldn't have pursued her."

"True," Doris said.

And they certainly wouldn't have gone through all that trouble and expense to wire her glasses, Schwartz thought.

"Problem is, we don't have a thing on them," Schwartz said. "As you can imagine, the cameras at that subway station are broken. It was the middle of the night, so there were no witnesses or at least none that have come forward. There are no fingerprints, no footprints, no clothing fibers, nothing. The only thing we know is that whatever it was, it was important enough or valuable enough to go after her and kill her."

"But they didn't get the key."

"No, they didn't."

"She jumped."

Schwartz wanted to smack herself on the head. Of course, she jumped. Why didn't she put this together earlier? "You're right Doris. Absolutely right. They would have grabbed her, snatched the key, and then pushed her into the path of the train. It wouldn't make any sense to kill her without first getting the key."

"She must have jumped onto the tracks when she realized that she wouldn't be able to get away. She sacrificed her life for that key."

"Yes."

"That's a big sacrifice," Doris said her eyes filling with tears. "I'm going to hang up now. I'll think about it some more and call you later."

For what things would someone give up their life? Doris thought. For an ideal, for truth? For honor, equality, freedom? For the hope of a better world? For love? All sacred values. Values that inform, shape, and direct a life. Values that lift a life from the mundane to the heavens.

What was it for Elizabeth? What sacred value made her jump in front of a train? What was worth her life?

She didn't know. Doris looked out the window and considered anew the barren, cold branches twisting in the wind. She wiped her eyes and sighed. She still thought she was right about the root cellar. She knew it didn't make any practical sense, but it still felt right to her. She opened her file drawer and hunted for the contact information for the architectural plan bequest. William Hopkins, a junior at NYU majoring in linguistics. That explained his attention to the details of the bequest. There was also a fair chance she could reach him in between classes.

"Hello, is this William Hopkins? This is Doris Sullivan. I am the director of the New York Historical Society."

"Oh yes, well, hi," William stuttered nervously.

"Thank you for picking up," Ms. Sullivan continued. "I wanted to thank you again so much for your family's bequest to the Historical Society. Even though we are going slowly and meticulously through the documents, we have already found some notable documents."

"That's wonderful to hear," William said having regained his composure.

"There are some documents that appear quite old and could be of great historical significance. We're working to authenticate them now but, as you can imagine, it's a painstaking process."

"Oh, of course, I'm sure it is," William said. "I just took enough of a look to see if certain documents were responsive to the bequest, but I didn't really go much farther. I thought it better to have the experts do it."

"Thank you for that, William," Doris said. "And I'll tell you, it's not very easy for us either," she laughed. "One question, if I may though, is about a set of architectural plans. Do you know which documents I'm speaking about?"

"Yes, I do. There was only one set of architectural drawings, right?"

"Yes," Ms. Sullivan said. "Do you happen to know anything about the background of the drawings? Where they came from? How they might have been procured?"

"Actually, I do. That set came from my great uncle's storage locker. I think it was part of a folder that had some handwriting on it. I remember it said 'Lt. Samuelson' on it, but I can't find the folder now or I would have included it. It got misplaced somehow during the consolidation of all the documents."

"OK. Are there any other, I guess we can call them 'companion' documents or housings that any of the documents came in that you have? Even if they're tattered or in poor shape, they still might be able to give some context for authentication purposes."

"Oh, sure," William said. "I think I still have all of those. I'll drop them by in the next few days."

"Wonderful. Thank you so much," Ms. Sullivan said. "I will look forward to receiving them, and thank you again, William."

"My pleasure."

Doris was delighted she had made that call. As conscientious as William was in assembling the bequest, it was clear he had made a huge miss in not including the companion documents and housings that would help the Society authenticate the documents. Still, she couldn't fault him. At twenty years old, he'd certainly done a better job than any of his family before him.

But there was something else that stuck in Doris's mind. She opened the file drawer and took out the bequest document inventory. She scanned the entries. Yes, there it was. "Lt. Samuelson." He appeared as an entry in seven categories. She pored through the entries. There were requisition forms, invoices, schedules, and various kinds of administrative forms. It looked like

Lt. Samuelson was a staff aide to some government official or officer. She saw the initials "AH" on a few requisition forms, but she knew she might just be imagining
what she wanted to see instead of what was true. It wasn't
until she came to an invoice with Alexander Hamilton's
signature that she knew she was right.

21

PIERCE DIDN'T LIKE what had just happened. The more he thought about it, the more unsettled he became. What was she doing looking at his computer? She had never done that before, and he saw no reason why she had to do it now. More importantly, why was her personal email open with a spreadsheet that looked like one of his models? He thought more about what he had seen on her screen. He had only glanced at it for a second, but it looked like one of his spreadsheets, worse yet, one of his gold spreadsheets, just a bit clunkier. He thought about running it by Timothy but decided against it. No reason to concern him and risk losing his confidence, especially with only one buy to go. He needed to take a better look, but he had no idea how he was going to do that. He certainly couldn't hack her email, and she was too smart to be tricked. Maybe a surprise attack would work. He stirred in the rest of the cinnamon, put a lid on his coffee and headed back to the conference room.

"Hey, Sarah," he began. "Why were you looking at the spreadsheet on my computer, and why did you have one of my models up on your personal email?"

Sarah swiveled around to face him. She thought he might have seen her personal email open earlier, so she had used the time wisely. She was ready for him.

"I told you," she said. "I was trying to figure out where the spreadsheet fit into my analysis. I didn't want to wait until you got back from lunch to have you email it to me."

"Fine," Pierce said. "What about your email, your *personal* email?" he emphasized. "Are you using your personal account for bank business? Is that something I should share with Mr. Bardack?"

"That wasn't bank business," Sarah said sharply. "If you want to go tell on me for opening my personal email during bank hours, go ahead, but that's as far as any of it will go."

Pierce was getting flustered. He was supposed to be on the offense, not the other way around. "OK then, why did you have one of my spreadsheets in your personal email?"

She couldn't believe her ears. He had said one of his "models" earlier. Did he just say, "my spreadsheets?" Did he really think it was his spreadsheet? The spreadsheet created by Jessica Hamilton Madison was so similar to those constructed by Pierce that, at a glance, even Pierce thought they were the same.

"Not that it's any of your business. That spreadsheet is not your spreadsheet. It's not bank business. It's my personal matter and none of yours. I am not going to talk about this anymore."

Pierce walked back to his computer and sat down. All that for nothing. He tried to recall exactly what the spreadsheet in Sarah's email looked like since the chance of him getting it now was about zero. It looked like a replication of one of his gold models, but slightly cruder. The elegant microbuys he crafted in his spreadsheet appeared bulkier here, although the shape was still present. It reminded him of reverse engineering. More like a spreadsheet that had been built from the end to the beginning, capturing the buy cycle that had already taken place, instead of from the beginning to the end as he constructed them, plotting the arc of the buy cycle that was going to happen.

Smug Pierce, Sarah thought. Usually so full of bravado and ego. He didn't look so good now. Was there really something more than just a coincidence between Jessica's and Pierce's spreadsheets? She studied him more carefully over the top of her computer. He was sweating—something she'd never seen before. She suspected he took all precautions possible to avoid that happening as it was so inconsistent with the self-assured, capable persona he was trying to project at the bank. Nevertheless, he was sweating now. He was also fidgeting. Something else she'd never seen him do.

Pierce abruptly stood up and left the conference room. The minute he was outside the room, he called Timothy.

"Hi, Timothy, do you have a quick minute? Are you Midtown by chance?"

"Hi, Pierce. No, unfortunately, still in Washington. What's up?"

"Give me a few minutes. I'm going downstairs, and I'll call you back."

Pierce caught the express elevator and was across the street and in the park in six minutes. For once, he didn't notice the beautiful fall colors or appreciate the resplendent barrels of mums dotting the walkway. He reflexively pulled his jacket tight about him and strode to his favorite café table behind the carousel.

"Timothy? Me again. Yeah, I just wanted to run something by you and get your take on it. I think it's nothing, but just wanted to be sure."

"Always a good idea, Pierce," Timothy said jovially. He was in a great mood. They were almost there. He was finally allowing himself to stick just a toe into the future. He could smell the sea breeze, feel the sun on his skin, taste the rum as it slipped down his throat. He could hardly wait. "How can I be of service?"

"Well, I was working on some compliance deals this morning with Sarah Brockman. I think I've even mentioned her to you on occasion. Priggish. Stuffy. Mean. We were working through the numbers on some deals, and she was giving me a hard time, as usual, on compliance. But when I walked past her screen to go to lunch, she had, what looked like, one of my models up on her screen in her personal email. Plus, although I only caught a quick glance, it really looked like one of my gold buy spreadsheets. I know this all sounds incredible and a little crazy. That's why I wanted to run it by you."

The color drained out of Timothy's face. He felt like he had just been run over by a semitruck.

"OK, OK," Timothy said almost hyperventilating. "What exactly did the spreadsheet look like, and what do you mean it was in her personal email?"

"Just that. When I walked by, I could see that her personal email was open. It was in there. It looked just like one of my buys, just a little blockier. Like it had been reverse engineered."

"OK. Thanks," Timothy struggled to get the words out. "I'll call you later."

Timothy kicked himself. He was the only one in the full loop, the only one entrusted with all the pieces. He was also the one charged to know much gold was in the world. As the Treasury official in charge of the depositories, he knew, more than anyone else, how much gold was in the U.S. gold depositories. He knew how much was in the global gold stores, and the long term and short-term projected output from mining. He knew how much gold was circulating from other sources. He knew all these things because he needed to know. It was his end of the bargain. And it was during this process, that he had met Elizabeth Hamilton Walker.

At first, he thought she was a reporter. He had received a call from the manager at the West Point Depository. It wasn't their regularly scheduled conference day and time, so he had paid close attention.

"Hi, Mr. T. How are you doing?" Devon had begun.

Timothy hated that Devon called him that, but he was helpless to do anything about it since Devon thought it was hilarious.

"Fine, Devon. How are you?"

"Good, Mr. T. I just wanted to tell you about something weird that happened a few hours ago. I was finalizing the ledger for the recounting in vault twenty-two and had been at it for a few hours so when 1:00 PM hit, I thought I'd go out for lunch. I was checking out at the front when I noticed an attractive woman over to the side chatting up Marcus. They were clearly having a nice time, and she seemed quite settled in, as if she'd been there for a while. I excused Marcus and brought him into the side room where I asked him what had been going on. He said she had shown him her DOD ID card, driver's license, and visitors pass clearance, and he had logged her in. Marcus said she had just been asking basic questions everyone asks like depository amounts, how the gold is kept, you know, the usual. She asked Marcus if he had ever seen any of the gold and been back in the vaults. Of course, Marcus wanted to impress, so he admitted that he had even though that's a breach of protocol."

"I'm sure you had a chat with Marcus about that," Timothy said.

"Yeah, but didn't write him up, first offense and all. Anyway, this is where it gets interesting. She told Marcus that she had heard about a legend of hidden treasure. That iron chests filled with bullion had been stored at West Point when it opened in 1802 and then transferred to the gold depository after it was built in the late 1930s. She wanted to know if he had ever heard of such a thing. Marcus, truthfully, said no."

"Quite fanciful. Sounds like a reporter or an outlier treasure hunter," Timothy said.

"I thought so too, so I walked him back out and talked with her myself. I asked her if she was a reporter and she said no, just an 'interested citizen,' which made me uncomfortable because she was sure acting like a reporter. She asked me the same question about the iron chests and I, of course, asked her if she had made a Freedom of Information Act request. She said she didn't have time and could we just help her out informally. That was all I needed to know and told her politely that we weren't allowed to do that and that she needed to submit a FOIA request."

"That's right, Devon. Good to direct her to submit a FOIA, but I don't think she's going to get anything with that anyway."

"Me either. That was a long time ago. I doubt there are any records left, let alone any iron chests filled with gold." Devon laughed at the absurdity of the image of iron chests sitting around with gold in them.

"It does seem a bit farfetched. I wonder what she meant by 'she didn't have time.'"

"I don't know. That's why I thought she was a reporter or somebody on a deadline."

"Yeah, very strange," Timothy said. "I'll check her out and make sure she's not a reporter or other person who might be of concern to us. What does the logbook say?"

"Elizabeth Walker, 390 WEA, Apt. 14C, New York."

"OK. Thanks for the call, Devon. Talk soon."

It seemed odd to Timothy. Odd. Not necessarily concerning, but he started a background check anyway. Pretty basic stuff. Mrs. Elizabeth Hamilton Walker. Worked for the last four years at Seidels, in marketing.

Lived her whole life in New York City. Recently married, no children, descendent of Alexander Hamilton. He paused. Descendent of Alexander Hamilton, the first Secretary of the Treasury. West Point. Iron chests. 1802. It began to seem odder. He had many tools at his disposal. He decided to use them.

"Good day, Dmitri. I have a project for you."

"Always a pleasure Mr. Murphy. I'm at your disposal."

"Thank you. It may be nothing, but again, it may not. I can't afford to take any chances. I need surveillance on a Elizabeth Hamilton Walker, 390 WEA, Apt. 14C, New York. The best of the best. I don't care about the cost. It has to be undetectable. I don't know what's the latest and greatest in the spy world. I will leave that to you."

"I understand. I will send you updates by our usual channels."

"Yes, thank you."

That's how he knew Elizabeth went to 48 Wall Street. At first, he thought she was attending an event there. Renovated in the early 1990s and situated at the corner of Wall and William Streets, the building was a premier event space for all kinds of public and private affairs. He had been there many times himself and had enjoyed each one.

Elizabeth had walked into the lobby right at noon and stopped briefly at the table exhibit for the lunchtime program put on by the Museum of American Finance. The Museum had been housed on three floors of 48 Wall for many years until it was displaced by a flood, but it still had some legacy rights to the open space, which it used to sponsor all kinds of financial programs. It always struck Timothy as perfect kismet that the only independent public museum in the United States dedicated to preserving, exhibiting, and teaching about American finance and financial history was located in the same place as the Bank of New York, one of the first banks in the country and founded by the first Secretary of the Treasury. Rebuilt in the Neo-Georgian and Colonial Revival style in 1927 to 1929, it was designated as a city landmark and registered in the National Register of Historic Places. A particularly delightful set of facts about the building, which Timothy had just learned a few weeks ago, was that in a fitting tribute to the Bank's founder, the cornerstone had been laid on January 12, 1928, the 171st birthday of Alexander Hamilton, with the building's opening occurring on January 12, 1929, Hamilton's 172nd birthday.

Built over the original raised basement, there had been rampant speculation in the financial community that the "necessary vaults" that had been built "for the business of a bank," were still existent in the basement and might contain untold riches and treasures. But that fervor had died off many years ago due to lack of evidence and access, and now it was only the occasional *Secrets of New York* ghost hunter who retained any motivation—until now.

Elizabeth warmly greeted the man behind the table, and he came around it and gave her an equally warm hug.

"It's great to see you, Elizabeth," he said. Timothy was pleased with how seamlessly the eyeglasses video recorder Dmitri had installed caught the exchange.

"Hi, Ben," Elizabeth replied. "I was hoping to catch you. How's the talk going?"

"Oh, just wonderful Elizabeth. You know Alexander is so popular right now thanks to Lin-Manuel Miranda. What a fabulous opportunity for us to educate the public about finance, in colonial times and now. We're delighted to have this bump."

"Yes, hopefully it will help fundraising for the museum too. I hope you find a new home soon."

"Me too."

"Well, Ben. I have a meeting, so will have to dash, but it's been lovely seeing you. Take care," Elizabeth said as she pivoted and turned to one of the side doors in the lobby.

She opened the door slowly, knowing the room was small and cramped by a desk almost at the door. No one was there.

"Hello," she called out.

Rustling and scurrying greeted her from the adjoining room.

"Well, hello Mrs. Walker," a rather portly man said as he entered the room brushing crumbs off his shirt with a napkin. "Please excuse me, I was just finishing lunch."

"I'm sorry, Mr. Kentley. Is this a bad time? Would you like me to come back later?"

"No, Mrs. Walker. It's fine. Just give me a moment."

He was back in less than a minute, napkin and crumb free.

"Thank you for seeing me and allowing me this privileged access. As I explained on the phone, it will just take a few minutes. I greatly appreciate your help."

"My pleasure," Mr. Kentley said. "This way."

He led her to a door at the farthest end of the lobby. Nondescript and partly hidden under the grand staircase, it was hard to see. Mr. Kentley took a set of keys from his pocket.

"We keep this door locked for obvious reasons," he said. "There are still those occasional 'treasure hunters' who think there might be something valuable in the basement. We certainly don't need any ridiculous commotion like that around here."

"Certainly not."

"Watch your step," he said as he opened the door and motioned for Elizabeth to go down.

For all its creepy exterior, the stairwell was well-lit and in good repair. Elizabeth proceeded down the stairs as Mr. Kentley closed and locked the door behind them. The three flights of stairs ended abruptly in a large, almost empty, room. Unlike the refurbished stairwell, the floor, ceiling, and walls of the room were a haphazard mix of stone, brick, concrete, and patching material. There was evidence of water damage that had been mitigated, but not corrected, and a trace of mildew. The room wasn't just neglected and forgotten but felt abandoned. Intentionally so.

Elizabeth stepped gently to the floor.

"I told you it was a bit of a mess," Mr. Kentley said. "There's no reason to keep it up. No reason to spend any money on it. We had to spend the money on the stairs for OSHA even though we told them no one ever comes down here."

"They take their job seriously, I guess. So are those the vaults?" Elizabeth asked, pointing to the far wall.

"Yes."

Elizabeth walked across the room. She could feel the unevenness of the floor beneath her feet and the weight of history pervading the room. There were two large vaults against the far wall.

"They look old. 1800s? Are these the original vaults for the Bank of New York?"

"Yes, we believe so, although no one has ever had them authenticated. That's something the building ownership is considering doing and then, of course, donating them to either the Museum of Finance or the Museum of the City of New York, but no one has got that far on it yet. I think they're concerned about the cost of having to move them, which would be significant."

Elizabeth looked at them carefully. "Do you mind if I touch them?"

"No, go ahead."

Elizabeth moved her hands over the cold, hard metal, feeling the indentations where the Bank's identification numbers had been cut into the side, the grooves formed by years of twisting the dials, opening and closing the handles. She used her phone light to look inside the vaults. Some dust, a paper clip, and a crumpled envelope were inside. She reached for the envelope, smoothed it, and opened it. Nothing. But then she hadn't expected to find anything. Not in these vaults anyway. She quietly looked for Mr. Kentley. He was still across the room by the staircase, checking messages on his phone. He had no idea that she had been researching him, and the other building management's agents for weeks, and that she had determined that he was the most likely to have the information she was after. She had chosen him. Now she would see if she was right.

"Mr. Kentley," she said. "I can't begin to tell you how appreciative I am that you allowed me access to these vaults. Vaults that my forefather installed. Vaults that represented security and safety not just for the Bank, but for the financial future, and really the future existence, of the United States as well."

"It's my pleasure, Mrs. Walker," Mr. Kentley said. "It's not often that I get to meet a direct heir to Alexander Hamilton."

"Well, thank you, Mr. Kentley. It's been my honor and privilege. I try to do all I can to uphold the family name."

Mr. Kentley smiled and nodded obsequiously. "And a fine job you're doing too, I might add."

Elizabeth moved closer to him, in a conspiratorial, rather clubby way. "I can see that you're the one who controls the show here. You're the true person in charge. That's obvious."

She saw the response she was hoping for. Mr. Kentley straightened up to full size, puffed up by the flattery.

"Why yes, Mrs. Walker. I have been in charge for over ten years. I know everything there is to know about this building and the tenants." He leaned closer and said, "I know things even the owners don't know."

Just as she thought. He was the one.

"As I said, I'm so grateful to you for showing me these vaults, but I was wondering if you could show me the others as well. I know it's a bit unusual, but I need to answer the questions raised in these newly discovered family letters. It's my responsibility. And I'm sure that if anyone has access to the other vaults, it would be you." It was a bluff she had used many times before, boldly asserting assumed facts. In truth, she had no idea if there were any other vaults or whether there had ever been any other vaults.

Mr. Kentley took the bait. "Well," he said. "When I first started this job, the building was still finishing the last of the renovations, the unimportant ones, the ones not seen by the public. They involved some of the crawl spaces on the main floor and the basement. One day there was a lot of activity. Four bigwigs came in, I think they were the building's owners, and they had some workmen with them with tools and a bunch of equipment, even some welding stuff. They all went down into the basement. At lunchtime, food was delivered, and they called up and asked me to bring it down. I guess I came down quicker than they thought and when I was at the bottom, I heard one of them say: 'Nothing, huh? What a shame.' I scooched over just a bit and was able to see into the adjoining room. There were two really old safes in there, wide open, with nothing inside. It looked like they had just been opened. Everyone was standing around and a few guys were peering inside the safes. There was a little dust and smoke that had been stirred up from forcing the safes open. I scooted back to the stairwell and stood there waiting. In a minute, one of the guys came out, and I pretended that I had just come down. 'Thanks,' he said. And I went back upstairs. So, if you're asking me if there were other vaults here, the answer is yes. If you're asking me if they had anything in them, the answer is no."

"Thank you so much for telling me, Mr. Kentley," Elizabeth said. "Is there any way I could see them now? Just to cross all my t's?"

Mr. Kentley paused. He wasn't supposed to know about the safes. He wasn't even supposed to know about the adjoining room. The door had been built into the wall. It wasn't really hidden, but you could easily miss it if you weren't looking carefully. He had never been through that door in all the years he had worked in the building. At first, he had been intrigued and wanted to take a look for himself, but he was afraid of getting caught and losing his job. Plus, he had already seen inside and there was nothing to see. After a few years, he had completely forgotten about the room and, he suspected, everyone else had too. To his knowledge, no one had ever removed the safes or done anything with them. In all likelihood, they were still there, just the way they were ten years ago and just the way they were over two hundred years ago. He didn't think there was any harm in showing Mrs. Walker, and she was so nice, he thought. And an heir to Alexander Hamilton.

"Sure," he said. "Follow me."

They walked across the room, and she could see a small doorknob, painted the same color as the wall, protruding from the wall. "It's hard to see, isn't it?" Mr. Kentley asked.

"Yes, very. You probably wouldn't even see it if you didn't know it was there."

Mr. Kentley turned the knob and the door opened easily. There was no light in the room, and Mr. Kentley fumbled around on the wall before he found the switch and flipped it on. The room was immediately bathed in a garish, cold light from the sole dangling lightbulb in the center of the room. The room smelled musty and dank, and the floor had a light coat of dust on it. It was clear the door hadn't been opened for a very long time.

"Wow," Elizabeth said. "No one's been inside here for quite a while."

"Yes. Maybe that day was the last day."

There were two antique safes with their doors ajar. Elizabeth approached and looked in. Nothing. She had suspected that would be the case, but the confirmation was hard to accept. She had exhausted both of her leads and was at a dead end. She believed what Alexander had written. She knew he had set aside a trove to fund a renewed fight for democracy if it should become necessary. More than anyone, he understood that money would be needed to win a fight like that. But, of course, through the generations of his heirs, even as the committed caretakers of the democracy with which they were entrusted, things happened. Papers were lost or given for safekeeping to a few and forgotten by the many. Or maybe the location was never written down at all in an abundance of caution and just meant to be told to each upcoming generation. In any event, the location of the trove was presently unknown. Elizabeth sighed.

"Thank you, Mr. Kentley" Elizabeth said. "I was hoping there would be something more. But all I see are two empty antique safes."

"That's all I see as well, Mrs. Walker."

"Thank you again, Mr. Kentley," Elizabeth said walking back to the stairwell. "I appreciate your help. I think I'm able to close my review of the family letters."

"Glad to be of service," Mr. Kentley said as he labored up the stairs.

Upon reaching the lobby, Elizabeth thanked him again and took leave of him, the Bank, and for a moment, the entire situation. She was tired, frustrated, and angry. All this had been thrust upon her. It had never been her choice, just a quirk of birth. But she had never been angry about it until now. How could her ancestors be so careless? How could they lose the location of the trove? But even as these thoughts swirled mercilessly around in her head, she knew it wasn't true. Her ancestors were not that stupid or careless. But they were cautious and vigilant. They had been the victims of deceit, lies, and blackmail. There were prying eyes all around. They wouldn't have written the location down in the society's logbooks or letters where someone could find it. They wouldn't have written it down at all.

She walked down to Fort Clinton at the tip of Manhattan. She let the bracing ocean breeze wash over her and clear her head. She was missing something. The clues were there, she knew it. She just hadn't yet put them together.

22

S ARAH HAD MOVED out of the conference room and was back in her office cradling a giant mug of coffee, studying the spreadsheets. It was already late in the afternoon, and she knew the coffee would keep her up probably much too late, but she didn't care. She decided to try a forensic matching and see if the spreadsheet was really tied to gold buys that had occurred in the last few months. Ralph had already verified the macro thesis. There had been massive aggregative gold transfers in the last six months. Almost indiscernible until you stepped back and looked at the whole picture. She was just starting to do a historical matching when her cell phone buzzed.

"Hi, Ralph. Yes, I was just starting to do that. It seems like we're so on the money, so to speak. I'm almost wondering if we should share this with Detective Schwartz."

"Possibly," Ralph said. "I don't know. I don't really trust the police, and I feel like we'll lose control of what we're doing. I'm not sure we have enough to give them. I mean there's really no evidence, just theories."

"I know what you mean. Let's hold off a bit and see what we can do on our own."

"I want the key."

"What?" Sarah asked. "The key?"

"Yes, that's why I was calling. I just had this overwhelming feeling that we should have a copy of the key that was found in Elizabeth's pocket. I mean, she died for it, right?" He said, the words catching in his throat. "It must be important."

"I agree. I hadn't really thought about it. We can't get the original key, of course, but I wonder if we could make a copy? Detective Schwartz freely let me hold it when I was in her office the other day. I bet we could bring some soft wax in and impress the key in it. Then we could get a copy made."

"Yes, that's a great idea," Ralph agreed. "It must be important, and right now it's our only chance. Soon, it won't be so easy for Detective Schwartz to check out the evidence bags each day. They'll probably be going into a more permanent location. Plus, she won't have a need for them either, especially the key. The more I'm talking about it, the quicker I think we need to act. I wonder if we can get in to see her today? If both of us go, I bet we can distract her enough to impress the key without her seeing us, especially because she won't be on the lookout for it."

"OK, sounds good," Sarah said. "What pretext? Why should we say we want to come in?"

"Well, I just found the train ticket to Montauk along with a restaurant tab and some kind of museum stub, so we could go in to drop them off."

"Good, but why would I be going? It doesn't take two people to drop off a few pieces of paper."

"That's true," Ralph said.

"I have a few recent receipts from lunches and dinners Elizabeth and I shared in the last few months, not that they're relevant, but I could drop them off as well. I'll go by my apartment and get them. I'll call her when you're in her office and when I'm close to the precinct and see if I can just 'pop by.' That will also provide a little distraction to impress the key in the wax."

"OK, let's go for it. See if it works."

*   *   *

Detective Schwartz replaced the receiver, a quizzical look on her face. What seemed insignificant to most, did not seem so to her. Ralph Walker wanted to drop some receipts by from Elizabeth's trip to Montauk. Nothing suspicious there, but when she said he could just drop them at the front desk, he stammered something about that being the only copy and that he would be more comfortable giving them to her personally. Strange, the detective thought. Wonder where this is going. She decided to let it play out. He was at her office door in less than an hour.

"Good afternoon, Mr. Walker. Thank you for coming in," the detective said. "Have a seat," she said motioning to the client chairs in front of her desk. "How are you?" He seemed nervous. He kept organizing and then reorganizing the slips of paper in his hands, even though there were just a few, and glancing out the window.

"I'm OK," Ralph said. "Not great. Can't really sleep or eat much. Having trouble focusing on anything. Mostly just numb." His voice trailed off.

"I'm sorry."

He handed her the slips of paper. "One thing, if you don't mind, Detective?" He asked. "Would you mind letting me hold the key that Elizabeth had in her pocket when she died? I know I didn't recognize it when you showed me pictures of it a few days ago, but I just want to touch it, hold it, if you don't mind. Just hold the last thing Elizabeth held before she died."

"Of course," Schwartz said as she made her way to the evidence bag. She had just retrieved the key and handed it to Ralph when her cell phone rang.

"Hello? Oh hi, Ms. Brockman."

"I've been looking for receipts, pictures, texts, emails, etc. like you asked for that could help show what Elizabeth had been doing and where she'd been going in the last few months. I have some pictures and things that would be hard to email to you, so I figured I'd just drop them by. I'm actually right down the street at the moment, so I'll just come by if that works for you?"

"Why yes, of course, Ms. Brockman. If that's not too much trouble."

Detective Schwartz glanced at Ralph as he studied the key. She didn't know what was in the works, but something was going on.

"It certainly is a beautiful key," Ralph said. "It's very old, isn't it?"

"Yes, we had it authenticated by the Met. It was made around 1800."

Ralph wasn't prepared for the rush of grief and pain that swept over him as held the key. He gently turned it in his hands, tracing the scrollwork on the bow and the hard edges of the teeth. He let the heavy weight of the key settle in the palm of his hand. It was warm. It should have been cold, resting as it had been in the plastic bag on the cold filing cabinet, but it was warm. He could feel her. He could feel Elizabeth. He could feel her love through this key. The tears rolled softly down his cheeks, and he didn't try to stop them. He looked up to see the detective studying him, but kindly and without judgment.

"You can feel her." Schwartz said.

"Yes."

"I'm sorry," the detective said again.

"Me too."

Ralph closed his palm around the key and looked up to see Sarah standing in the doorway.

"Hi," she said. "Is this a bad time?"

"No, not at all," the detective said. "Ralph came in a few minutes ago. I know you know each other, so I didn't think he'd mind if you dropped by as well."

"Of course not," Ralph said as he stood up to give Sarah a hug. That was her cue. The plan was to accidentally sweep whatever was on the detective's desk to the floor as she reached to hug Ralph. The ensuing commotion caused by catching and picking up papers, they hoped, would be enough for Ralph to impress the key. Even better though, was coffee. Sarah had seen an almost full cup of coffee in a paper cup sitting at the edge of Schwartz's desk when she walked in. Even better. Sarah moved quickly to embrace Ralph, knocking the cup filled with coffee all over the detective's desk.

"Oh, no!" Sarah and the detective yelled almost in unison.

"Grab the papers!"

To the untrained eye, it looked like all three were trying to stop coffee, catch papers, and begin mopping up the mess, but, in truth, Ralph had turned, quickly pulled the wax from his pocket, impressed the key, and put the wax back—all in the blink of an eye, except that Detective Schwartz's eye did not blink. She saw it all. She decided not to say a word. Ralph and Sarah needed the key for something. She would roll with it for now and find out what was going on when the time was right.

"I'm so sorry," Sarah said, still dabbing the papers. "What a clumsy move."

"I think we're OK," the detective said. They finished what they could and put some papers to dry on the windowsill.

"Here are the things I came to drop off," Sarah said as she handed a clip of papers to the detective. "Sorry again."

"It's fine. Thank you both for coming in. I appreciate your help."

As soon as they were on Central Park West, Ralph pulled the wax mold from his pocket.

"It looks great!" Sarah exclaimed. "We should be able to get a key made from this easily."

"I think so too," Ralph agreed. "I'll go to the key shop on my way home. I've got to take Bodie out."

"Of course, thanks Ralph. Talk later."

23

D MITRI CLOSED HIS eyes for a moment against the late afternoon sun and took a long drag on his cigarette. It was that time of day when sunglasses helped or didn't, and he had decided to go without and squint. Nevertheless, he could easily make out Sarah and Ralph in front of the precinct across the street talking quietly and then parting. Sarah walking briskly down Central Park West, her hair swinging from side to side, Ralph going the other way.

He finished his last cigarette and started rolling his balls, his mind drifting back to last fall. The more he watched Sarah, the more he noticed the similarities between her and the girl with the chestnut hair. The girl who was still his. His in his memory. He knew the girl had a name, but he had picked out a private name for her, just for him. Mary, Mary, full of grace, beauty, kindness, and forgiveness. Unbounded forgiveness for all in need for everything they had done, even him. If he saw her again, he thought she would forgive him, but he wasn't sure he would ask her. He could still see her long swinging hair, her uneven smile, a smile so much like Sarah's. He started thinking about Sarah. The same smile, the same walk, the way she tossed her hair. They could be sisters. He wondered if she would like a gift too. Just a small token to let her know someone was near, watching, protecting her from harm. A secret friend. He had picked up his tool kit at the apartment. He wanted something small to start with so he could increase the size of his gifts later. It always worked better that way. He started looking around the park. Something small. Something furry. He had been suspended so many times at school for this when he was younger. But when he got older and had moved on to bigger things, nobody seemed to care. It was as if a door had closed, and he was on the other side. By high school, he mostly stopped going to school and eventually dropped out. A few weeks after his eighteenth birthday, he got the call.

The KGB. Even now, decades after the SVR name change, they were still the KGB to him. He grew up with them—with the comic books, the graphic novels, the movies. He read all the articles, searched the newspapers, scoured the internet for anything he could find about them. He idolized them and wanted to be them. Eventually, he was.

It had been a good run, he thought. At least until it wasn't. He moved deeper into the park, where the bushes were thick, and took out his tool kit.

At 5:00 PM, Timothy was still kicking himself. He knew Sarah Brockman and Elizabeth Hamilton Walker were good friends, but he had barely thought it necessary to set surveillance on Elizabeth, let alone on Sarah. All he had found out about Elizabeth was that she was looking for some kind of lost treasure, as nonsensical as it sounded, and that she had acquired a key from Hamilton Grange that night. Her death was a horrible mistake. It wasn't supposed to have happened. He had asked Dmitri and Yugov to watch the camera feed and provide him with updates. He had never asked them to tail her and certainly not to intimidate her. But he wondered if someone else had. After the accident, Dmitri had sent him a curt text detailing that she had fallen in front of an oncoming train, but that was it. When asked for more explanation, he failed to respond, again and again. Radio silence, and this from someone who had always been available to him, at all hours, for all things, even in the middle of the night. Yugov too. The fact that both had now gone missing was worrisome, hugely so.

Even more troubling was the fact that he was the one who made the decision about Sarah. He was the one who decided that she didn't need to be watched, that Elizabeth would never have taken Sarah into her confidence, that there was no need to worry since Elizabeth was dead and the key remained with her. But now, he thought it was an enormous error in judgment. What did Sarah know? What was Sarah doing with one of Pierce's spreadsheets? How did any of this fit together?

He was getting sweaty and worried. He was one buy away from freedom. A lifetime of freedom. He couldn't let this slip through his fingers. He had only had Dmitri and Yugov and now he had neither. Espionage was not his usual line of work. He didn't know where to turn.

He picked up the phone.

"Pierce? Hi, it's Timothy. I'm going to need you to do one more thing for me."

"Of course," Pierce said. He had been waiting for Timothy to call back after he had hung up so quickly. "What do you need?"

"I need you to help me out with Sarah. We need to find out what that spreadsheet is all about. It's too random, bizarre really, that she has one of your spreadsheets, or one that looks like one of yours, in her personal email. It's probably just a strange coincidence, but it is very strange. We only have one day until our last buy and then we're done, and our futures secured."

"I don't know what else I can do," Pierce said plaintively. "I already asked her. I tried to find out what was going on, but she closed me down completely. Pretty well dared me to bring it up to Bardack at the bank."

"OK," Timothy said. "Just do your best to poke around. We only have one day."

"One day can be a very long time."

Yes, it can, Timothy thought as he hung up. He felt impotent and scared. He knew who had authorized the tail on Elizabeth. He knew who Dmitri and Yugov really worked for, and it wasn't him. He wondered if they were watching Sarah and everyone in Elizabeth's orb just to be sure. He wondered if they were watching him.

Of course, they were. The stakes were too high. They were watching Sarah and Ralph and Pierce and him. They were watching all of them and probably many more he didn't even know about. But they weren't just watching, they were ready to act in any way necessary. He felt his stomach turn over. Maybe Elizabeth had fallen in front of the train, maybe she had been pushed, but they were the obvious cause of her death. He hadn't signed up for this. He was just the one who moved gold. He didn't threaten anyone, and he certainly didn't kill anyone. But maybe the law wouldn't see it that way. Maybe the law would see him as part of all of this. He decided to try and calm down. None of this would come out anyway. The police would either determine Elizabeth's death to be a suicide or a crime, but they would never find out who pushed her. Dmitri and Yugov were that good. They left no trail and, in fact, they were probably out of the country by now anyway.

He mixed himself his 5:00 PM martini and sat down in his favorite overstuffed chair overlooking Times Square.

He loved his apartment. He loved being up so high looking down at the hurly burly cacophony below. He felt like
a medieval king on his hill considering his lowly subjects.
He ate two of his Castelvetrano olives as he waited for his
martini to take hold. Whatever it was, he reasoned, it
couldn't take him down in a day. Funny, he thought, as he
took another sip. His whole life was going to come down
to twenty-four hours. He watched the bustle below him.
Elmo and SpongeBob were getting into it again and the
superhero team had zeroed in on an Asian tourist group.
Surround and conquer. Plus, Wonder Woman looked
particularly hot today. Money in the bank.

His phone started vibrating wildly, or so it seemed to
him, as he started to feel a little buzzed himself.

"Hello?"

"Hi, Timothy, it's Macky. Sorry to call so late but
wanted to tell you that Fort Knox is finished. I emailed
you the spreadsheet."

"Thanks. And thanks for the call. I haven't seen it
yet. Is it just what we were expecting? No surprises?"

"No surprises."

"Thanks, Devon. Have a good night."

He loved knowing there were twelve troy ounces to
one troy pound of gold; not sixteen ounces as for everything else. Metals were special and gold the most special,
particularly to him. He had spent a lifetime in Treasury,
his entire twenty-five-year career. And overseeing the
depositories was the thing he had enjoyed the most. He
closed his eyes and could see gold bars, high stacks of
them, secured in armored cars, moving into position, for
transfer at 4:00 AM the day after tomorrow. He could see

the confirmation of the resulting deposits into his Maldives bank accounts, shortly after. He could see himself calmly gathering up his two suitcases, turning off the lights, and walking out the front door for the last time. He could see himself boarding his flight to the Maldives. Settling into his recliner, cognac in hand. He could see himself on the beach, day after sun-kissed day. He would make it, he thought confidently as he poured another martini. He would make it.

But Pierce wasn't so sure. He had somehow made it back to his office and closed the door, but his anxiety was exploding, consuming him, feeling like it was reaching a point of no return. Bile started rising in his throat as he thrust himself into his desk chair. He was sweating profusely, his body running from hot to cold, his head spinning. He thought he might pass out. He never should have agreed to this scheme. He never should have taken it on. He never should have tried to grab such a big brass ring. He wondered if he was having a heart attack or if it was possible to die from anxiety. It had all been borne he knew, from illegitimate yearnings—for power and prestige for himself and redemption for his family. For a family who had suffered so much. Misunderstood and maligned. Set unfairly forever in the headstones of history by those with poisoned pens filled with hate. Not heeding the selfless striving to help a nascent nation and the good works done. Only seeing errors and missteps, self-dealing, and greed. He knew the truth. He needed to make sure the world knew it too. He lay flat on the floor, his body starting to calm. The sweat cooling, forming beads on his chest. After a while, he was able to sit up and sip some water. His heart stopped racing, his mind started to clear. He knew what he had to do.

He started searching addresses, Google, social media, and all the threads that led from there. Within five minutes, he was dialing.

"Hi, Ray, guess who?" Pierce said.

"Whah, I dunno," Ray said sloppily as he wiped the pizza sauce from his mouth.

"It's Pierce. Pierce from Clayburg High. I'm so glad I found you. Great you're still living on Staten Island."

"Hey, Pierce! Nice hearing from you. How ya been?"

"Good, Ray. Good. I've been meaning to drop by, but you know how it goes. I wanted to ask you though if you're still doing detective stuff? You know, tails and things, like before?"

"Oh yeah, Pierce. That's what I do. Same thing. Since high school. Makes me a livin' ya know. It's alright by me."

"That's great news, Ray. I have just a quick, easy little project for you if you have time."

"Oh yeah, Pierce. For you, no problem."

"Thanks Ray. It's just a one-day tail on a colleague of mine who I think might be trying to undercut me at the bank. Nothing major. I just want to know where she's going for a day or so until we have our personnel reviews. I heard she might be in with the bank president and trying to slide in ahead of me. I also heard they've been seen around town, if you know what I mean."

"Gotcha.'"

"So, Ray, nothing needed during the rest of today at the bank. I'll watch her here and follow her to make sure she goes home. We have so much work to do that I can't imagine she'd do anything other than just work and go home. You can pick it up in the morning if you're good with that."

"OK, got it."

"I'll text her name, address, and work photo so you know what she looks like."

"I'll start at her apartment at 6:00 AM to make sure I don't miss her. Do you want photos if she does go and see someone?" Ray asked.

"Oh yeah, absolutely."

"I got great equipment, good in all kinds of light."

"Wonderful. Like I said, shouldn't be a big deal. I just want to make sure all my hard work isn't going to waste."

"Smart, Pierce. Nobody better."

"Thanks."

Pierce gathered himself together and went back into the conference room. Sarah had changed her seat so now he couldn't see her laptop screen as he walked past. Well, she's not dumb, he thought, and she's never going to tell me what's in that spreadsheet or why she has it. His only hope was to tail her and see if he could learn something that way.

"How are we doing on the Reggia compliance?" he asked.

"*I'm* doing well," Sarah said. "How far are you?"

"Jumping back in," Pierce said. They worked for an hour in silence before Sarah excused herself.

"I have an appointment," she announced as she headed for the door.

Too bad he hadn't asked Ray to start tailing her immediately, he thought ruefully. But he didn't think there was a chance she would leave the bank with so much work still to be done.

He waited before she had turned the corner at the end of the hall before rushing to his office to grab his coat. He made it to the front door just as she started down the subway steps at the corner. B line, uptown. He moved down the subway steps in a sea of people and got on the train a few cars behind her. He pressed himself into the small space right inside the door where he could see everyone entering and exiting her car. Sarah got off at 81st Street and within a few minutes, he was trailing a few hundred feet behind her. She was walking fast, but not hurriedly, and he could easily keep her in view. Walking to the river, she turned down Broadway to The Apthorp and went inside. With a well-timed sprint, he entered the lobby just as the elevator stopped on the 14th floor. He couldn't be sure Sarah had gone to the 14th floor, of course, but the lobby was clear. He approached the doorman stand to see if he could sneak a glance at the sign-in sheet, but it had already been returned to the drawer.

"Can I help you?" the doorman asked perfunctorily.

"Ah, ah yes," Pierce said quickly as his brain churned. "I'm meeting my agent for a showing. Is Eric Smith here yet?"

"No Eric Smith. You can wait over there," the doorman said suspiciously motioning to a set of chairs at the far end of the lobby. "Isn't it rather late for a showing?"

"Ah, no." Pierce mumbled. "He's really booked. This is the only time he had today. Thanks." Pierce started walking to the seating area but knew he couldn't be there long. He fielded a pretend call on his phone.

"Oh?" he said rather loudly to be within earshot. "Rescheduled? No problem. I'm here, but I have some errands on the Upper West Side anyway, so no biggie."

As he turned around and started heading back to the lobby door, he noticed the tenant mailboxes on his left. He could feel the doorman watching him, making sure he was leaving the building. He knew the boxes were ordered by floors so as he came up to the higher floors, he slowed down to button his coat and rejigger himself for the cold outside.

"Walker—Hamilton 14C." The name leaped out at him. He knew about the reopening of The Grange and that there was one last Hamilton descendant who was living in New York City. He also vaguely remembered overhearing someone at the bank gossiping about Sarah and her friend "the Hamilton." What he didn't know was that she was dead. He never watched the news or read the papers, mostly relying on the pop-up feed on his browser, and although he knew about the subway accident, he had missed the story identifying the victim.

She's just visiting her friend, Pierce thought as he walked out of the building, down 79th Street to Broadway. Although why she would make a social call when there was so much work to do was puzzling. He called Ray and asked for another one of his guys to help with surveillance. Sarah was busier than he thought.

* * *

She had been rubbing Bodie's belly for the last few minutes and was already feeling more relaxed. She let the "maybe I should get a pet" idea wander through her brain for a few seconds before she hard-stopped it with the knowledge that she was never home and a bona fide plant killer.

"OK," she said, turning to Ralph. "Where are we at?"

"I think I've finally made some progress," Ralph said. "I think we can say that Elizabeth and Jessica were right. Someone has been buying enormous amounts of gold over the past six months. Not just trying to corner the market but consume the market. I was able to use Jessica's model and track some of the buys. The raindrop buy program makes it more laborious to track, but still possible if you keep following the trail. It looks like the buys are aggregating in three sources, two that are international, and one here in the States although I haven't been able to pinpoint the source yet."

"That's fabulous, Ralph," Sarah said excitedly. "Huge. So Elizabeth was right. Someone is hoarding gold."

"Yes. And it's surprising that the Fed or Treasury aren't onto it, or maybe they are and they just haven't been able to stop it. In any event, it looks like they've almost accumulated all the global gold left to accumulate. Whatever they're planning, it looks like it's almost done."

"Whatever it is, it can't be good for the United States and probably the world. How could it be? Plus, we know Elizabeth and Jessica thought it was a code red emergency and Elizabeth thought it serious enough to activate the purpose of the society for the first time in history."

"First time in history," Ralph said. "Elizabeth had to do all that, and by herself."

"Yes," Sarah said. "She did. And what was she thinking about the key? Was Elizabeth trying to figure out who was doing the buying or was she trying to find Alexander's stockpile?"

"I think she was looking for the trove," Ralph said as he stood up and retrieved the key from the side table drawer. "It looks like a key that would fit an old, solid lock. A lock that would protect a trove. I think she thought finding the trove was her best chance since everything was moving so quickly. I think she was looking for the funds Alexander had stashed."

"Well, she got the key. It must be the key to the trove. That's why she died rather than give up the key. But did she actually find the trove? We don't know, and we have to know."

"We've got to do another search. Would she have written it down? Is it somewhere in her computer? I don't know. I just don't know." Ralph was getting upset and anxious. He started pacing the room, looking randomly in drawers, in books, under the planters on the windowsill. Sarah could see that he had had enough for the day.

"Ralph," she said gently. "Why don't you take a break? Take Bodie out for a long walk. Take a bath. Take a breath. We can pick this all up in the morning."

"OK," he said gratefully. "Thank you. I think I'm losing it." He went into the other room and returned with his coat and Bodie's leash. "I'll walk you out."

"Thank you," Sarah said as they rode down the elevator in silence. Ralph continued to Riverside Park while Sarah went the opposite way. Within minutes, she was on Central Park West, walking quickly, letting her arms swing, allowing the movement to lift her and free her, if just for a few minutes. It was a habit she had developed in LA, during that difficult time. It was a strange habit to have started in LA, she knew, a city notably averse to walking at all. But it had released her from the worries and cares of running her small personal injury law firm and later, had sustained her through all the fall-out from the case. She had even inspired Sam to shake free of his car on occasion. Sam. A sigh escaped her.

Her eyes started stinging with tears and she walked faster, New York fast, past the New-York Historical Society. She paused. What was Elizabeth looking for there? She assumed Detective Schwartz had followed up Elizabeth's ticket stubs and contacted the museum. Had she found out anything? Maybe she and Ralph were wrong in not sharing what they had with the police. After all, investigating crime is what police do. For all they knew, maybe the police were far along in the investigation and teaming up and sharing their information might be the rocket fuel needed to find Elizabeth's killer and even find the trove. Maybe she and Ralph were just being arrogant fools. She turned back uptown on Central Park West. The precinct was just blocks away. She expected that Detective Schwartz might still be working, and she could just check in and see how the investigation was going. But she realized she couldn't do any of that without Ralph's approval, and that couldn't possibly happen until tomorrow. Her mind was spinning. She was exhausted too. She decided to take her own advice and get some rest.

She dragged herself up the five flights of stairs and rounded the last landing. A beautiful, ribboned box was at her door. What a lovely surprise. Most likely early Thanksgiving cookies from Mrs. Andrews in 3A although no card was attached. An annual treat, they were always a welcome gift. She took the box inside and set it on the table as she took off her coat and changed into her pajamas. A little warm milk and a cookie might help her relax even more than a deep pour of Cabernet. She waited until the milk was steaming in the pan and opened the box gently, trying to save the ribbon for reuse later. As she slid the ribbon off the box and opened the lid, she knew something was wrong. There was a smell. Not a cookie smell. Something else. She looked in the box and screamed.

She dropped the lid and vomited all over the table. She grabbed a kitchen towel and held it tight over her mouth. Someone was knocking at her door.

"Sarah? Are you OK? I thought I heard you scream."

It was Leyla, 5B, next door. Sarah held the towel tighter over her mouth, thinking hard.

"Sarah? You OK?"

"Sorry Leyla," she finally yelled across the room. "A giant cockroach just ran across my dinner. So sorry. I'm fine."

"Are you *sure* you're OK?" she asked again.

"Yes, thank you, Leyla. Sorry again."

"Well, OK. If you're OK."

Sarah could hear footsteps and her neighbor's door close. She ran to the bathroom where she vomited again in the toilet. She lay down on the cool marble floor, her head resting on the bathmat. Deranged. Sick. She knew who did this. She couldn't call Ralph until tomorrow, and she wouldn't call the police. It was a warning, and it meant they were on the right track.

She stayed on the floor a long time. Eventually she stood up, cleaned herself up, and went back into the kitchen. She got a thick, black garbage bag out of the closet, put on her dish gloves, and swept the lid, the box, and all its contents, into the bag. She threw her gloves in after them and tied it first with six garbage bag ties and then looped rings of packing tape around the top. Around and around, as tight as she could. Changing quickly into sweats, she took the bag downstairs to the dumpster where she threw it in as far back and as deep as she could. Going back to her apartment, she opened all the windows and took out another pair of gloves, the Clorox, and scrubbed the table, the counter, the floor, and the chairs until she couldn't scrub anymore.

25

Detective Schwartz was still working and expected to be for a few hours more. She picked up the phone on the first ring.

"Hi, Scott. Nice to hear from you. Business or pleasure?"

"Afraid this one is business, Deb. Nice to hear you as well. I figured you'd still be at work with everything that's going on. I just wanted to let you know that Dmitri and Yugov are back in the city. You got picked up in the interagency alert bulletin because they were tailing Sarah Brockman. She's one of your contacts in the Elizabeth Hamilton Walker case, right?"

"Yes."

"You know Dmitri and Yugov. They come and go. We watch them all the time. We know they're into all kinds of bad and yet we can never pin anything on them. But we've had enough of them. My boss finally got his requisition approved for some extra cash to do a proper investigation. We're finally going to get them I hope."

"You will, Scott," Deb said approvingly. "Nobody better than the FBI—when funded," she added. "Do you know why they were tailing Brockman and are they still tailing her?"

"No and yes," Scott said. "They're still watching her. We don't know why yet. I can tell you she just left Ralph Walker's apartment. He was Elizabeth Hamilton Walker's husband, right?"

"Yes, that's right. Interesting. Brockman and Walker are working on something together. I was going to let it play out, but now I'm concerned about Brockman's safety. Dmitri and Yugov are vicious and cruel. They're the kind that tortures a mouse before killing it."

"Yeah, especially Dmitri. Twisted. Sick. I was just reviewing the files we have on him. Something's really wrong with him. I want him gone. I want them gone. I want them behind bars for good."

"Me too. Can you add me to the real-time contact list? I need to know if they're getting too close to Brockman or Walker. I have a bad feeling about this."

"I understand. You've already been added, Deb."

"Thanks, Scott."

"There's also been some chatter with Russia. Both Dmitri and Yugov. Encrypted. Haven't got it broken out yet but should be able to in the next few hours. We already have the phone numbers, but they're burners so aren't going to be of any use."

"Any idea who it is?"

"No. But probably no one new."

"Right. Thanks again, Scott. Really appreciate your help."

"Anytime."

"Bye," Deb said as a note alert popped up on her phone from Scott. "They're also watching Ralph Walker. Yugov's on him now."

"Thanks," Deb typed. "I wouldn't have had the manpower to do this. Much appreciated."

"You're so welcome," Scott replied. "We're just starting to get the surveillance up and running so coverage will be spotty for a few days, but we'll give you everything we get."

"Thanks again," Detective Schwartz typed as a new text appeared.

"Hi, Deborah," it said. "Doris Sullivan here. Please check your email immediately. Kindly call when done."

Detective Schwartz gave a thumbs up emoji and opened her email. There was a cover email from Doris with the re: line "Root Cellar" and eight attachments. Oh no, Schwartz thought. Doris was still on that root cellar wild goose chase. Schwartz didn't think there was anything to it, and she found it hard to believe that this was an emergency needing immediate attention, but considering the credibility of the source, she dived in.

She opened the attachments one by one. By the sixth, she was getting frustrated. Why didn't Doris tell her in her cover email what she was supposed to be looking for? The attachments were just requisition requests and invoices for various materials, mostly wooden beams, planks, joists, nails, fasteners and other building hardware. As Doris had indicated, it looked like requisitions and payments for materials to build a root cellar. Probably the root cellar Doris believed had been added to The Grange. The only other commonality Detective Schwartz could see was that they were all initiated at the behest of a Lt. Samuelson and signed off by "AH."

Finally, she made it to the last attachment. It was a log of all the requisitions and invoices with check marks next to the entries. The last entry was the most recent and had no check mark next to it. Requisitioned by Lt. Samuelson, it was directed to the Bethlehem Locksmith Co. for a "strong steel lock and key." Two clear signatures graced the bottom of the page: Lt. Stephen Samuelson and A. Hamilton.

Schwartz breathlessly Googled examples of Alexander Hamilton's signature to compare. Undeniable. A perfect match.

"Doris?" she practically yelled into the phone. "How did you find this? Is this The Grange root cellar? Is Elizabeth's key for the root cellar?"

"Isn't this exciting?" Doris said gleefully. "Yes, I think so. You know, I couldn't let it go. I had to play my hunch and was lucky. I was able to reach that terrific kid who brought in the bequest, and he remembered that the folder had Lt. Samuelson written on it although he had misplaced the folder during the transition of the documents to us. After he gave me that name, I just put the requisition requests, invoices, and log entries together. I think Alexander Hamilton directed Lt. Samuelson to build a root cellar or similar structure, probably at tax-payer expense, and that the key you have fits into the lock for that structure."

"Plus," Doris continued. "Based on the amount of materials, it's a substantial structure. Probably the size of a large family's root cellar. Providing, of course, that it's the same key."

"This is amazing, Doris! Amazing! Thank you so much for your hard work. I'm sorry I doubted you. You were right all along. So where does this leave us? A structure, about the size of a root cellar, but perhaps larger, was built at Alexander Hamilton's behest, accessed by a key that was hidden in the piano at The Grange."

"A key that Elizabeth found and died for," Doris added.

"Yes," Deborah said somberly. "But where is the structure? Did Elizabeth know? Is there any chance that there really was a root cellar at The Grange that was just overlooked in the descriptions of the property?"

"At first I thought so," Doris said. "Because it made sense. It was the obvious choice, but now I'm not so sure. I've studied so many pictures of The Grange, from so many different angles, and haven't found one that shows a root cellar. Plus, when The Grange was moved to 287 Convent Avenue in 1889, there was no reference to a root cellar, and there was no reference when it was moved to St. Nicholas Park. But that all flies in the face of the fact that there had to be a root cellar at The Grange. The ice trade really wasn't established in New York City until the 1830s, and the Hamiltons had to have some way to store their vegetables, fruits, and other perishables. They had to have had a root cellar."

"There was a subterranean basement though, right? At The Grange? That could house a locked room that operated as a root cellar?"

"Yes, and that's the likely answer, but why was Hamilton's aide involved, and a lieutenant no less, for a root cellar at his home? That doesn't make sense."

"I agree," the detective said as an alert popped up on her phone. "Doris, I'm sorry, I have to look at something. But I can't thank you enough for all you've done."

Dmitri and Yugov were both moving. Dmitri uptown on 8th Street, Yugov to the river. Both had left their targets.

26

Aᴛᴇʀ ʟᴇᴀᴠɪɴɢ ᴛʜᴇ Apthorp, Pierce had positioned himself at the corner of 79th Street and Broadway where he could watch the front door and follow Sarah when she left. He didn't have to wait long. Within minutes, Sarah, a man, and a dog, made their way out of the building and down 79th toward Riverside Park. He quickly walked to the far corner and watched as they said their good-byes. The man and dog continued on to the park. Sarah walked to Central Park West and eventually down into the subway, where he easily followed her onto the train, and to her apartment. She looked tired, he thought, and so was he. He had planned to log a few more hours at the bank, but headed home instead, grabbing his favorite Indonesian noodle dish on the way. He had a bottle chilling in the fridge, but it was too early to drink it yet. He had one last thing to do.

He quickly ate his dinner as he waited for his computers to boot up. He thought he would be excited to reach this final step, to make this last buy, but he could feel the anxiety rising in his body, threatening to overwhelm him. Timothy was nuts. How exactly was he supposed to find out what the spreadsheet Sarah had in her personal email was all about? And why was he asking him to do that anyway? He had never agreed to any kind of spy, cloak-and-dagger thing. He had just agreed to buy gold. He was starting to get sweaty again. What if he had made a huge mistake, about all of it? It had seemed like the perfect offer. He would help himself, help his family, and help the country. But maybe that was just it. Maybe it had been designed to be perfect, too perfect. The thought made him sick to his stomach.

He lay down flat on the floor and let the anxiety wash over him. It was a trick he had learned through the years that could sometimes short circuit a full-blown attack. His mind rushed to Timothy. What did he really know about Timothy, a guy he met in a bar? *In a bar.* A guy who had so captivated him that he had quickly become one of his closest friends? A guy who had brought him into one of the most massive financial undertakings in a century? He looked up to see his mother looking down on him. Her soft, flaxen curls framing her face, making her smile seem ever more beatific and gentler in the photograph. It was his favorite picture of her, taken nine months before she died. Part of the family curse they had said, to have died so young and so quickly, unexplained still, in most part. He could remember her soft, warm touch, that she always smelled like roses. He would never stop missing her, longing for her. He started to breathe. Deeply and fully, his breath began to slow the tide and calm his anxious heart.

It was most likely nothing. Sarah had a spreadsheet that looked like one of his gold buys in her personal email, and she was aggressive about protecting it. That was it. Anyone with a solid finance or accounting background could have constructed that spreadsheet with a little work based on his *Financial Times* article. That's why he had written it, so people could use the models he designed in addition, of course, to improving his visibility at the bank. So that made sense. It was the protective part of how she reacted that didn't.

Maybe she had her own side hustle that she was engaged in while working for the bank. There were many rules about banking and personal interests that employees like Sarah needed to comply with for all the reasons. Maybe she was afraid of getting busted. Protecting her own self-interest—that made the most sense to him. He knew she had received a great deal of acclaim after the big insurance case she solved, but he didn't think it had yielded much cash. Otherwise, she wouldn't be working where she was and living where she was. And, since she was approaching her forties, she was probably looking to set aside a little nest egg.

Satisfied, for the moment, he turned to his work. All his screens were up and running. He opened his programs and started a scan. The global markets were looking good. He started populating his chart, animating his graphs; he could see the projections being realized, dropping neatly into place. He had been right about the timing of this last buy. Still though, considering that it was a two-hour process, he controlled himself; he wasn't out of the woods yet.

He was done by 1:00 AM. He double-checked all his graphs and spreadsheets, and with one push of a button, the buys began. It would take an hour to complete the miniscule buys in numerous time zones. Millions of digital dollars moving, digital gold moving, racing through the digital financial highways. This part always felt strange to him, even as a quant jock. It was hard to feel the numbers tied to anything real, let alone gold and currencies, but they were real, nevertheless. He watched the buys tick in for a while. He had dreamed about this moment. Dreamed how it would feel to have his future virtually assured, but it felt nothing like his dream. It felt more like a nightmare.

He opened his laptop. When he first considered Timothy's offer, he had done an extensive background search on him. He had Googled him to the last page, following all the threads and researching anything that looked even remotely suspicious. He had checked for aliases, inconsistencies, even the tiniest flags, and nothing had come up. Timothy Patrick Murphy was exactly as he said: a forty-seven-year-old single man, raised on the East Coast with a lengthy career in the Treasury Department. He liked football. He liked to travel, but only to the typical places and only top notch. He liked to drink cocktails, in bars or alone, but again, only the best. Macallan, Stolichnaya, Patron. He hated beer and wine and shunned the softer set who did. He liked refined things, comfortable things, beautiful things. His childhood had been a struggle, coarse and ugly. An ill-equipped mother and absent father had left him with a sense of lack and scarcity that he hoped would finally be filled with the money he would receive. He would buy only the best for himself. Eat the best, clothe himself in the best, become the best. He would become his vision of a true gentleman.

Pierce continued his research. Nothing had changed. Timothy was just the same. He was still posting pictures of himself in luxurious surroundings with beautiful, high-end clothes. He was still posting pictures of food on Instagram.

The computer screens flashed and beeped. The buys were done. Pierce texted Timothy: "The eagle has landed."

Timothy awoke with a start. He had been dozing after his two martinis, waiting for the text.

"Fantastic!" he texted back. "You have done a great service to your country and done it well. Everyone will be so pleased. This buy just wraps it up. The transfers of the gold bars are already set and ready for 4:00 AM tomorrow. All at once for security and safety. Less prying eyes. All those buys, over a year. Everything you wanted is going to come true. I have all your routing information for the transfer. Get some rest."

* * *

From far uptown in the underground apartment by the Hudson, Dmitri and Yugov took off their headphones and turned off the screens. Dmitri reached for one of his burner phones.

"Done," he said.

"Good," came the terse reply.

Yugov swung his chair around to face Dmitri.

"Aren't you glad Sergei made you do the install on Timothy right away?" He said with a sneer. "*That* was a good decision." He swung back, got up and walked to the front door. "I'm out. See ya."

Dmitri counted the footsteps walking up the stairs. He knew Yugov was heading to the clubs in the East Village and would be gone for most of the night. He started his assembly. He had everything he needed for a perfect, high-end install. After double-checking his equipment, he took off his shoes and crawled into bed, knowing he could catch the few hours of sleep he needed before he went to work.

*   *   *

Sarah awoke with a start. The image in the box tormenting her dreams. She looked at her phone. 2:00 AM. She got up and opened the blinds. The street below was quiet. The après-theater bar scene was over. The tourists had boozily wound their way back to their hotels. Only the locals were left. She watched as an older couple made their way down the street, carefully helping each other navigate the uneven pavement and mounds of leaves piled high waiting to be swept away in the morning. They were laughing loudly, enjoying their night and each other.

Sarah turned away and hurried back to the warmth of her bed. She was scared. The box with its gruesome contents was a warning. A heinous warning. They knew who she was. They knew what she was doing, and they wanted her to stop. But, of course, it was already too late. She was already in too deep. They had shown that by sending such a forceful message. They would kill her anyway. In their minds, even if she did stop, she already knew too much.

There was only one way out. Only one way to live. They had to win. She turned on the light, retrieved her bedside notebook and started reviewing everything she and Ralph knew. Elizabeth and Jessica were right. Someone was buying up the world's gold and not just cornering the market but hoarding it. Financially, it was aggressive, but politically, it was hostile. There was something frightening going on. She didn't know what it was or who was behind it, but she knew it was bad. Really bad. And it all pointed to one thing. She was sure Elizabeth was looking for Alexander's cache, and finding the key may have confirmed for her that she found it.

She went to the closet and pulled down the box. Once again, the musty smell of the old documents overpowered her as she opened the lid. She carefully spread out the contents of the box on the table, minding the delicate fasteners on the books and Alexander's fragile, deteriorating letter. She scavenged in the drawers for any forgotten tea bags and threw an ancient English Breakfast tea bag into a microwaved cup of hot water. She started in with a fresh eye, a surprisingly focused eye, given the hour. She was looking for any clue as to where the key might fit. Sarah studied the actual sized pictures of the key Ralph had texted her. It was important to him that he keep the copy he had made from the mold, and she fully understood. A picture was fine for her purposes.

She reread the charging letter from Alexander to his family, hunting for hidden clues, but there were none. She then went to the earliest entries in the logbooks. There were heartbreaking entries right after the funeral, not so much about democracy and the purpose of the Society as much as they were entries better suited to a diary. Entries of entreaty and grief, pouring out from the unremitting crush of a family's broken heart. There were various pedestrian entries in those first few pages too, that related to Elizabeth taking care of the family's business and her assumption of its head, but there was one particular entry that caught Sarah's eye. It was in the same bold hand that she believed was Elizabeth's. It was more of a calendar entry than anything else. "Cellar inspection with Lt. Samuelson, July 28, 1804." It seemed odd not only because a lieutenant was involved in what was obviously a domestic issue but also because The Grange had been completed two years prior. Any issue with a cellar would have been resolved by 1804. Still, that was all she had.

She started pulling up any information she could find on cellars in the late 1700s. Within an hour she knew that The Grange was highly likely to have had a cellar, that it probably had a lock, and that the key Elizabeth had in her pocket when she died was exactly the kind that could fit it. But she didn't recall ever seeing a cellar in any of the pictures she had seen of The Grange.

Her head was buzzing. She glanced at her screen. 4:12 AM. She had to get some sleep, or she would be useless the rest of the day. She poured herself a double shot of Jameson and headed for bed, pausing to close the blinds on the way. The wind was chasing the autumn leaves down the sidewalks and into doorways, bending the branches of the almost bare trees, casting eerie shadows below. She thought she saw one shadow pass into another, someone at her building's door. But a second look told her she must have been mistaken. She climbed into bed and was asleep within minutes, just as the shadowy figure five floors down, quietly jimmied the lock and came in.

27

BODIE WAS ALL over him, licking his face, making the quiet little whimpers that told Ralph he had to go out. The sky was bright, and the street was bustling. He must have slept in. He checked the time. 9:00 AM? He never slept until 9:00. He texted Sarah. No answer. He called. A sleepy voice answered.

"Oh, hi, Ralph. Geez, what time is it? 9:00? I can't believe it. I have to tell you what happened last night. But why didn't Mr. Mandelman wake me up? He always wakes me at 7:00 AM. I've got to check on him. I'll call you right back."

"OK. I've got to take Bodie out though, so I'll try you from the park."

Sarah walked quickly over to the open shaft. "Mr. Mandelman," she called down. "Are you there? Are you OK?"

No answer. She heard a slight scuffling sound. She tried again. "Mr. Mandelman, are you there? Are you

OK?" Nothing. She started anxiously slipping on her sweats and loafers just as she heard a voice coming up the shaft.

"Yes, Sarah. Fine. Just a little tired today." Mr. Mandelman sounded tired, but there was something more.

"Are you sure you're OK?" she asked again.

"Yes," he said more forcefully. "I'm fine. I'm sorry I missed our 8:00 AM wake-up call."

Sarah felt like electricity was shooting through her veins. She took a deep breath. "No worries, Mr. Mandelman. I'm sure we'll have our 8:00 AM alarm tomorrow." She backed away from the shaft and moved to the farthest end of the apartment dialing "911" as she did.

She heard footsteps racing down the stairs. Loud, jumping steps two at a time, clattering down the stairwell. She ran to her door and threw it open. A man was bolting through the foyer, the door slamming hard behind him. Sarah sprinted down the steps to Mr. Mandelman's apartment. She burst through the door, terrified of what she'd find.

He was there, facing her, ankles and wrists tied to a kitchen chair, a grotesque gash across his face. She ran to him and started undoing his painful ties just as she heard the police at the front door.

"Are you OK? Can you wait a minute while I let the police in?" Sarah asked Mr. Mandelman. "Maybe they can still catch him."

He nodded firmly and Sarah dashed down the stairs. She swung open the door for the two police officers waiting on the stoop.

"I called you, I saw him. He's big, all in black, with a backpack. I couldn't see his skin color. He ran out of here about a minute ago."

"Is the vic OK?" The taller officer hurriedly spat out the words. "EMTs here in a minute."

"Yes."

"Go, Jake, go east. I'll go west. Head for the subway entrance. I'll call in the description."

The officers took off down the street as Sarah ran back up the stairs and into apartment 4A. She continued untying the ropes that had gouged deep, ugly tracks into Mr. Mandelman's skin.

"Water," he said. "Please."

Sarah filled a glass with water and handed it to Mr. Mandelman who drank it greedily.

"Are you OK?" she asked as she knelt next to him. "The EMTs will be here any minute. Can I help you to the couch?"

"Yes, Sarah. Thank you." He could barely get the words out through his tears. "You saved me."

"Excuse me," came a voice from the hall. Sarah looked up to see a third officer standing there. "May I come in?" he said.

"Of course," Mr. Mandelman said. "Thank you," he said as the officer helped him to the couch.

He took out his field notebook and pen and turned to Sarah. "I'm Officer Hollister. Is there anyone we can call for, I'm sorry, what is your name?"

"Herman A. Mandelman," he said.

"A daughter? Son? Any relatives close by?" Officer Hollister continued.

"My daughter," Mr. Mandelman said. "She lives in Jersey City now." He gave the officer his daughter's cell phone number.

"Can you tell me what happened?" he asked.

Mr. Mandelman took a deep breath. "I was asleep in my bed," he said. "I don't know what time it was. I woke up to hands grabbing me, shoving me out of bed, really rough, lots of force. I couldn't tell if it was one person or two, but later I saw it was one. Then he tied something across my mouth hard. Vicious. I could taste blood. I thought he knocked a tooth out, but it was just the tie digging into the sides of my mouth. I cried out, and he hit me across the face. I could feel his ring slice across my cheek. I'm not sure if I passed out for a moment, but maybe I did. Then he put a pillowcase over my face and shoved me out of the bedroom and into the chair. He tied me so tight in the chair, my feet and hands were getting numb. I tried to tell him, but my mouth was gagged. He seemed to understand because he came over and got up real close to my ear and whispered how painful it must be for me. I couldn't see, but it sounded like he was smiling saying it. He said he wouldn't be long, but that I would be. That he would leave me, just like that and no one would find me until they smelled me.

Mr. Mandelman paused and took a sip of water. "He started moving all over the apartment, moving chairs, pulling things from shelves, and then it would get really quiet and I would think he was gone, but then, all of a sudden, he would do something again. As you see, this is a small apartment in a walk-up building. I don't know

what he was thinking he was going to find here."
Mr. Mandelman took another sip and rubbed his wrists.

"Then I heard my beautiful angel, Sarah. I had forgotten about my Sarah. When I heard her voice, I thought I had a chance."

At that, Sarah went over and sat next to Mr. Mandelman on the couch, taking his hand in hers.

"I could hear the man stop and listen. The next thing I knew, he ripped the pillowcase off my face and cut the tie from my mouth. He hissed into my ear again and said that I better say that I was fine or I'd be dead in a heartbeat. And that I better be convincing. He waved the bowie knife he had used to cut off the tie in front of my face for emphasis. That's when I came up with the 8:00 AM alarm."

"Yes, it was brilliant," Sarah said. "I wanted you to know that I understood, so I said '8:00 AM' again."

Sarah turned to Officer Hollister. "Mr. Mandelman has been my 7:00 AM voice alarm for quite a few months now, ever since the building opened up the water pipe shaft for repairs months ago. It's a beautiful way to start the day. He hasn't missed a day so when he did, I thought something was wrong."

Sarah looked at Mr. Mandelman, "It was truly brilliant. He had no idea."

"No idea," Mr. Mandelman agreed. "After you said good-bye, Sarah, he started stuffing things into something, maybe a bag or backpack. He was behind me so I couldn't see, but that's what it sounded like. Then he opened the door and took off down the steps. I heard the entry door slam on his way out. I figure he just blended into the street and was gone."

"You figured right," Officer Hollister said. "We sent a couple of sets of patrols down your street and a few side streets, but no one has come up with anything suspicious. Do you have any idea what he looks like? Any description?"

"He was all in black with a black full-face mask, but when he waved the bowie knife in front of my face, I could see that his hand was white. He's big, over six feet tall, I'd say, and seemed strong but not bulging muscles. Nothing distinguishing. Probably the way he wants it."

"So, what do you think he was after? I know you'll want to do an inventory as soon as you feel a little better but look around. Do you see anything missing?"

Mr. Mandelman's eyes roved all around the main room and kitchen. He got up gingerly and went into the bedroom, looking in drawers he passed by.

"All that I can see that's missing right now is my watch and my cufflinks that were on my bedside table. I don't know why he was here for so long. It doesn't make sense."

"No, it doesn't," Officer Hollister agreed. "I think this is enough for now. Here's my card," he said handing the card to Mr. Mandelman. "Please call if you think of anything else. Do you have a superintendent in this building? I'll let them know they need to rekey the lock downstairs."

"No super," Mr. Mandelman said, "but the building management number is in the foyer. We would sure appreciate it if you could call them."

"Of course, my pleasure," Officer Hollister said heading out the door. He looked at his phone. "EMTs here in two minutes."

"Oh, wait," Mr. Mandelman said. "He's a smoker or at least hangs out with a lot of smokers. I could smell old smoke on him when he came close to me."

"That's helpful," Officer Hollister said. "Anything else?"

"No, I can't think of anything else right now. I appreciate your help."

After the door closed behind them, Sarah patted Mr. Mandelman's hand. "I'm so sorry this happened to you, Mr. Mandelman. Is it OK if I give you a hug?" she asked.

"Thank you, please," Mr. Mandelman said reaching over. "Thank you, dear friend."

* * *

Wish I could have just killed him, Dmitri thought as he slid glumly into the last available subway seat in his car, his heart still racing from his getaway. How could he have known the two of them shared a daily wake-up call? Messy exit for sure. He would make two subway transfers, carefully avoiding the Port Authority with all its cameras and MTA police, and switch his coat for the brown one he'd brought in his backpack. The NYPD would never find him—or at least they wouldn't find him right now. It would have been so much easier if he could just have taken the old man out before starting the surveillance install on Sarah's apartment, but Sergei was adamant. Sergei thought another dead body might really provoke even more police action. He was still furious about the attention Elizabeth Hamilton Walker's death had stirred up. Another death could be the final nail in the coffin.

At least he had done a good job on the install and finished it even though it had taken longer than he had planned. He had pulled the permits from city planning and knew the water shaft had been opened, but he couldn't be sure it hadn't been fixed and closed again until he got inside the old man's apartment. The open water shaft made the install almost child's play easy and, by using Mandelman's apartment, it also reduced the chance that anyone would suspect who the true target was. Now that they had complete surveillance of Sarah's apartment, they had a better chance of finding out what was going on. It was a huge win for the team, and, he hoped, at least a small shot of redemption for him.

* * *

It was 10:45 AM before Sarah left her apartment, making her hours off the pace for the day. She was still weak and shaking from everything she had been through and felt terrible for Mr. Mandelman. She wasn't sure what to think about that. It all seemed so random but also explainable. Old people were common targets for all kinds of crimes and certainly burglaries. The burglar had probably identified Mr. Mandelman as an easy target and watched him for some time or at least long enough to know which apartment was his. But on the heels of what had happened to her, she wondered if there might be some connection. Ralph didn't think so. As worried as he was about what had happened to her, he didn't think the two had anything in common.

"Are they getting the new locks for the front doors put in today?" Ralph texted again.

"Yes, yes, they promised."

"What about new locks for your door? A deadbolt. Maybe a door lock barricade. I looked up 'best door security' and that came up. Looks invincible."

"Yes, they're doing that too. A deadbolt for sure today. I'll ask them about the barricade. OK?"

"OK."

"There's something else I want to talk to you about. Hang on. Calling."

Ralph picked up on the first ring and Sarah dove straight in with what she'd found. "Hi, Ralph, I found something interesting last night before all this happened. It was one of the first entries in the logbook and was about a cellar inspection with a Lt. Samuelson on July 28, 1804. It's written in the handwriting that I think is Eliza Hamilton's. I did some quick research late last night and the key would fit into the kind of lock that was used in root cellars then. It's likely that The Grange would have a root cellar and that it would be kept locked. It could be Alexander's trove. Maybe that's why Elizabeth went to the museums the week before she died—to do some research on a Grange construction, to see if she could find it. Maybe she was on this trail."

"Good thought," Ralph replied. "How about if we split up and check them out? I'll go to the Museum of the City of New York, and you go to the Historical Society, if that's OK with you. I have a contact at the museum. Might be useful or it might not, but worth a try."

"OK, great. I'm about finished with the compliance projects. I'll tell Pierce he has to finish them up. I am senior to that twit after all. Then I'll head over."

"Perfect. Talk later."

"OK," she said as she rounded the corner of the bank's lobby.

"Good morning, Sarah."

It was Pierce.

"Good morning." She looked up to see him standing a few feet away, waiting for the elevator. He didn't look good. His eyes were red, his hair and clothing were a disheveled mess, and even his skin looked pallid. He looked either sick or exhausted. She took a few steps back.

They squeezed on the express elevator and then split off to their respective offices. Sarah answered a few emails and completed her final review of the Reggia compliance. She was out of the bank by 1:10 PM, and on her way up Central Park West to the Historical Society.

Detective Schwartz saw the FBI alert come up on her phone and called Doris Sullivan.

"Hi, Doris, it's Deb. I'm wondering if you might be able to help me out on something?"

"Oh, hi, Deborah. Of course. What is it?"

"We've had the good fortune to have the FBI watching one of our contacts in the Elizabeth Walker case as it concerns another matter that they're working on. They just alerted me that my contact is heading into the Historical Society as we speak. Her name is Sarah Brockman, and I don't know what she's doing there. The FBI can tell me where she is, but they can't tell me what she's doing. Are you willing to do a little detective work?"

"Yes," Doris said excitedly. "You know how much I want to help find Elizabeth's killers. Any way I can help, I want to."

"OK, thank you. I'll send you a picture of her so you know what she looks like. She just walked into the building now. Just see if you can figure out what she's doing there. It must be some kind of research, and it could have something to do with Elizabeth's case. Since Sarah knew that Elizabeth visited the Historical Society the week before she died, I'm hoping the two are tied together."

"Got it. OK, I just got the picture. I'll head downstairs and see if I can find her."

"Thanks very much, Doris. Let me know when you can."

*　　*　　*

By this time, Sarah had passed through the main exhibition rooms and had made her way to the Klingenstein Library. Doris recognized her easily. It looked like she was doing some keyword searches on the library computers. She decided to go all in.

"Excuse me," Doris said as she approached Sarah. "Can I help you find something?"

Doris didn't have a name badge on or, luckily, her director's pin, but she looked officious in her St. John knit and expected that Sarah would assume she was just an ordinary employee of the Historical Society.

"Oh, yes," Sarah said gratefully. "I don't have much time, so I would appreciate any help I can get. I'm looking for information about early-1800s root cellars in New York. Specifically, whether Hamilton Grange had one."

The director gasped. She tried to cover up her surprise, but Sarah looked at her intently.

"Is this an unusual request?" Sarah asked.

"Ah, no," Doris said, having regained most of her composure. She didn't know how much she should tell Sarah. Detective Schwartz hadn't given her any direction about what to do should something like this happen. "It's just that I've been spending a lot of time on The Grange since it opened. Researching all kinds of historical facts and objects for the National Park Service, so it's just such an unusual coincidence."

The director knew she had to get some immediate guidance from Detective Schwartz. She pretended she had an important call and excused herself, moving into the stacks, out of hearing.

"I'm with her, Deborah," Doris said. "She asked for help researching whether The Grange had a root cellar."

"You're kidding!" Detective Schwartz said. "She must be on the same track we're on but coming at it differently. Ok, so point her to all the generally available research on root cellars and The Grange. Don't tell her anything about the bequest information. She may have other facts we could use. Just stay with her and see what you can find out. Does she know you're the director?"

"No. She thinks I'm one of the librarians."

"Perfect. Text me status updates if you're able."

"Will do."

By this time, Sarah was back on the computers searching 1800 New York root cellars.

"Sorry for the interruption," Doris said. "Having any luck?"

"Not much," Sarah said. "Just finding general information about root cellars, but the pictures are helpful. It looks like they were mainly dug into a hill, about four feet down, and made of stone. Mostly in a half circle design, rounded top, flat on the bottom. It seems that most were not in the basement of the house since the first-floor fireplaces kept the cellars too warm."

"Makes sense," Doris said. "How about searching 'architectural plans for The Grange' or even 'John McComb Jr.' who was the architect for The Grange?"

"Good ideas, thank you. I'll try that."

"Not too busy today," Doris said. "I'll help."

"Thank you."

The two stood side by side at the terminals searching, sharing ideas, exchanging polite banter. Sarah was getting more relaxed and comfortable with Doris after that initial misstep.

"This is such an interesting project, at least to me anyway as a historian," Doris chuckled. "What's the project for, if you don't mind me asking?"

Sarah froze. She should have figured out a lie beforehand. Her mind raced. She remembered a notice she received from some kind of bulk mail newsletter.

"Ah, ah," she stammered. "I'm a graduate student at the City College of New York working on my master's in

Urban Planning. I wanted to understand how the sustainability of the past could inform the future. Especially in light of all the roof-top gardens being built and the shifting movement to green, even in urban environments."

She was good, Doris thought. Quick on her feet. No dummy there.

"That's fascinating," Doris said. She thought the two of them were getting along very well, so she decided to push it. "So why specifically The Grange? Wouldn't any 1800 New York root cellar do?"

Gotcha, Doris thought as she turned the table. She looked intently at Sarah. But Sarah wasn't one to be caught twice.

"I think I can gain more cachet with those I'm hoping to persuade if my project is tied to someone who is so respected and honored."

"What if you find out that The Grange never had a root cellar? Do you have any reason to think that it did?" That was it, the million-dollar question. Doris kept typing, feigning nonchalance, as she looked sideways at Sarah.

"No," Sarah said a bit too quickly. "I just figured it would. If it didn't have one, I'll just switch gears to another Federalist luminary. Not a big deal."

The nascent detective in Doris was disappointed, but she decided there was a way she could help them both. She pretended to check her watch.

"I have a few more minutes. Let's look just at The Grange. If there was a root cellar, I don't think it could be part of the house. The house was moved two times.

It was first moved from its original location, at what is now the south side of 143rd Street between Amsterdam and Convent Avenues, to allow for the implementation of the Manhattan street grid. The Grange was in foreclosure and had been condemned for destruction. St. Luke's bought it and moved it, I think about a half block east and two blocks south next to St. Luke's. The last move was in 2006 from that location at 287 Convent Avenue to the present location in St. Nicholas Park.

"Yes, I remember reading about it," Sarah said. "It was quite a neighborhood event and, I understand, an engineering masterpiece."

"It was," Doris agreed. "Here, look at this," she said as she stepped back from the screen. "The original porches and other exterior features were removed for the move. They just moved the house."

"They probably wouldn't have moved a root cellar if it was attached to the house or under the house."

"I think that's right."

"Thank you very much," Sarah said turning to Doris. "I appreciate your help. It seems clear that I need to pick another Federalist hero for my project."

But what was really clear to Sarah was that if there had been a root cellar at The Grange, it would be at the original location, either as part of the foundation or as a stand-alone construction apart from the house. The logbook entry had said "cellar inspection with Lt. Samuelson." That made it seem like it was a separate building and, even though the original estate was thirty-two acres, it would necessarily still be close to the original location of the house for the proximity to its kitchen.

It was getting dark. She texted Ralph an update but got no reply. Probably still at the museum, she thought. She'd try him again later from the bank.

* * *

Ralph was still at the Museum of the City of New York. He had walked across the park and up Fifth Avenue to the museum. He had always admired the neo-Georgian building. With its red brick and marble trim, it epitomized classic New York to him as it had to Elizabeth, who had loved not only the museum and building but the Weinman statue of Alexander out front. She felt Weinman, solely among all the other sculptors, had captured the quiet nobility and resolute will of Alexander, and she always paused for a deep moment at his statue before going in. Ralph did the same.

He made his way into the first-floor galleries and the New York core exhibit. Filled with documents, objects, and thousands of still and video images celebrating over four hundred years of New York history, it was one of his favorite places in the city. But the more he toured the exhibit, the more he realized nothing as mundane as root cellars would be featured in the museum. It had the original handwritten version of Emma Lazarus's "The New Colossus," a cross-section of a wooden water pipe laid by Aaron Burr's sham utility, the Manhattan Company, and the Tiffany silver shovel used to break ground for the subway. It had significant artifacts, not root cellars.

He was feeling deflated. He walked up and down the document stacks and jewel cases, looking at the robber barons, stock certificates, railroad shares, and James Fisk's and Jay Gould's attempt to corner the gold market in 1869. Amassing gold. Nothing new in human history. But what if Elizabeth had come here not to research a possible root cellar at The Grange as Sarah thought, but came, instead, to figure out who was buying the gold. He knew many of the curators of the Museum of American Finance were on loan to the Museum of New York until a new location for it could be found. That was how he happened to establish his financial contact here.

Fisk and Gould had tried to corner the market. What if a multinational company was doing the same thing now—or worse, a country? He found a small nook and opened his laptop. He started researching the latest news surrounding gold. Who was buying gold? Who was hoarding gold? His finance jock brain was on fire.

His screen flashed with all the commercial gold bug blogs and their alarmist articles detailing the threats posed to fiat currencies, chief among them, of course, being the U.S. dollar. He scrolled past their elaborate conspiracy theory articles with the "buy gold here" button at the end and skimmed gold bug websites expounding the risks posed by fiat currencies including their fanciful intimation of an impending international monetary crisis. But the deeper he got, the more he thought they were right. He started seeing news articles detailing how Russia and China were accumulating physical gold. Reports of them stacking many tons of gold each month in amounts far greater than could be explained by annual mine output or publicized transactions. Disturbing blog posts about Russia and China already taking steps toward bypassing the dollar. China's opening of a renminbi clearing bank in Russia and Russia's central bank opening its first ever foreign branch in China. Concerns about movements by both countries to peg the yuan and ruble to gold bullion that would supplant the U.S. dollar as the dominant currency, weaken the dollar, and cause economic chaos. Articles, carefully hedged, written by experts about how these actions could ultimately threaten the financial dominance of the United States and, by extension, national security.

Ralph pushed back his laptop and took a breath. He felt light-headed and a little sick. Was Elizabeth researching this? If all this was true and not disguised gold bug chatter, it was terrifying. Were Russia and China waging a war against the United States without firing a shot? A war that could decimate America quicker than bullets or bombs. A stealth war—perfectly designed to deal a surprise and crushing blow. He needed air. He flung his laptop in his backpack and headed for the door.

"Ralph Walker, is that you?" said a booming voice behind him.

Startled, Ralph whirled around, almost clocking Mr. Edmund Pierpont III with his backpack.

"Oh, I'm so sorry," he gasped trying to catch his breath. "Edmund!" he cried, embracing him. "I'm so very happy to see you. I was going to go looking for you in a few minutes. How are you?"

"Great to see you too!" Edmund said finally releasing him from his bear hug. "Well. How are things with you?"

It was a simple question, a standard greeting, but, while he had been on the receiving end of that many times since Elizabeth died, this one caught him broadside. "Elizabeth is dead," he choked out. "She's the one who got hit by the train in Harlem a week ago." He started sobbing uncontrollably as Edmund wrapped him again in his ample, gentle arms and led him to his office.

By the time they got there and sat down, Ralph was better. "I'm sorry," he said. "It's just still so fresh."

"Don't apologize," Edmund said sitting next to him on the small couch. "I can only imagine." But Edmund, who had been an outreach minister for teens at risk for many years before turning to finance, probably could. He had seen terrible things and beautiful things. Because of his size, standing at six feet, five inches, and girth, he had been able to inspire and, when needed, intimidate, and help in ways that others couldn't. They called him "Bear," and he had loved it all. But after about fourteen years, he became tired. Not really burned out, just tired. He went to doctors and psychologists and tried to fix his fatigue, but nothing worked. Nothing, until he went to Cboe. He was visiting a cousin in Chicago. An options trader, she had arranged a tour of the Cboe trading floor. He walked into the frenzy and excitement of live trading, and he was hooked. He felt rejuvenated, alive again. He had found the answer to his fatigue. His body was telling him that it was time to move on and move on he did. Within a few years, he had his finance degree, a job as a banker at JP Morgan Chase, and then ultimately moved into specializing in the history of finance. When he became a curator at the Museum of American Finance, he thought he'd reached heaven.

"Thank you, Edmund," Ralph said dabbing his eyes. "It just happens sometimes and then I just shake it off and keep going. I'm here because Elizabeth was here the week before she died. I think she was working on a project that got her killed."

"Whoa, Ralph. Really? That's serious stuff. Have you talked to the police?"

"Yes and no. I don't have much on this right now, and I don't want them running over what I'm doing and taking me out. Do you have a few minutes? Are you willing to help me?"

"Of course, of course. Talk to me."

"I think Elizabeth was trying to find out who has been buying and hoarding gold. From what I know, it seems to be an international player or players. They've been buying gold for a while, possibly undetected, since they've been using a relatively new technique that I call the rain method. Small, almost miniscule buys, like drops of rain, that aggregate into a very large pond. Since the Museum of American Finance is closed for now, I think she came here to do some research and perhaps talk to some finance curators."

"Interesting," Edmund said. "Let's take a look."

They adjourned to the computers in the private staff space. It was already getting near closing time, but there was a fundraising event starting right at 6:00 PM that was projected to go until 11:00 PM so they had plenty of time.

"Yes," Edmund said pulling up the curator appointment calendar. "She made an appointment with one of my new friends from the Museum of the City of New York. Gordon Elliott. Smart guy. He's got a master's in American History and a doctorate in Numerical Analysis/Approximations with a subspecialty in Statistics. He was on the Columbia University faculty for many years, but then had some run-in with the department chair and quit. He can be quite stubborn when it comes to his professional opinions."

"Do you mind calling him?" Ralph asked. "I know it's after museum hours, but this is all really time-sensitive."

"Not at all," Edmund said as he pulled up the contact list on his phone and started dialing.

"Hi, Gordon. Edmund here, thank you for picking up."

"Of course, Edmund. What can I do for you?"

"I have a friend here, Ralph Walker, who just wants to know if you know anything about Elizabeth Hamilton Walker? He's her husband."

"Oh, yes. The police were here asking about her too. They wanted to know what research I was helping her with and whether she found anything. They also asked if she seemed unusually stressed or agitated. I think they even asked if she seemed 'overwrought,' which I thought was rather strange. I told them exactly what I'm going to tell you now. She is a smart, gracious, and lovely woman who was not 'overwrought' in any way. She just seemed like she was in a hurry. She was interested in the status of the global gold market. She was most interested in recent gold trading and global gold reserves, and notable changes in either. We started on some foundational research and made a follow-up appointment for the next week, but she never came back.

Edmund saw Ralph's face crumpling, his eyes filling with tears.

"Thank you so much, Gordon," he said quickly. "So you just got into basic gold market trading, right? Nothing really specific."

"That's right. Like I said, she was in a hurry. She kept looking around her. She didn't have the time to do what she wanted to do. That's why we made the follow-up appointment."

"Got it, Gordon. Much appreciated," Edmund said ending the call and turning to Ralph.

"Let's get on this, Ralph. Elizabeth was obviously onto something."

"I know. But are you OK doing this, Edmund? Especially on your own time?" Ralph asked.

"Nothing better," Edmund said. "I live for this kind of stuff," he said pulling up some of the proprietary folders from the finance museum.

"Don't worry," he said seeing the look on Ralph's face. "It's OK. Even though many of the finance museum curators are here, we're really working for both museums. We're trying to keep the finance museum up to date while helping out with needs at the Museum of the City of New York. I am absolutely within my rights to share any of this with you."

After a few minutes, Edmund said: "Yes, I see what you mean. It does look like Russia and China have been amassing significant amounts of gold. And that's just the gold we know about. They seem to be taking further steps to back their currencies with gold bullion. Russia, in particular, has acquired so much gold in the last few years in relation to its total ruble supply that it is almost on a de facto gold standard now. If this is Russia and China's plan, the U.S. would be forced to immediately follow suit in order to prevent a catastrophic fall in the value of the dollar and try to preserve the dollar's reserve currency status. Looks like financial Armageddon to me."

"Me, too," Ralph agreed. "Do you think we have the tools to trace it? I mean trace the gold buys? If we could do that, I'd have enough to go to the police. Right now, all we have are theories."

"Maybe. I don't know. Worth a try. Are you hungry? I'm starving. I'm going to pop up to the fundraiser and see if I can appropriate some dinner."

"Yes, sounds good. Thanks, Edmund, and I really mean it. Thanks for everything. I'll keep working."

Ralph skimmed a news article about recent Russian gold buys and called Sarah.

"I've been looking for you," she said. "How's it going?"

"Oh, sorry. I've been in a little deep. First chance I've had to call you."

"No worries, what's up? Are you still at the museum?"

"Yes. I think Elizabeth came here to try and find out who was making all the gold buys, not anything about the root cellar. I think she may have been working with one of the finance curators on loan from the Museum of American Finance. I am working with one right now. Remember I said I had a contact here? Well, I found him, and he's helping me dig deeper into the source of the gold buys. We're making good progress."

"Fantastic," Sarah said. "That makes a lot of sense. I made some headway too, but not as much as you. The upshot is that, if there was a root cellar at The Grange, it's probably at The Grange's original location in Harlem and is either embedded in the remnants of the foundation, if any remains, or in a separate building close to where the house was located. Lots of ifs, I know. Not very promising. It sounds like you're on to something big though. Great work, Ralph."

"Thanks. Where are you?"

"I'm back at the bank. I have a midnight filing deadline on a compliance matter. I tried to punt but got closed down. Pierce is here too. You know how much I like the guy, but he's good at cranking stuff out. Plus, maybe I can get some more intel on those spreadsheets. Let's talk later."

Ralph had just turned back to his screen when Edmund walked in with two enormous plates of delicious looking food.

"I overdid a little on the shrimp," he said. "But they'll never miss it. The bar was packed. Benefits of working at a museum," he laughed as he handed Ralph his plate.

"Indeed," Ralph said as he bit off the tail of the shrimp. "Indeed."

* * *

Gordon Elliot was still sitting on his couch trying to figure out what to do. It was the same lie he had told the police, and it had been just as successful. And it wasn't *really* a lie, he thought generously, as much as just a failure to disclose. The truth was Elizabeth had met with him that day and what had happened was as reported. What he failed to tell was that she had met with him many times before that and that on this last occasion, she took the box with her.

The relationship with Elizabeth had been uncomfortable from the beginning and never improved. He had inherited the relationship from Jessica Hamilton Madison, one of his oldest and best friends, so it struck him as a bit perplexing that they didn't get along better. Especially since he had become instant friends with Jessica. They had met right out of business school. Jessica coming from Wharton and he from NYU and both landed in retail banking at the New York branch of Commerzbank Frankfurt. Thrown into the fire together, they had a lot in common and routinely shared coffee or a glass of wine as they tried to navigate the mysterious world of Wall Street finance. But, after a year, it became clear that Jessica was going to make it, and he was not. With a decided lack of social graces and ability to "suffer fools," as he said, he was strongly encouraged to move on to a different employment choice. Within a few months, he was an associate professor of finance at Columbia. Although his lack of people skills didn't help his student reviews, his writing was good and his math skills unparalleled. The department directed him increasingly away from any student interaction at all and into writing articles for mathematical journals and financial publications. A prestige bump for the university and just fine for him. But, eventually, even that turned sour and he found himself out of academia and at the Museum of the City of New York. He had hoped to land at the Museum of American Finance, but his reputation preceded him, and they wanted nothing to do with someone as strong-minded as he.

It was a better fit than he had hoped. He was able to use his American History degree, of course, but found many applications for his math sensibilities as well. The curators, well aware of his history and skill set, sent anything even vaguely math related his way. Over the years, he had been asked to calculate the daily tonnage of cargo that passed through the port of New York in the late 1700s, the total labor cost to build the subway tracks, and even the gallons of beer consumed during the annual Fifth Avenue St. Patrick's Day parade. He was hip deep in this last project when Jessica Hamilton Madison appeared at his door.

It was a month before her death. They hadn't stayed in the closest contact and, of late, had only met for an occasional dinner. He was surprised by how gaunt she looked and how nervous she seemed. She needed help replicating models she had seen in an article in the *Financial Times*. He assumed it was for an article of her own but after many meetings and hours spent working together, he learned it was much more. In their last meeting, a week before she died, she brought the box with her.

"Gordon," she said, when they were alone in a private conference room. "This box contains irreplaceable and hugely significant historical documents. They're the originals. There are no copies. I think someone's watching me and following me, and I can't keep these documents safe anymore. Can you? Can you keep this box in a fireproof vault and keep the documents safe? Can you do it in secret? And, if anything happens to me or to Elizabeth, will you give them to the museum?"

He was the perfect person for the job. A recluse and contrarian who enjoyed bucking the system at every turn, he was delighted to accept. He placed the box in a fire-safe vault with other artifacts and waited. He didn't wait long.

"Mr. Elliott," Elizabeth said as she approached him at the funeral. "I'm Elizabeth. I believe Jessica told you I would be in contact should something happen to her."

She looked tired, Gordon thought, and sad, but still easily recognizable from Jessica's description.

"Hi, Elizabeth. I'm sorry."

"Me, too. I'm sorry for you too."

Elizabeth pulled a tissue from her pocket and dabbed her eyes. "Is it possible to come by the museum tomorrow? To look through the box?"

"Yes, of course. I'm free all day. Any time is good."

"Thank you."

"I'm sorry," Gordon said again. As sorry as he could be.

Elizabeth was at the museum by 11:00 AM the next day and spent hours in a private room going through the contents of the box. This was the start of a pattern that continued for many weeks. She would come in, retrieve the box from Gordon, and work on it for hours. He would check on her periodically to see if she needed anything, but she never wanted to be disturbed. The visit the week before her death was different. She came in at her usual time, retrieved the box, and began her work. At 4:30 PM she asked to see him.

"Mr. Elliott, thank you. I appreciate all the help you've given us and for keeping this box safe. Can I ask you a question?" She moved the letter from Alexander closer to Gordon.

"Do you see the words 'Revenue Cutter Service?' Do you see anything different about them?"

Gordon leaned in to get a better look. "Yes," he said. "It looks like the letters are slightly larger and darker than the rest of the letters, although it may just be a function of aging."

"Yes," Elizabeth said. "I think so too. I've looked through the documents in this box countless times. I know them like the back of my hand, but I've never noticed this before. Maybe it's because I was never really looking for anything like this, but I think they're different too. I think they're intentionally different."

Gordon peered again at the writing. "Yes, I think so too."

"Thank you. I'm going now but I'll be back. Will you please put the box back where it's safe again?"

"Yes."

"Have a good evening."

"You, too."

Elizabeth was back two days later.

"Hi, Mr. Elliott. I'm sorry to have to ask you this after all you've already done, but do you think you might be willing to help me just a little more? I could use some help with maps of the city and waterways in the late 1700s, assuming there are any?"

"Sure, there are maps and yes, I'm happy to help."

"I know Jessica trusted you completely." She looked at him pointedly. "I know she told you about the trove. I think the clue to finding it is the Revenue Cutter Service. I think Alexander hid the clue in his letter, in the actual words, so I went to the Cutter Museum in Montauk yesterday. I saw lots of pictures of winches, cranes, and other equipment that the cutter boats had onboard in the late 1700s for moving cargo. It looks like strong equipment. I think it could transfer a lot of weight. And I think it did. I think the equipment was used to move the forfeited cargo to the trove. Which brings us back to: *Where is the trove?* And this is where I could use your help. The cutter captains had limited access to horses and carts. They generally did all their work with their cutter boats or with smaller boats. So, they must have off-loaded the cargo directly from their boats into the trove, probably either from the Hudson or the East River."

"Makes sense."

"Which means that the trove needs to be right next to the water where the boats could reach. It also needs to be someplace private where they wouldn't get caught."

"That's why you need the maps. I think there are maps that show the boat landings on the Hudson or East River. I don't think there would be that many landing sites in the 1700s but I don't know."

"Plus, it has to be a site that's not accessible by other means. For privacy again."

"That should cut the choices down. I'll get the maps, take a look, and get back to you as soon as I can."

"As quickly as you possibly can. Please."

Gordon worked almost round the clock. In the end, there was only one landing that had all the criteria. Only one.

*   *   *

Sarah walked back into the conference room. She could feel him even before she saw him. Pierce. He still looked pale and sickly, maybe even more so. She continued to her laptop and sat down.

She could feel his eyes on her.

"What?" she said.

"What do you mean?"

"Why are you staring at me? Do you have a question about this filing, or are you just staring at me to be creepy?"

He was calm now. Unnervingly so. "I'm not staring, Sarah. I was just wondering what kind of side hustle you have going that the bank doesn't know about."

"What are you talking about, Pierce? Are you just talking trash to be annoying, or do you really think you have something on me to run to Bardack about?"

Pierce studied her over his laptop. "I know what you're doing, Sarah. I know all about you. I know you're in violation of bank conflict rules." He had decided that his best chance was to attack. He knew it was unlikely that he would learn anything, but he was hoping that the pressure would slow her down long enough to get the last pieces in place. According to Timothy, the gold shipments were arriving in the depositories tomorrow morning at 4:00 AM. The gold he had been buying for all these months. Once the gold missing from the depositories was replaced, no one was going to care how.

Sarah glared back at him. "I'm not even going to respond to that," she said. "Why don't you put all your energy toward getting this filing done instead?" She turned back to her screen and started typing.

"Sorry, no offense Sarah," Pierce said. "I just think you should be careful."

Indeed, she thought as she opened another file from Ralph. Interesting stuff. Ralph and Edmund were on a roll. It seemed clear that Russia and China had been aggregating gold for years. It also appeared that they had stepped up their purchases exponentially over the last eighteen months or so, but tracing the actual buys was more challenging.

"Hi, Ralph and Edmund," Sarah typed. "Terrific work! Out of the park, guys! How's the raindrop model playing out? Are you able to track the buys?"

"Not so far," Ralph replied. "They're so small, it's tough. Edmund has access to the historical buy charts though so I think we can do it with enough time. We've got to see exactly who is buying. I mean names, people, not just countries."

"I agree," Sarah typed. "But we don't have much time. Whoever was after Elizabeth is after us too, right now. Plus, we might have information that can help the police. We have more solid information, not just thoughts and theories. I think we have enough to go to the police."

"I think so," Ralph typed. "And I agree. They're watching us, waiting for us to lead them to the cache. The more I think about what happened to Mr. Mandelman, the more I think you're right. There might be a connection. It doesn't make sense. I don't think it was just a burglary. He's right under your apartment, right? And that water pipe cut is still open? I bet they installed cameras and other surveillance. They might be there right now, waiting. It's not safe there. I think we go to the police first thing in the morning, and I don't think you go back to your apartment tonight."

"But the box is there. We have to get it. My apartment isn't secure, no doorman. They just rekeyed the front door, and my apartment but still—it's not completely safe. We need to get the box and bring it to your apartment even for these few hours."

"You're right. Where's the box?"

"In the bedroom closet, on the top."

"OK, that's good. I don't think they would have cameras in the closet."

"And it's a big closet. I can walk into it and close the door."

"Alright. I'll call three of my water polo buddies to meet you at Connolly's. We have to assume you'll be tailed. Have a drink. Invite the guys back to your apartment for another. I'll tell them to be rowdy and carry on. You can slip into the closet and put all the documents in a suitcase and then all of you head over to my place. I'm good on the couch."

"OK," Sarah typed. "Plus, I'll say things about how they're going to be working in my apartment for the next two days fixing the shaft. They probably won't buy it, but at least it's an explanation for me leaving with a suitcase."

"Alright. Let's do it. How much more time do you need at the bank?"

"Forty-five minutes, then I'm good. I'll be at Connolly's at 8:00 PM."

"OK. You'll know the guys. They're big," Ralph typed. "See you later."

"Thanks. You good?" Sarah typed.

"Yeah, concerned. Worried about you. Not going to admit to scared, not yet."

"Me neither."

Sarah looked up to find Pierce studying her again. He knew she'd been at the Historical Society this afternoon: Ray had told him that. Ray had also said that she was researching 1800s root cellars, specifically at The Grange, and that she had lied to the librarian about why she was doing it. Gold, root cellars, The Grange, Hamilton. Treasury Secretary Hamilton. Elizabeth Hamilton Walker. Sarah. They were all connected, Pierce knew, and he, along with his gold buy model, was somehow connected too. He watched her as she typed. She was probably working on it right now. If he knew how to hack into her computer, he would, in a heartbeat. But he didn't, and he didn't know anyone who could. He knew his rising anxiety was getting the best of him and messing with his judgment. He knew he was going down the rabbit hole but didn't know how to stop it. He resigned himself to watching her type.

"So Sarah," he finally said as he saw the filed compliance document pop into his inbox. "What's your plan?"

Sarah closed her laptop and stood up. Pierce looked more off than he had earlier. Deranged wasn't quite the word, but it was close. "I'm leaving, Pierce. That's my plan. See ya."

She grabbed her coat and walked quickly out of the building and down the street to Connolly's. Ralph's friends were already there, having a drink at the bar. Big and brawny, they were easy to spot. They were also very nice. She ordered a vodka tonic and sat down. Within minutes, she could feel some of the tension in her body start to evaporate as they laughed and joked and tipped a few more. Within thirty minutes, they were on their way. They packed themselves into a taxi and headed over to Sarah's apartment.

The new lock system on the front door worked smoothly and was a welcome upgrade to the building, but the lobby felt eerie and strange to her, like she had just returned from a long trip. Her apartment felt the same. Nothing seemed out of place, but it felt that way. It felt like things had been moved, even by just a hair. It felt like things had been touched. It felt like someone had been inside.

She poured a couple of shots for the guys and retrieved her suitcase from under the bed, chattering about the shaft repair and accompanying disruption, as she went into the closet and closed the door. She pulled the box down from the top shelf and started loading the documents into her suitcase. Everything was there, even the handkerchief. She sighed in relief. Maybe she was just being paranoid. The box was in plain view. If anyone had been in her apartment, they would easily have found the box and taken it. Nevertheless, she was thrilled she had it now. They hailed a cab and made their way uptown to Ralph's apartment. Squashed into the middle of the backseat, it was hard to see if anyone was following them, but when they got out, she took a thorough look around. No one. Was she just exhausted, paranoid, and now a little drunk? Maybe she and Ralph had overreacted. Maybe no one was after them at all.

The night doorman checked the list, called up, and sent them up. Ralph was standing in the open doorway when they arrived.

"So glad you're here," Ralph said. "And it sounds like it all went without a hitch."

"Yeah. No problem. Easy. I wonder if we're just being paranoid," Sarah said once they were in the apartment. "I didn't see anyone following us, and I didn't see any signs of intrusion in my apartment. Plus, of course, the box, and all its contents was still there."

"I don't know if we're overreacting, but I don't really care." Ralph said. "It can't hurt to be careful tonight and protect the box, especially if we're taking it to the police tomorrow. Elizabeth entrusted it to us. We've got to finish the job." Ralph could see that they'd all had a little something to drink—some of the guys, a bit more.

"Why don't we all just say good night and get some rest. I can't thank you enough," he said, turning to his friends. "You guys are awesome, helping me out on such short notice. Just the best. See you Thursday," he said as he opened the door to show them out. "Thanks again." He turned to Sarah.

"You take the bed. I'm good on the couch. Been on it plenty of times," he joked. "I'm going to take Bodie out for his final walk and then we'll crash. I think a good night's rest will do us both a world of good."

"Yeah, you're right. We're not a hundred percent."

Ralph took down the leash, grabbed Bodie and some bags, and headed for the park. He didn't see the man tucked into the alcove of the building next door or the man walking his dog behind him. He didn't see them following him down the steps and into the dark, dimly lit park. One far behind the other, but both in line behind him. He didn't see them pause when he paused or quicken their pace when he did. All he saw was the full moon, bright over the Hudson, shimmering on the water, reminding him of the love he had lost forever.

"THAT GUY SHE'S with just walked the dog," Ray said as soon as Pierce picked up. "I think they're in for the night. You good to pick it up in the morning?"

"Yeah, Ray. Thanks," Pierce said. "I appreciate all your help."

"Hey, Pierce? Just one more thing. I know this is weird, but I think there was someone else tailing him."

"What do you mean?"

"Just that," Ray said. "I noticed a guy behind me walking his dog, which, of course, ain't nothin' in the park, but every time the target turned, he turned, and every time he stopped, the guy stopped and waited. It just seemed weird, that's all. Figured I should tell you."

"Thanks, Ray. Thanks for telling me. Probably nothing, but I'll keep an eye open tomorrow just in case." He popped a little purple pill, turned off the ringer and crawled into bed feeling almost instantaneous calm wash over him. Just a few more hours and it would be over he knew, but it still felt like an eternity to him. His eyes grew heavy as he watched the last party boat of the night cruise by filled with revelers, expertly navigating the East River, awash in the light of the moon.

Timothy enjoyed one last look at Times Square. Midnight and still hopping. He would miss New York, but he was going for something better. He opened his browser and checked the trucks' locations. All had tracking on, so it was a quick look. Every truck was right where it should be, in time for delivery. He finished packing his suitcases, closed the blinds against the brightness of the moon, and went to bed.

Dmitri lit up a cigarette. He took the collar and leash off the dog and ran him further into the park where he would be found or not. Yugov's dog. Borrowed while Yugov wasn't at the apartment to stop him. Serves him right, he thought, after his constant vicious attacks and efforts to turn the team against him. It wasn't his fault the dog slipped the collar.

He felt better after that. Yugov loved that dog. He would be enraged when he found out Dmitri had lost him. A self-satisfied smile crossed his face as he waited on the bench. Thirty minutes, forty-five. Another fifteen minutes, he thought, and he could assume Sarah and Ralph were in for the night. He started thinking about another, larger gift he could leave Sarah. Someone who wouldn't be missed. Port Authority Bus Terminal was a good start or Lower East. He would leave just a few samples at her apartment later to remind her that he was still here, close by, watching. Her secret friend. He had already checked out the new door locks. They were basic and cheap. Nothing he hadn't seen before.

He turned up the volume on his earpiece so he could check Ralph's apartment before he got on the train. All quiet. Yugov had taunted him about how long it took him to do the install on Sarah's apartment, an easy, beginner's install, he said, that shouldn't have taken until morning. But what Yugov didn't know, and what Dmitri wouldn't tell him, was that Dmitri had also used his snake cord to attach a miniscule microphone to the bottom of Sarah's phone. He could hear everything within about a twenty-foot radius of the phone, which was about everything he needed to hear.

29

S ARAH SLEPT FITFULLY, her dreams filled with figures shrouded in black, veiled faces, talking but not so she could hear, walking in the foggy, damp darkness of the night, following a lantern to the top of a wooded hill. She awoke with a start. 8:15 AM. No sound from the living room. She got up and peeked through the door. Ralph and Bodie were still asleep, Ralph on the couch and Bodie in his dog bed to the right. It had been a late night. She moved about quietly, getting ready for the day.

"Sarah?" Ralph said softly. "You up?"

"Yes," she called. "How'd you sleep?"

"Not great, you?"

"Same. I'm going to take Bodie out, be back in a few."

By the time she had made coffee and some eggs and bagels, he was back.

"So, what do you think?" Ralph asked between bites of his bagel. "How do you feel about it all?"

"I don't know. I don't know if we're being paranoid or cautious. I don't know if we've let our imaginations run wild. I do know that I want to check out the original Grange location for the root cellar. I know it's a long shot, but Elizabeth was working it, so maybe not. Then I think we should go to the police. They will probably think we're nuts, but it feels like the right thing to do."

"I agree. There's one really promising thread of research Edmund and I were following last night. Edmund is already working on it again this morning and has been texting me some good stuff. If it pans out, it might make the police take us a lot more seriously. I should probably keep working on it with Edmund while you run up to The Grange, but I'm not convinced you're safe going up there alone."

"It's Convent Avenue. Busy street, and I'll take the train, so I'll be with lots of people at every step."

"Still though. What if someone is following us? They could follow you there." Ralph put his bagel down and leaned across the table. "There is one thing we could do to make it safer."

"Go ahead."

"Remember Prohibition? I don't mean personally, of course," as he chuckled, "but the era?"

"Yes, tough time in a city that likes to drink."

"Exactly, so everyone just found a way to drink anyway. One thing they did was tunnel. Law enforcement would set up shop in front of the large apartment buildings on the Upper West Side and Upper East Side, mainly on Central Park West and Fifth, and wait until certain well-known violators headed out. Because they were so easily followed by the IRS and DOJ agents, they were having a tough time running their bootlegging operations and making the big bucks they wanted to make until one of the bosses came up with the idea of tunneling. Mostly just short tunnels connecting the apartment buildings with 'safe' access points where they could get out on the street without being seen. Everyone started doing it. They paid off the superintendents and the doormen who helped them move the dirt out and the materials needed to construct the tunnels in. It worked surprisingly well and took the government almost until the end of Prohibition to figure any of it out. Anyway, long way to get to my point, which is that some of these tunnels still exist. Most have caved in, I expect, or are in danger of caving in, but some are not. The one that leads from this building is not."

"Wow, Ralph," Sarah said. "Fascinating."

"Right? I doubt Elizabeth ever told you about my poker nights, but I'm friendly with the doormen here, and we usually play poker every Wednesday night. They told me about the tunnel. The doormen and some of the supers all over town know about these tunnels, and sometimes even use them. I've been in this one myself. It's in great shape since the builders used concrete instead of just dirt and beams. It's solid. I think it would be a great way to escape any detection from the front door in case anyone is watching."

"I agree. Great idea, Ralph. Where does the tunnel come out?"

"On 80th, just across the street. It's short, but it works. It comes out in what looks like a garden shed at the community garden. You know that small, kind of

left-over space? That's it. You just have to pull the bar up
that crosses the inside of the door when you come
through. It closes naturally when you close the door, so
no one can get through the tunnel from the opposite
direction. I think the doormen rejiggered it so they
didn't have to worry about anyone sneaking into the
Apthorp."

"OK. I'm in. Sounds great. Plus, I love this. I've
never been in a bootleggers' tunnel before."

"There's a first for everything."

"It's almost 9:00 AM, good time to head out."

"I agree, plus Reggie is on duty now. He's one of my
poker buddies. He'll know where the key is for the tunnel door, and he'll show you to the entrance. I'll call
down and let him know you're coming. I don't think
he'll have any problem letting you use the tunnel."

"I'll keep you in the loop as to what time I'll be at
the police station. Let me know how it's going with
Edmund."

"I will. Just a minute," Ralph said as he moved to the
side table and opened the top drawer. "Take Elizabeth's
key. I hope you have a use for it," he said handing it to
her. "Now, let's do this."

*   *   *

Reggie was just as helpful as Ralph had said, and the
tunnel was just as described. Sarah beamed her phone's
flashlight around the walls and ceiling as she entered.
Plastered in concrete, with just a few cracks, it looked
solid even after almost one hundred years. The worst
part was the smell. Dank and fetid, with moisture

seeping from the floor, it smelled like a mausoleum. Sarah covered her mouth and nose and hurried through. Within minutes, she was at the exit. She pulled the bar up and was out of the tunnel and into the shed. With an easy push to the door, she was outside. She stepped away from the door and let her eyes adjust to the morning light. There was no one around. No one had seen her exit the shed. No one except Pierce.

Pierce had overslept. He had intended to be in front of the Apthorp at 7:00 AM to track her when she left Ralph's, but he had smacked the snooze button one too many times and was just getting off the train at 79th Street when he saw her. He considered it pure luck or maybe a sign that he was on the right track. She looked around quickly before heading into the subway. He followed her back down. Uptown local, going to Harlem.

He watched her from the back of the train. Busily typing and scrolling on her phone with her ear buds in, she was taking advantage of the few Wi-Fi spots they passed through on their way uptown. He didn't care. He was happy to just sit. He studied the people in his car. Most of them looked tired, many were sleeping. At this hour, the car was filled with workers on the overnight shift, going home to sleep the day away. The man to his left had his eyes closed, his hat pulled way down. The smell of musty old cigarette smoke that oozed from his bulky winter coat struck Pierce as particularly nauseating this early in the morning, but he was so tired, he just couldn't care. All he wished was that he could sleep too, but he knew that wasn't an option. He searched in his pocket for the caffeine pill he had popped in before he left his apartment. By the time they reached the next stop, he felt fine.

Sarah started moving toward the doors to exit the train, and he quickly fell in line behind. He was off the train and starting up the station stairs just as Sarah reached the top. She immediately yanked her phone from her pocket and stepped to the side. As soon as he reached the top of the stairs, his phone started buzzing too. Texts were shooting up on the screen. Voice mail alerts. Calls were coming in. Video posts. Sarah was tucked into a nearby doorway, thumbs racing over her phone. She couldn't scroll fast enough. Texts, calls, voice messages, tweets, Facebook posts. Her phone was blowing up. CNN, MSNBC, ABC, BBC, Bloomberg, were all over the airways, scrambling to get the news out first.

"BREAKING NEWS: RUSSIAN PRESIDENT AND CHINESE PRESIDENT HOLD SURPRISE JOINT NEWS CONFERENCE, ANNOUNCE GOLD-BACKED CURRENCY."

The financial community was hysterical. "Financial Armageddon! The end of U.S. global dominance!" And from the Post: "The dollar is dead!" She tapped into the Bloomberg feed. All her favorite talking heads were on air, some obviously broadcasting from their apartments, discussing the significance of the move to gold-backed currency and imminent collapse of the dollar as the world's reserve. She flipped to MSNBC, CNN, ABC. Finance and banking experts were blanketing the screens, dissecting the move, trying to digest it, trying to appear calm while others did not even appear to be trying. "The dollar is doomed!" the MSNBC anchor said before being replaced by a more disciplined colleague.

Gold.

Sarah was right. It had all been about gold.

Dmitri was right. It had all been about Sarah.

He pulled his hat even lower, insulating his ear buds from all the background noise, as he watched the news feed on his phone. Perfectly positioned in a doorway just off the subway entrance, Dmitri could watch Sarah, Pierce, and the news feed at the same time. Now Dmitri knew why they had told him only a small part of it. The trove was real. It wasn't just crazy speculation as he had often thought. Maybe Elizabeth had known where it was. Maybe now Sarah knew as well. But one thing was clear to him—he knew that if he could find the cache of gold, he would be redeemed. He would be spared. He would live.

Sarah twisted her earbuds deeper into her ears and flipped back to Bloomberg just as Bloomberg cut to the Treasury Secretary's press conference.

The press room was overflowing. Reporters were lining the walls, crouching on the floor, squeezing into any available space. The noise was deafening. But the podium was empty. Eventually the Secretary came out. Standing ramrod straight, he grasped the podium with both hands until his knuckles turned white.

"This announcement doesn't in any way affect the global dominance of the United States," the Secretary said unable to control the quiver in his voice. "We are, and will always remain, the world's reserve currency."

The Secretary paused for a moment, the sweat beading on his forehead. Releasing his death hold on the podium, he squared his shoulders and announced loudly: "The full faith and credit of the United States remains rock solid and indestructible. The U.S. dollar is as strong or stronger than it's ever been."

With that, he turned and walked swiftly off the stage, staring directly ahead, determinedly ignoring the reporters and their shouted questions, focused solely on getting to the door.

*   *   *

Sarah closed her browser and looked around. Some people were checking their screens or were on their phones, but no one seemed particularly concerned. She flipped to CNN. The White House correspondent was covering reports that countries were calling to immediately repatriate the gold they had stored in U.S. depositories. Belgium, Switzerland, France, the UK, Iran, Mexico, Romania, Libya, Ecuador, Azerbaijan, were all demanding repatriation. The countries were reportedly calling the president directly, demanding their gold.

CNN cut to the reporters covering the president live at a presidential library fundraiser at the St. Regis hotel in Washington, minutes from the White House. Reporters, who had been milling about absently in the hallways, were suddenly on their phones and then thronging the ballroom, moving directly to the front of the stage, pressing in on the president as he concluded his remarks.

"Mr. President, Mr. President!" the reporters shouted. More reporters streamed into the ballroom, elbowing their way forward and shouting for recognition. The president appeared baffled as his aide rushed to his side and whispered in his ear. Reporters were pressuring the stage, squeezing in, shouting his name, shouting questions.

"Is it true that countries are calling to immediately repatriate their gold?" one reporter shouted louder than the others.

"The full faith and credit of the United States is as strong as it's ever been. Built on a bedrock of trust for centuries. The world's reserve currency for a reason."

"Yes, Mr. President, but are countries calling to repatriate their gold?"

"We are the most trusted nation in the world. Our economy is the strongest. Always has been, always will be." At that, the president waved to the reporters, and moved to the steps.

"Mr. President?" a squat, seasoned reporter called authoritatively, squeezing forward.

"Are countries calling to repatriate their gold? The American people have a right to know."

The president stopped and turned from the stairs. His face grew hard. "If any country wants to take their gold back from the safety of the vaults of the United States of America, let them do it. Go ahead. Repatriate away."

"Is there enough gold to cover the requests?" the reporter asked, listening on his earpiece.

"Gold? Is this about gold?" He said tersely. "We have all the gold we need."

Only he didn't.

Timothy saw the deposits hit his bank accounts at 7:00 AM. He watered his plants, put his pajamas in his suitcase, and walked out the door. He didn't lock the door, and he didn't leave it open. He closed the door gently and left the key on the table in the hall. He easily caught a cab and was at JFK in fifty minutes and through security in twenty-five. He watched the early morning chatter on the television screens around the terminal. Frothy, saccharine, good morning chatter meant to soothe the masses and provide comfort and predictability to the start of their day. He imagined how different it would be in a few hours. But he wouldn't care. He would be 40,000 feet above the Atlantic, winging his way to paradise. He saw the frantic calls come in from his depository managers at Fort Knox, West Point, Denver—9:45, 9:49, 9:50, 9:52, 10:00 AM. Starting as soon as the announcement hit the air. Every few minutes. They saw what was happening. They knew repatriation requests were coming. They knew countries would want their gold and that American citizens might too. They also knew how much gold they had. He ignored them all.

He thought about Pierce. Again, he felt a little pang of discomfort, of remorse. When they couldn't reach him, he knew all the depository managers had called Treasury, had called the Federal Reserve. They had to call. What were they to do? They needed help, guidance, directions from someone with authority to handle this financial cataclysm. They had to protect themselves. The thought that American citizens might even storm the depository gates would not escape them. And when even Treasury couldn't find him, they would know something was gravely amiss. They would alert the authorities, but even the authorities wouldn't find him. His alias and his documents were impenetrable.

But they would find Pierce. He had made sure of that. He had left just enough of a trail that they would. And, in truth, the gold had shown up at 4:00 AM just like he had told Pierce, just not at the depositories. It had shown up where the Chinese and Russians had wanted it to show up. He had also made sure of that. He wrote one last text using his new disposable phone as he settled into his luxurious first-class seat. He watched out the window as the airplane breached the clouds and flew into the bright morning sun, leaving whatever was left of the old Timothy behind.

Sarah put down her phone. She was starting to feel panicky. She saw it all for what it was, a stunning coup by the world's two other superpowers. A massive, surprise attack, designed to inflict maximum damage on the United States while catapulting Russia and China to power. But she knew that the United States would be able to cover the repatriations and other fall out with the gold reserves in the depositories. That would buy America time to regroup and reposition. It would be ugly, but it was doable. She called Ralph. He didn't answer. She texted him. No answer. She started to get panicky again. She scanned the street. People were still checking their phones, but not frantically so, drinking coffee, eating pastries from the street carts, talking and walking, bundling up against the weather.

Pierce was glad he had worn his Yukon coat. He was sitting on a bench not far from Sarah, watching the feed, trying to figure out what to feel. He thought he was OK. Timothy had told him that the gold he bought for the United States would make its way into the depositories this morning. That should be enough gold to make good on the debts to the other countries who wanted to repatriate their gold as well as stabilize any national or international banking concerns. He continued to think it all the way through. By the time he was done, he had decided that he might be the hero in all this. That he might be the one who history books would credit with saving the financial system of the United States by replenishing the gold reserve. It was an electrifying thought. Yes, of course, that was how it was going to go. The financial powers of the nation would realize what he had done, and so well too, and give him the shout out. Probably on national TV. He was getting flushed and almost salivating at the thought. What would his father say? What would everyone on Staten Island say?

He flipped through the various channels watching the dramatic coverage including agitated and widespread speculation, bolstered by years of suspicion, that there was no real gold in the depositories. But they didn't know what he had done.

Then, in a millisecond, all the cameras were outside—in the Financial District, all over Midtown, even the Upper West Side and Upper East Side. People were streaming into the streets from the offices and apartment buildings. Thousands of people were emptying the buildings, shouting, screaming and running, running to the banks. They were jamming the lobbies, crying for gold, demanding gold for their dollars. The city was exploding. Pierce looked up. People around him were pocketing their phones, looking around frantically, starting to run.

He checked his feed. Facebook and X's rapid-fire posts were swamping the screens:

"YOUR DOLLARS ARE WORTHLESS! RUSSIA AND CHINA HAVE ISSUED GOLD CURRENCY. GO TO BANKS! TRADE YOUR DOLLARS FOR GOLD NOW! YOUR DOLLARS ARE ONLY PAPER! PAPER! THERE IS NOT ENOUGH GOLD. ONLY THE FIRST FEW WILL GET GOLD. THE REST WILL GET NOTHING!"

The president was back on the networks telling everyone to be calm, that it wasn't true, that it was just Russian and Chinese propaganda blanketing social media, trying to harm the United States, but no one was listening to him. They were listening to TikTok, Facebook, X, WhatsApp, YouTube, Tumblr, Instagram, PayPal—screaming to dump the dollar for gold as soon as possible before it was too late. New Yorkers were listening. So were the people in Chicago and Los Angeles, Atlanta, and Detroit. In every city and every town, people were listening and pouring into the streets, rushing to their banks, packing their lobbies. Panicked mobs started breaking out—overrunning the banks, breaking windows, tearing down counters, demanding their gold.

A text popped up on Pierce's phone. He sighed in relief; it was Timothy. He devoured it:

Sorry to have to put this in a text but I'm 40,000 feet somewhere over an ocean right now. I expect everything is going rather badly at this particular moment, to put it mildly. So sorry it has come to this because I like you, really I do, and if I could've done this another way, I would have. To be blunt, the gold you thought you were buying for the United States was really for the Russians and Chinese. I expect the Feds have figured this out by now. They think you're a traitor, that you sold out the United States, and they're after you with everything they have. Dreadfully unfair I know, but they think you're responsible for all of this, everything. Especially since they probably saw the huge deposit to your account today. The country's financial foundation is shattered and they'll need someone to blame. Sorry. Really I am. But you know how the world works, right? I would run if I were you. Run now. Do not pass Go . . . – T

Pierce felt the bile rising in his throat. How could Timothy do this to him? How could he do this to him? As if saying it over and over again in his head would provide an answer. He choked back tears of rage, shame, and the deep pain of betrayal. He was dead. The Feds would certainly get him. He looked up to see Sarah gesturing frantically at the phone. "What?" she said. "What was that?" Maybe she was his last chance. Maybe she was on to something with root cellars, Hamilton, gold spreadsheets, something that could save him. Maybe she knew something about gold; gold that could replace the gold they think he stole. Gold that could cover, stop the panic. He knew if he ran now, he wouldn't get far. Without a working alias and a plan, he didn't have a chance. Sarah was his last hope.

Sarah was yelling into the phone now not able to hear what Ralph was saying. Finally, she did.

"No, no!" Ralph shouted into the phone. "It's in Weehawken. The Palisades. The Dueling Grounds. Hamilton Park." Ralph was almost wheezing from lack of air, trying to get the words out. "Bodie must have knocked this page off the roll that had Angelica's picture on it when he was hunting for treats. He was just doing that again and his tail swept it out from under the bottom shelf. It's the Dueling Grounds where Philip and Alexander dueled. Dug into the Palisades, I think, like a bunker. Run to the subway. I'll get directions for you and text them to you. I'll get the police and meet you there."

Sarah ran. Through the streets of Harlem, the cold wind burrowing deep into every opening, flapping her coat wide as she ran. Her phone was buzzing as soon as she got to the entrance. Train to Port Authority, bus via Lincoln Tunnel, short walk. Got it. She could hear the train coming as she raced down the steps and through the turnstile. She could hear the wheels whirring, see the cars rocking. She could feel Elizabeth's terror and her courage.

She moved to the front of the train quickly and got in position to dash to the Port Authority. It made perfect sense. Alexander knew the Weehawken Palisades and the densely wooded and schist bedrock they contained. He knew the dueling grounds. He knew the specific wooded ledge, twenty feet above the Hudson where his beloved son, Philip, was shot and where, as fate decreed, he would be shot as well. The ledges were only accessible by boat either by a row across the Hudson or by a stop on the Hudson by the cutter captains. He knew that many ledges were twenty to twenty-five feet above the Hudson, an easy hoist up from the ship's deck, even with heavy cargo. He knew that these things would allow his work to be done in private, away from prying eyes. He knew that building anything on the cliffs or razing them would be next to impossible and that a bunker dug into them could last forever.

As soon as the doors opened, she was off. Moving expertly through the midday crowds, she was on the bus and headed through the tunnel within twenty minutes.

And so was Pierce. With his bulky winter hat pulled low over his eyes, scarf and baggy Yukon thermal coat, he was unrecognizable. He hung back, waiting for her to board the bus, and then rushed on at the last second, claiming the last seat at the back. She was furiously texting and wiping the now drying sweat from her forehead. He studied the bus map. There was no stop that stood out. No landmarks, no locations he knew. He had no idea where she was going. He tried to breathe. He could feel the anxiety rising in his chest, making his breath shallow and strained. New sweat mingled with the cold sweat and trickled down his back. He started to shiver, almost uncontrollably, and pulled his coat tight about him. His seat mate looked at him with concern.

"You OK, man?" he said.

"Yeah," Pierce choked out. "Just need my medication." He reached into his pocket and found his last China Girl. It was a little larger than the rest in the batch, and he had bought it as a step up to try when his anxiety was busting off the charts. He popped it under his tongue. The relief was almost instantaneous. He started to breathe, he stopped sweating and shivering.

His seat mate looked over again. "That's some cool juice, you got there," he said. "Took you right back down."

"Yeah," he said. "Yeah." He was feeling better. He knew what he was doing was unsustainable. He knew it would kill him in the end, but for right now, it worked. And that's all he needed. He needed it to work.

They were coming out of the tunnel. The bus rocked and shuddered as it crawled up from the entrance, cutting off from the 495 freeway and making its first stop. The bus stopped again on Bonn Place and continued down the street, taking a left on King Avenue. By this time, there were six passengers left on the bus, Sarah being one, and Pierce reflexively slumped down in his seat, trying to make himself small and inconspicuous. Sarah checked her phone and got ready to get off. He did the same. When the bus took a right turn onto Hamilton Avenue, he knew. The Dueling Grounds. He had been there as a kid. He had a friend who was mad about Revolutionary War sites and who cajoled his parents into taking him to just about every one of them. Sometimes the parents allowed a friend to come along on these expeditions, and on this one, he had. He remembered the site had a bronze bust of Hamilton, set on a marble pedestal with a plaque or two, but like a typical boy, the main thing he remembered was the death rock, the rock where Hamilton reputedly laid his head after he was shot. The bus stopped midblock, just up from the site. As Sarah was moving to the front, he quickly moved to the middle door, pushed the exit strip, and made his way to the bus bench where he waited for Sarah to get farther down the street.

He was feeling good. Maybe a little too good. His anxiety was completely gone, replaced by a kind of euphoria that swept him to unfathomable heights and absolute clarity he'd never experienced before. He knew Sarah was going to Alexander's cache. He knew it contained gold. He knew she would give the bars to him if he explained to her what happened. He knew she would save him and save America just like Alexander Hamilton had done before her. He quickened his pace.

He started following her. She was almost at the statue. She paused for a moment in front of it and then started off down the steps into Hamilton Park. The gold was most likely stockpiled in some kind of bunker, he thought, protected from weather and thieves. He had to talk to her in private. He knew he could convince her. He knew she would listen. He knew she would understand why he did what he did and that she would save him. He started jogging to the park steps. But he couldn't remember which steps she took down. They all looked the same to him. He felt confused and a little dizzy. The euphoria had evaporated as quickly as it had come. He sat down next to the statue, next to the rock where

Alexander had laid his head. He wanted to lay his head there too, just for a moment, just for a rest, but the rock was enclosed by a wrought iron fence, and there was no way to get in. He stretched his hand through the fence posts and touched the coarse, uneven face of the rock. Surprisingly cold, mercilessly unforgiving, an accusatory tombstone. He wrenched his hand back as if it had been burned and stood up. He picked the closest flight of steps and started down. The brush was dense and dry, the leafless white oak, beech and ash trees formed a canopy of brittle skeletons in the sky. Only a thin dirt trail cut through it. He started in. He was surprised at how quickly the wild of the park closed in. The city faded away. He felt completely alone. But he wasn't. He could hear bushes cracking, footsteps in the dry leaves ahead. He wasn't far behind Sarah. He moved, as quietly as he could, stepping ever so gently, avoiding, as best as he could, the mounds of dry leaves, twigs and empty seed pods scattered along his path. Even so, he heard her stop and listen. He stopped. She started again. He started, then stopped again.

Someone was behind him. He heard twigs cracking underfoot, leaves crunching. He whipped around, hoping to catch the intruder, but there was no one there.

He felt dizzy. The wind picked up, swirling the leaves into whirling dervishes on the path, making the empty seed pods dance. Confusing him. Scaring him. He heard footsteps starting to run behind him, recklessly crashing through the brush, unheeding the destruction and the noise, gaining on him with each step.

He tripped on a root and fell hard onto the path, rocks and dirt grinding into his hands, the bark etching deep scratches in his face. He rolled over covering his head, knowing the intruder was right behind him. He braced for the attack. But there was no one there. He picked himself up and ran for the opening in the trees up ahead. If he could just make it there, he somehow thought he would be OK.

He burst into the clearing, gasping for air, terror splashed across his face.

"Sarah, Sarah, please help me," he cried as he saw her at the far side of the clearing, before falling to his knees.

Sarah spun around, turning from the brick face of the vault. "What! What are you doing here, Pierce?" she screamed. "What do you want?" She stepped back to the wall, flattening herself against it in fear, looking frantically around for a stick.

Pierce slumped to the ground. He covered his hands with his face and cried.

"Sarah, Sarah, you have to help me." He was choking, desperate to get the words out. "I've been tricked and betrayed. The country has been tricked and betrayed. Everyone thinks I did it, but I didn't. I was lied to by a person I thought was my friend. They think I stole the gold, but I didn't. The Russians and Chinese stole it. They've got it all. We've got to cover what's supposed to be in the depositories and buy some time or our financial system will collapse. The Russians will win. The Chinese will win, and we will all be crushed." He uncovered his face and looked at her. Sweat, blood, tears, and dirt streaked across his face. The pleading in his eyes almost too painful to bear. But in the pain, she saw the truth, and she believed him.

She quickly turned back to the vault. It looked more like a hill with a door than any kind of cellar. It was large—broad and deep, with grasses, shrubs, and all kinds of plants carpeting the exterior. It blended in so perfectly with the surrounding forest that she understood why it had been bypassed all these years. Only the door needed to be hidden, nature and time had done the rest. Covered with vines and crisscrossed by branches, the door was concealed so completely that she had found it only because she believed it was there. She had found Alexander's cache.

She pulled the key from her pocket and cleared the vines enough to find the keyhole. Made of steel, it had weathered the elements for over two hundred years, but it looked rusty and corrupted, and her heart sank.

She inserted the key into the keyhole and tried the key, but it wouldn't turn, not even a hair. She tried jiggling it, moving it this way and that, but there was no use. It wouldn't budge.

What were they thinking? How could she and Ralph have thought that a key they had made from a wax mold would work? She felt naïve and just a bit stupid, but just a little. After all, they had found the cache and whether Elizabeth's key worked or whether the authorities would have to force the door open through other means just meant delay, not defeat. She returned the key to her pocket just as a harsh, ugly voice cut through the forest.

"I'll take that," Dmitri said stepping into the clearing, his gun pointed at Sarah. "Now!" He started walking toward her, apparently unaware that the key hadn't worked, and also seemingly unaware of Pierce who, lying prone on the ground was easy to miss. He was holding his stomach and moaning, clearly out of play.

"Give it to me!" Dmitri said again, more stridently as he approached Sarah, backing her further against the crumbling bricks, forcing her into a hollow. There was nothing she could do. She knew he would kill her anyway. With a mighty heave, she threw the key as deep into the thicket as she could. She knew it wouldn't stop him, but it would slow him down, perhaps long enough for Ralph and the police to arrive. She knew it would be too late for her.

"You fool!" he shrieked as he reflexively dove for the key. But it was long gone, and he was furious.

"That was a very stupid thing to do," he said coldly making his words seem even more abhorrent. "You will die for that."

Sarah prepared herself for the bullet. In her heart, she knew it was always going to come to this. There really was no other option. Once she and Ralph had kept the box and decided, almost by default, to not turn it over to the police, this was the inevitable and inescapable end. Another killing at the Dueling Grounds she thought, only this time, there was only one gun.

She looked up in time to see Pierce stagger to his feet. Weaving, almost falling to the ground, he lunged at Dmitri, throwing every ounce of his small, anemic frame at a man twice his size and twice his strength.

Pierce let out a horrifying shriek as he rammed his body into Dmitri's back, destabilizing him, sending the gun skittering along the dirt path. Dmitri turned and clawed viciously at Pierce. Tearing at his eyes, punching him, pushing him, kicking him, forcing him backward toward the trees, toward the Palisades cliff.

Sarah ran and picked up the gun and levelled it at Dmitri. "Stop or you're dead!" she screamed. "Put your hands up, hit the ground, now!" she yelled. "Now! Or you're a dead man!"

Dmitri had Pierce at the edge of the cliff, the ground crumbling around his feet, rocks giving way, crashing down the slope. Dmitri glanced sideways. He saw the gun. He saw Sarah's steady hand. He saw the brutal resolve in her eyes. But as he dropped his hold on Pierce, he gave him a slight, almost imperceptible, push as well. A small push, that wouldn't have unseated a bigger man or even most small men. But Pierce was spent. He had nothing left. His right foot trembled over the edge, and he pulled it back, onto the edge of the cliff, only to have the crumbling earth give way beneath him, sending him plunging over the Palisades edge.

He saw the bedrock cliffs rising to meet him. His family destiny flashing vividly in his mind. Pierce Burr. He was just like Aaron Burr, just like all the other Burrs. He couldn't escape his family legacy no matter how hard he had tried. The world would believe Pierce Burr had betrayed his nation. A Burr like all the rest. A "greatly immoral, unprincipled, voluptuary" Burr as Hamilton had called Aaron only this time it would be applied to him. Another Burr, once again bested by the Hamilton legacy. The soul rending pain of this knowledge was harsher than the rock he saw out of the corner of his eye.

A rock not unlike the Hamilton death rock, made of bedrock, made to last forever. He looked up as he fell, up to the blue sky, unusually blue for November he thought. He saw the leaves fluttering in the sky above for a split second before his head hit the rock. Beautiful leaves. Golden leaves.

The police were on the scene moments later. Sirens blaring, lights, loudspeakers blasting, they came from the service road at the other end of the park and screeched to a stop at another clearing, just behind the wall.

"Drop the gun! Put your hands up! Lie down, face first! Don't move! Now! Do it! Now!" Detective Schwartz shouted over the loudspeaker. Sarah threw the gun a few feet away and dropped to the dirt, Dmitri dropped down as well. Schwartz and Ralph raced into the clearing, followed by another seven officers, guns drawn and ready. Two ran to guard Dmitri, two others ran to the edge where they had seen Pierce fall, and the others fanned out to check the woods. Ralph ran to Sarah.

"Sarah, Sarah," Ralph said, choking back the tears. "I'm so sorry. Are you OK?" He kneeled next to her as the detective motioned the OK for her to sit up.

Sarah sat up slowly, light-headed, weak from what she'd just been through. She laid her head on Ralph's shoulder.

"I'm sorry," he was saying. "So sorry. I almost got you killed. I should have realized how dangerous this all was. I just saw the page Bodie swept out with notes scribbled all over it. The only thing that stood out was "Weehawken?" Everything I had been looking at these past few days, the research, the box, came together and clicked. And I called you. I wasn't thinking. I could've gotten you killed. I'm so sorry."

"There's nothing to be sorry about, Ralph. You were right. We found it. It's here. And, even if you weren't right, we both made the decisions. Through all of this. We were in this together. And what about the police, Ralph? Bringing the police in was everything. Everything. I had no idea what I was going to do. I had the gun, but what was I going to do next? I didn't know," she said as she watched the police come back from their search and congregate in the clearing.

Sarah watched Detective Schwartz in the middle of the group. She had been on the phone ever since she had determined that the perimeter and the suspect were secure. She walked over to Sarah.

"Sarah," she said. "You are amazing. I am astonished by what you did. And by what Ralph did. I know nothing was by the book, and I'm sure there will be some minor repercussions, but they will pale in comparison to what you two have done for Elizabeth and for this country. Ralph told me everything on the way over. I tried to get the New Jersey police here first, but they were not fans, even coming from me, so they will have a lot to explain later."

Detective Schwartz looked up to see the EMTs walking into the clearing. She motioned them over to the two officers at the side of the bluff where Pierce had fallen and looked expectantly at Sarah, but Sarah shook her head.

"No thank you, but I'm fine. Just tired," she said.

Schwartz nodded and paused. "I hear them," the detective said studying Sarah. "And now I see them," she said as they looked up the wooded hill to Hamilton Avenue where they could see government cars and vans, news vans, other official looking cars, nondescript cars, all descending on the Dueling Grounds. "The FBI is coming," Schwartz continued. "Treasury, the Federal Reserve, DOJ, CIA, I don't even know who or how many, but they're all coming. They're coming for Dmitri, and they're coming for the cache. The reporters are coming, of course, because they track the police band, hard to keep them away. They're all coming and there's nothing I can do to stop them.

At that, Sarah stood up and faced the detective. "You can find me for any follow-up that you need to wrap up your case. For anything that I am obliged to do. But," she said as she waved her hand across the throng of people, cameras, lights, microphones, news trucks, and reporters descending into the park. "This, I am not obliged to do again."

She looked long and hard at the detective, then reached out, hugged her, and walked away.

And she didn't look back. She didn't see Detective Schwartz run to the cache and pull Elizabeth's key from her pocket. She didn't see how the key turned in the lock, but she heard the door creak and groan as it swung open, and she felt a hush so deep from those gathered, that she turned around. The wind picked up, rustling the last of the season's leaves in the trees, releasing them from their moorings. Leaves falling from the old-growth beech and ash trees, twisting and turning in the wind, before floating, like golden parachutes, into the open cavern and onto the refrigerator-sized stacks of gold on pallets, crowding the entrance, going back farther than she could see.

She started walking again. Through the trees. Trees that had been there for centuries. Trees that had seen a democracy rise, a democracy fall to the brink of extinction and yet rise again. She wondered what Alexander would have thought about all of this. Restoring truth, validating honor, standing for courage and fairness and equality. They had fought against those who sought to use their power to crush and destroy. They had fought for justice, for liberty, remaining steadfast, loyal, and true. Unwavering and unyielding to the end.

She hoped she'd done the first Hamilton proud—and the last one.

ACKNOWLEDGMENTS

I CONTINUE TO be humbled and amazed by how much goodness there is in the world. When I consider all the people who helped bring this book to light, I am dumbfounded—by their talent, skill, kindness, and generosity of spirit. Thank you all.

To that end, I extend my deepest thanks and gratitude to my sister, Kaarin, for her love, friendship, brilliant edits, and unceasing support and faith in me, and in this book, through the many years it took. Cheers!

To my husband, Jerry, with deepest love and appreciation, for his unflagging support, enthusiasm in and for this project, his strong advocacy in support of the appropriate placement of a comma, and for the time and space to do this thing that matters so much to me.

To Gwen, my sister and friend, who has always lent a ready ear in support of and in encouragement for this process, and the rest of life as well.

For my parents, Elisabeth Jirgensons Swenson and Richard Karl Swenson, of blessed memory, whom I will hold forever in my heart for their unconditional love, guidance, and support, and for instilling in their daughters the "give it a go" attitude that has made our lives so incomparably rich. In an interesting twist, and while in the middle of writing this book, I happened upon a thesis my father wrote circa 1950 on the banking system and finance in the United States in which he stated: "That a man of Hamilton's ability was available at this time is something for which we should be everlastingly grateful." The legacy fascination continues.

To Claudia Cross, my superb agent, advocate, sounding board, and friend—thank you. It means the world to me that you loved the story and characters from the beginning, but that was just the beginning. Your editorial comments to the manuscript made it so much better, and your professional judgment and emotional acuity made everything work. Thank you for being a tireless advocate for me and for the message of this book.

To Marcia Markland, my stellar editor at Crooked Lane Books, thank you also for loving the book from first read, and carrying the torch for it at every turn. But mostly, thank you for guiding this book to become the very best it could be. Your editorial suggestions were expert and carefully considered. I think you made it soar.

To the extraordinary team at Crooked Lane Books: Thank you to Rebecca Nelson and Nebojsa Zoric for the beautiful cover, to Thaisheemarie Fantauzzi Perez for navigating the editorial process, and to Dulce Botello, Mikaela Bender, and Cassidy Graham—the amazing marketing and publicity team bar none.

Thanks also to my publicist Emi Battaglia. You are not only skilled and talented but worked tirelessly to bring this story to the world. Thank you.

Thank you also so very much to my beta readers and early readers. Your kindness and time in reading and providing comments were invaluable to me.

My deepest appreciation is left for the last. Thank you, readers. Thank you, booksellers, librarians, educators, publishers, agents, reviewers, authors—everyone who loves books. Thank you for continuing to do so. You keep books alive.